D1714299

# THE SINGING SCORPION

**Center Point
Large Print**

**This Large Print Book carries the
Seal of Approval of N.A.V.H.**

# THE SINGING SCORPION

## William Colt MacDonald

CENTER POINT PUBLISHING
THORNDIKE, MAINE

This Center Point Large Print edition
is published in the year 2010 by arrangement with
Golden West Literary Agency.

Copyright © 1934 by Allan William Colt MacDonald.
Copyright © renewed 1962
by Allan William Colt MacDonald.

The text of this Large Print edition is unabridged.
In other aspects, this book may vary
from the original edition.
Printed in the United States of America
on permanent paper.
Set in 16-point Times New Roman type.

ISBN: 978-1-60285-751-3

Library of Congress Cataloging-in-Publication Data

MacDonald, William Colt, 1891-1968.
  The singing scorpion / William Colt MacDonald. — Center Point large print ed.
    p. cm.
  ISBN 978-1-60285-751-3 (lib. bdg. : alk. paper)
  1. Large type books.  I. Title.
  PS3525.A2122S36 2010
  813'.52—dc22
                                                        2009048594

# CONTENTS

# 1

## *El Escorpión* Strikes!

The clouds had been gathering all day and by eight o'clock that night the moon was obscured from view the greater part of the time. A steady breeze, blowing from the south, had strengthened to a chill, penetrating intensity that moaned around the corners of the R-Cross-L Ranch buildings and vibrated the leaves of the surrounding cotton-woods until they resembled the dry rustlings of impatient buzzard wings. In the R-Cross-L cook-shanty, dishes and hardware clattered against a dishpan. A short time later a stove door banged and the lamp in the cook-shanty was extinguished.

Rectangles of yellow light still shone from the bunkhouse and main ranch house. A door in the bunkhouse was flung open. Momentarily a man's lean height was framed against the opening, then he stepped out, into the darkness. After a moment a curving pinpoint of crimson struck the earth in a shower of brief sparks: cigarette butt. A voice called to the puncher outside some words that had to do with playing "just one more round."

"I'm hittin' the hay," came the stubborn reply, as its owner returned to the bunkhouse. "You hombres been begging for another hand ever since I cleaned your pokes. Tomorrow night'll do—"

His voice was lost in the slamming of the door. An instant later another head was poked outside and craned upward to see the sky:

"By Cripes! Johnny's correct. It does look like rain before mornin'. Gettin' sort of frizzly too. Shut-eye for me right pronto. I ain't forgot what Buck said 'bout buildin' up them tanks."

Two or three more of the R-Cross-L hands pushed outside to verify the weather report, then all headed back inside the building with words to the effect that the rain might bring warmer weather again. The door banged shut; the oil lamps were puffed out. Silence descended.

Now only the light shining from the main room of the ranch house remained to break the gloom that enveloped the buildings. An hour slipped past.

A half mile from the ranch ten riders, their clothing still damp from the Rio Grande crossing, guided their ponies along a narrow pass twisting between two steep rock walls. Saddles were still wet; horsehide steaming. Emerging from the pass the high-peaked sombreros and serape-huddled forms of the horsemen were silhouetted an instant against one side of the pass as the moon momentarily pushed through the clouds.

The horses' hoofs might have been muffled in blankets for all the sound that was made. They and their riders moved silently toward the ranch buildings with the ease of dark shadows. Again the moon was blotted from sight. A drop of rain splashed the hand of a rider near the end of the line, then another and another.

Some comment on this fact ran in guttural tones through the group. From the leader came a sharp reprimand in the same, low-voiced tongue. The horses moved closer together, plodded on until the trees surrounding the ranch buildings had been reached. Here the animals were brought to a halt beneath the cottonwoods. A few words were whispered in the Yaqui tongue. The leader, accompanied by one of his followers, climbed down from his saddle and started on foot toward the ranch house. The pair moved swiftly through the brush and trees, their soft steps carrying them across the gravelly earth with the stealth of Apaches. Emerging into the clearing surrounding the buildings, the leader halted to consider his next move. While he stood silent, mentally arranging certain plans, a low, almost noiseless, humming sound occupied his lips. Eventually he spoke three short phrases to his companion and moved on toward the ranch house. The Yaqui fell in behind a distance of ten yards. . . .

In the main room of the ranch house, Rufus Lockhart, owner of the R-Cross-L outfit, sat before the dying embers in the huge rock-built fireplace. The large, comfortable chair in which he rested was drawn up to a hewn-oak table on which stood, among other things, a shaded oil lamp, a nearly full bottle of bourbon whisky, an open box

9

of cigars and the ledger of ranch accounts which Lockhart had just put down.

The R-Cross-L owner was a big man with bushy, iron-gray eyebrows, a hawk-beak nose beneath which the bristly, sweeping mustache covered only partially the firm, straight-lipped mouth. His lean, muscular legs concealed in dark trousers and high-heeled riding boots were stretched out toward the fireplace. His woolen shirt was a dark plaid, open at the throat.

Lockhart sat a trifle straighter in his chair, ran powerful fingers through his shock of gray hair and twisted around to reach the cigar box. One of the doors leading into the room was at his back. As his hand touched the cigars, he hesitated, eyes narrowing, at the soft sound that had reached him from the rear. His gaze went quickly to the holstered six-shooter and belt, hanging on a wooden peg above the fireplace mantel, then he finished his movements and placed one of the cigars between his lips. The hand that struck the match was steady.

A spiraling drift of tobacco smoke left Lockhart's lips and, drawn toward the fireplace, was whisked up the chimney. Only then did Lockhart speak. Without turning his head he said, steady-voiced, "Well?"

The tones of the intruder, when he replied, were low and musical, "I'm afraid you won't think it's well, at all, Lockhart. This time there won't be any slip-up."

Lockhart nodded slightly. Still he didn't turn around. The man at his rear left the doorway. Wide, careful steps carried him into the room and around in front of Lockhart. He stopped near one corner of the mantel, the six-shooter in his hand covering Lockhart's body, and said,

"I won't bother telling you not to make a move or an outcry. On the other hand, suit yourself." This with a graceful, careless shrug of the shoulders.

Lockhart said steadily, "I had an idea it might be you, Janisary."

"You alone?" cautiously.

"Don't see anyone else here, do you?" Lockhart evaded.

For a moment the two eyed each other in silence—silence except for the low undertones of a soft Mexican air tunefully hummed by Janisary while he waited for Lockhart to make some move. Janisary was tall, with powerful shoulders. He might have been thirty years; something in his dark eyes set deeply above the high cheekbones spoke of additional years. A trace of silver in the dark hair above his temples augmented that fact. His mouth was a wide thin slash, formed by sullen lines of resentment in his swarthy features, his nose straight. By some he might have been considered handsome. This, coupled with a certain magnetic personality, doubtless was responsible for his success in many unquestionably devious pursuits.

Despite the steeple-crowned, gold-embroidered sombrero and red-and-black striped serape draped carelessly over Gage Janisary's left shoulder, the man wasn't a Mexican. For the rest, his clothing was typical of the Southwest cow country: overalls, woolen shirt, scarlet bandanna knotted at his throat. His boots—that part which showed below the wide, turned-up cuffs of the overalls—were better than ordinary: soft, hand-tooled leather equipped with big-roweled silver-inlaid spurs. Twin cartridge belts crisscrossed at his hips. The holstered gun at the left was a mate to the one held relentlessly in Janisary's right hand, the trigger finger of which even now quivered with tension to release the death shot.

Lockhart wasn't missing any of this. He stirred slightly to ask: "Is there any need of waiting longer, Janisary?"

"I can't say that there is," came the low purring tones. Eyes wary on Lockhart, Janisary took a quick pantherlike step toward the cigar box, secured one of the weeds, scratched a match and lighted it. A haze of gray smoke swirled momentarily about his features, cleared away. He said abruptly, "Any idea where your son is, Lockhart?"

Lockhart stiffened a trifle. "Pete's down in Mexico some place."

"And how well I know that." A thin humorless smile touched Janisary's lips. "You see, Lockhart,

12

I've got him." The words were at the same time soft-spoken and brutal.

An expression of concern, pain, flitted across Lockhart's features. He fought to hold his voice steady: "That's bad news. Where is he?"

"In the Valley of the Singing Scorpion, if that helps."

"It doesn't. I've heard of—By God! Janisary, you're the Singing Scorpion!"

Janisary inclined his head in a short, graceful bow. "*El Escorpión,* at your service, Señor Lockhart—or rather, not at your service—"

"You devil! What have you done with Pete—"

"Nothing as yet. You don't need to ask; he's a Lockhart, like yourself. That ought to be enough for you—"

"But look, Janisary—the boy's never done you any harm. Just because you swore to kill me is no sign—"

"He's a Lockhart," Janisary said cruelly. "I pay my debts with interest. I wanted you to know that. I won't make your death any easier than I can help." A fanatical hate glowed in the dark eyes. Janisary added impatiently, "Enough of this. I've got to be on my way."

"It's been a mighty crooked way the last five years," Lockhart stated evenly. "I'd hate like hell to have on my conscience what you've got on yours."

"That's just a matter of opinion. Hell, I've—"

Janisary interrupted himself to glance toward the door through which he had entered. A flat-featured swarthy individual in flapping cotton garments and a cartridge belt was standing there. A few swift words in the Yaqui tongue were exchanged. Near the front of the house a door slammed shut. Footsteps approached the room. Another door at Janisary's right opened and a sleepy-eyed, yawning Mexican boy appeared.

The young Mexican started to speak, then stopped abruptly as he saw Lockhart's visitors. He turned back, stumbling in his haste.

Janisary's gun hand flicked swiftly to one side. His six-shooter roared. The Mexican boy crumpled in the doorway. Lockhart leaped up, trying to reach his own gun hanging above the mantel. The Yaqui Indian at his rear raised one arm, moving with the swiftness of a striking rattler. A streak of bluish light flashed across the room and stopped with a soft thud between Lockhart's shoulder blades.

Janisary turned back, raising his gun toward Lockhart, then halted as Lockhart's knees buckled, letting him to the floor. Janisary nodded quickly to the Yaqui who disappeared in the passage beyond the doorway. Janisary glanced coldly down at Lockhart, his queer humming sounding through the room, then stooped before the fireplace, seized a charred bit of wood. Straightening, he quickly sketched a crude like-ness of a scorpion on the wall above the mantel.

Flinging the charcoal to the floor, he leaped across the room and headed for the back of the house. At the open rear door he halted, leaning nonchalantly against the jamb, waiting. The Yaqui had already disappeared.

A gust of rain flung itself against Janisary's face as he peered through darkness toward the bunkhouse. There, someone was fumbling at the door latch. After a moment the door opened. A voice said, "I tell you I heard a shot. No, I wasn't dreamin'." The voice was raised, "Hello, the house. Everythin' all right?"

Waiting in the doorway, Janisary quite suddenly laughed, the sound carrying to the man at the bunkhouse. Janisary called back, "Sorry if I startled you, Buck. That dang Mex boy undertook to clean one of my guns without first unloading. Scared him plumb silly. Nobody hurt. Go back to bed."

It was all done in an excellent imitation of Rufus Lockhart's voice.

"Glad nobody was hurt." Relief was plain in the tones of the man at the bunkhouse door. "Glad nobody was hurt, Rufe. G'night." The door closed.

It was raining quite hard now. The footing was slippery as Janisary stepped down from the house and leisurely proceeded through the gloom to the waiting horses beneath the trees. He laughed as he strode through the darkness, humming a gay snatch of song in an undertone.

15

After a time muffled hoofbeats sounded through the night, then grew fainter and fainter until they had vanished, like blood sinking into wet earth, from all hearing. . . .

Rain drummed steadily against the windows of the main room in the ranch house. A gust of wet air swept through the open rear door, fanning the flame in the lamp chimney and bringing a reviving breath to the Mexican boy sprawled half inside the room. Rufus Lockhart lay as he had fallen across the hearth, his head almost inside the fireplace. A final flickering light from the dying embers cast a pale reflection on the ugly stain seeping into the stone.

The Mexican boy staggered up, one hand blindly smearing the shallow furrow at the left side of his head. He took two steps into the room, eyes searching out the silent form on the hearth with the knife haft protruding between the shoulder blades. Shrinking back, his swiftly averted glance fell on the sketch Janisary had drawn on the wall over the mantel.

Horror swept across the boy's bloody features. He took three slow steps to the rear as though to flee, but like one hypnotized he found it impossible to remove his gaze from the ominous drawing. A cry welled up in his throat, swelled, then found full utterance:

"*Madre de Dios!*" the boy shrieked. "*El Escorpión! El Escorpión* strikes!"

He ran, stumbling, through the house to the rear door, floundered through the mud and rain to the bunkhouse, pounded madly on the door. "*El Escorpión!* The Scorpion!" he shrilled wildly over and over.

# 2

# The Three Mesquiteers

Gage Janisary drew back the lowered shade in a second-floor room in the Lobo Tanks Hotel, and gazed along the winding dusty main street. Either side of the thoroughfare was lined with high false-fronted buildings and squat structures of adobe. The midday sun beat straight down. There weren't many pedestrians on the street. A few men lounged in the deep shadow beneath wooden awnings fronting the various stores. Here and there a cowpony or wagon waited at the almost unbroken line of hitch-racks that lined the roadway.

Janisary dropped the shade and sat down on a chair near the bed. An impatient tune hovered about his lips. After a time he rolled a cigarette, lighted it and stretched his lean form on the bed. Ten minutes passed before he rose and dropped the cigarette butt to the floor, placed his heel upon it. Again he drew back the shade and glanced along the street. This time he saw a rider just swinging into view, half a block away.

Janisary went to the door, opened it, strode along the hall to the top of the staircase that led below. He called down to the clerk on duty in the hotel office:

"I'm expecting a man about some cows. Send him straight up when he comes. The name is Crawford."

From the office came the clerk's reply, "I'll do that, Mr. Gage."

Janisary returned to his room and again closed the door. He uncorked a dark brown bottle that stood on the dresser, set out two glasses. Three or four minutes later a knock sounded on the door panel. Janisary crossed to his belts and guns hanging on the foot of the bed, drew out one gun, then went to the door and swung it open.

A big beetle-browed man with a month's growth of whiskers stepped quickly inside. His cowman clothing was covered with alkali dust. Sweat traced muddy streaks down his features and was lost in the beard. His pale blue eyes looked uncertainly at the gun in Janisary's hand, as he closed the door.

Janisary laughed softly. "Figured it was you, Tench, but I'm not taking any chances." He slipped the six-shooter back into the holster on the bed, went to the dresser and poured two drinks. "Wash out the dust before you talk."

Tench Crawford downed the drink at a gulp, looked eagerly at the bottle. Janisary nodded.

Crawford poured himself a second drink. Janisary had scarcely touched lips to his own glass. He sat down on the bed, kicked a nearby chair into position for Crawford. Crawford removed his sombrero and wiped perspiration from his narrow forehead. Finally, he said, "You got a heap of nerve, chief."

"You just finding that out?" Janisary smiled.

Crawford laughed. "Mr. Gage. Cattle-buyer. That's good for more than a chuckle. My God!" admiringly, "I don't see how in hell you got the nerve."

"Simplest thing in the world, Tench. Lobo Tanks is the last place they'd think of looking for me. What happened?"

"After you left us, I swung away from the rest of the boys, told them to get back to Malpaisaño pronto. I figured there wouldn't be no sign left, with all that rain, for a man to follow. I followed the ridges. With daylight, I saw Buck Patton and the R-Cross-L hands—"

"How do you know it was Patton—?"

"I was hid out on a shelf of rock. They passed right near me the second day. Seven riders, countin' Patton. So close, I could have reached out a hand to him. Heard one of the cowpokes call him by name." Crawford sighed heavily. "That Patton's a bulldog on a trail. Once he and his crew found sign, they stuck like—"

"I know Patton," Janisary said shortly. "What happened?"

"It's a damn good thing for you you cut loose from the bunch and holed up here."

Janisary frowned. "That sounds bad."

"You'll have to get you a new crew of Yaquis, Gage."

"Wiped out?"

"Every damn son of 'em. They fought like fiends when Patton cornered 'em. That'd never happened, only our horses was tired. The R-Cross-L ponies was fresh. I watched the battle from the top of a hawgback. Patton only took four men back with him. Two of 'em was bandaged. They'll never guess who killed Lockhart. Them Yaquis didn't get no chance to talk. You was wise, cuttin' loose—"

"They know who tried to kill Lockhart, all right—"

"Huh! What did you—"

"There's a rumor around town to the effect Lockhart didn't die—"

"Holy Gesis!" Consternation twisted Crawford's features. "And we're still hangin' around Lobo Tanks?"

"Take it easy, Tench. The town's changed a heap in the last five years. It's grown. There ain't half a dozen men know me. I've kept close to this room. I won't be going out to the R-Cross-L and Lockhart can't come here. Patton's away—"

"He's home by this time."

"I'm not worried."

"Ain't the town on the prod some? Lockhart was well thought of—"

"A town can cool off a lot in a week, Tench."

"Lobo Tanks can go plumb below zero and I won't feel comfortable." Beads of nervous perspiration dotted Crawford's grimy features.

"We'll leave tonight—after it gets dark. Now tell me, did you see Porky?"

Crawford nodded. "He's holed up in the hills, 'bout ten miles south of town. For once in his life he was right. Young Lockhart did bribe that Mex boy to get word to his father. Good thing Porky overheard that, or ol' Rufe Lockhart would have come a-ridin'—"

Janisary's eyes narrowed. "I'm commencin' to think Mex boys are bad luck for me. A Mex kid butted in that night at Lockhart's. I had to shoot him —but how about this Mex young Lockhart sent?"

"Porky caught up to him 'bout three miles from here—before he could get to the R-Cross-L."

"Porky question him?"

Crawford shook his head. "The Mex wouldn't talk, put up a fight. You know how quick Porky is on the trigger."

Janisary swore. "I know Porky is a damn fool," he snapped. "Then what?"

Crawford shrugged his shoulders. "There don't seem to be anythin' more. Porky went through the Mex's clothes before he buried the body. Didn't find any notes or anything."

"Good!"

"But here's somethin' sort of queer, chief. The Mex had Pete Lockhart's six-shooter."

"The hell you say!" Janisary stiffened. "I'm dam'd if I know how he got it. I took that gun away once—"

"Probably the Mex stole it—"

"You sure it was Lockhart's?"

"Accordin' to Porky it was the same gun. Had Lockhart's initials on the butt, P.E.L."

Janisary said slowly, "If it really is Lockhart's gun, somebody's double-crossin' me. I'll be damn glad to get a look at it. Porky didn't bury it with the body, did he?"

Crawford looked uneasy. "Reckon you're not goin' to like this, chief, though I don't see how it can make much difference. You see, Porky was sort of short of change. He needed money for food while he was holed up, waitin' for us. To cut a long story short, he sold the gun."

Janisary swore a violent oath. "Why, that unmitigated fool. Who bought it?"

"Porky peddled it to a gunshop in Lobo Tanks —here in town."

Janisary's voice shook with anger, "Crawford, you slope out pronto and buy back that gun. Do you hear? If it's been sold, find out who got it. But get that gun! Don't come back without it!"

"I'll do my best, but—but—"

"But what?"

"Well—" lamely, "—I don't see what difference it makes—"

"*You* wouldn't," Janisary sneered. "Cripes! You're as big a fool as Porky. A gun with Lockhart's initials, loose on the town that Rufus Lockhart practically owns. Oh, you damn idiot. And you can't see why?"

"Dam'd if I can," Crawford said meekly. "If anybody recognized it, they'd just think young Lockhart might have peddled it himself—"

"Keep your mouth shut! Can't you see what might happen? Undoubtedly, Rufus Lockhart knows the whereabouts of his son—"

"Lockhart could never find the Valley—"

"He'd know the general vicinity anyway. Suppose Pete Lockhart had already found that treasure. For all we know he may have pulled the lead on the cartridges in the cylinder and stuffed something valuable in the shells. Then put the leads back. You know, that treasure is supposed to be made up of gold and precious stones—"

"I still don't see—"

Janisary swore at his henchman. "Let word get out that Pete Lockhart has discovered a treasure down in Mexico, and you'll have the whole country on our necks. Yes, and the Mexican Government too. We've been pretty lucky. Nobody is likely to discover the Valley by accident, because nobody comes anywhere near it. But just let a treasure-hungry crowd of a hundred or so come snooping around—oh, hell, Tench, you make me tired. If you don't realize what it means now, you never will. You get out and get on the trail of that gun just as fast as God will let you—"

"But suppose there ain't nothin' hid in the shells—?"

"I'm not saying there is. In fact, I don't think there is. But I'm not taking chances of one single thing slipping past me. Now get!"

"Gosh, chief, I ain't so keen to be prowlin' around this town—"

Crawford stopped short, shrinking before the baleful gleam in Janisary's eyes. Janisary's voice trembled with anger: "You do as I tell you, Crawford, or else—"

The words weren't completed, but the threat in Janisary's voice was sufficiently ominous to persuade Crawford to back hastily toward the door, his face suddenly ashen. Behind him, one hand fumbled at the doorknob. He gulped out a few unintelligible words and disappeared in the hall.

"And hurry it up," Janisary snarled after him.

He stood at the open doorway a moment, listening to Crawford's retreating footsteps on the stairway. When the sounds had died away, Janisary strode across the room, jerked back the window shade. After a few seconds, Crawford's head and shoulders appeared under Janisary's line of vision, then again disappeared along the sidewalk, headed east.

"The damn fool," Janisary swore, "has gone the wrong way. That gunshop is west of here." He glanced diagonally across the street toward a gunsmith's sign painted above a shop. "Take him twenty minutes to find it, I suppose."

Janisary's disgusted gaze moved farther along the thoroughfare, shifted to the center of the road to a point where three riders were just entering the town. Had Janisary known the part these three were to play in his life, his next actions would have been different. As it was, his eyes passed over them with small notice, as he dropped the shade and sat down to await Tench Crawford's return.

The three riders pulled their horses to a walk as they neared the center of town. To all appearances they were just a trio of drifting cowboys, loafing their way across country. Certainly there was little in their clothing to distinguish them from the cowmen so familiar throughout the Southwest cow country: overalls, vests over woolen shirts, bandannas knotted at throats, high-heeled riding boots and roll brim Stetsons. One fact stood out: instead of the usual single weapon, each of the strangers carried two Colt's forty-five caliber six-shooters in the worn holsters that were attached to the twin cartridge belts encircling their slim hips.

Under the gray sombrero of the center rider was a rebellious thatch of brick-red hair. The nose in his long bony face was aquiline, his jaw square and sinewy. His eyes were a keen slate-gray with deep humorous lights which could, on occasion, change swiftly to the hue of cold, blue steel. At either side of the wide mouth with its straight thin lips, were tiny, upcurving lines that relieved the otherwise stern features. His name—one feared by outlaws throughout the Border Country —was Tucson Smith.

Lullaby Joslin, Tucson's companion on the right, lacked three inches of matching Tucson Smith's six feet plus in height. Joslin was lanky, his arms long and bony-wristed. His leatherlike features were long and dour. He was sleepy-appearing, soft-spoken. His clothing had a sloppy, ill-fitting look and his hair was as black and straight as an Indian's. To those who didn't know him, Lullaby Joslin's funereal appearance might elicit chuckles, resembling as he did a rather mournful-looking scarecrow. But these facts were quickly forgotten by anyone who had ever watched Joslin shoot his way out of a scrape. It was said his guns were swifter than "greased lightnin'."

The third man of the trio—Stony Brooke—was dark complexioned. He possessed a snub nose, innocent blue eyes and a good-natured grin. He wasn't as tall as his two companions, but what his muscular frame lacked in height was more than compensated by a barrel-like torso. It was freely predicted that Stony would laugh at his own funeral; certainly no one had ever known him to show the slightest sign of fear in the tightest sort of predicament. His main object in life, so he maintained, was to find some *real* excitement, and while he had already encountered sufficient danger—together with his two companions—to have more than satisfied any other man of thirty years, his adventure-loving soul still yearned for new ranges from which the use of gunpowder had not already vanished.

The West knew this trio by many names; the name which came most familiarly to acquaintances' lips was that of the Three Mesquiteers. Like Dumas' Three Musketeers, of fictional fame, these three were "all for one and one for all." Law officers termed them the best loved and at the same time the most feared trio throughout the Southwest. As one old-timer had phrased it, "If they's any bounty ever put up on Satan's pelt, Tucson Smith and his pards will shore collect it. Two minutes after they'd rode into th' Jaws o' Hell, they'd have th' devil an' all his imps reachin' frantic fer hymn-books."

"This town," and Lullaby Joslin straightened wearily in his saddle, "looks like it might have a decent restaurant. Seems like every place we lit on, past coupla days, ain't been able to offer nothin' but *chili* an' *tortillas, tortillas an' chili.* 'Course, it's Stony's fault. Always lookin' for the out-of-the-way places. S'help me, I'd like to put him out of the way, sometime."

"You and how many other ghastly spectacles?" Stony asked defiantly. He continued in earnest tones, "Now, look here, Lullaby, you know we can't find no *real* excitement, hittin' the big towns—"

"Who in time wants excitement?" Lullaby snapped back. "Me, I'm cravin' to settle down for a spell, like we planned. So help me, if I ever get where I can set again—"

"What'll you do—hatch aigs?" Stony snickered.

"Eggs—that's what I've been thinkin' of," Lullaby said gloomily, "ham-an'-eggs. I dream of 'em nights. I swear to St. Pete, if I ever see a platter of real honest-to-God eggs again, I'll cackle."

"What you been doin' the last coupla days?" Stony asked innocently. "It's sure certain you ain't done nothin' to crow about. You ain't done nothin' but beef about yore stomach—"

"Beef!" Lullaby said dreamily. "What I'd give for a big slab of beef just cooked to a turn, with the juice oozin' out—"

"You ought to pack a cow with you, cowpoke," Stony grinned.

Lullaby eyed him sourly. "It's bad enough," he stated, "just havin' a calf along, ain't it, Tucson— a billy-be-damned grinnin' calf?"

Tucson smiled. He was used to the eternal wrangling of this pair long since. He drawled lazily, "You two ride along and scout up a good chow place. I'll find you—"

"What you goin' to do?" Lullaby wanted to know.

Tucson gestured toward a gunsmith's sign a few doors ahead. "I'm goin' to drop in there and see if I can get an ejector spring for my right-hand gun. Stony damn nigh ruined mine with his experimentin' the other night. Took all the zip outten it."

Stony reddened. "Just the same, I'll bet Mr. Sam Colt would have paid me good money for the patent if it had worked."

"Yaah!" Lullaby chuckled his derision. "You and your patents. I note you didn't use your own gun—"

"But if it had worked," Stony was explaining earnestly, "we'd all been millionaires—"

"As it is," Lullaby snapped back, "only one of us was affected—an' I'm expectin' him to bray any minute—"

They walked their ponies along the street, still arguing, while Tucson guided his mount to a stop before the gunshop. He swung his lean form down from the saddle of the rangy sorrel, dropped reins over the hitch-rack and stepped inside the shop. The proprietor laid down a bit of gun mechanism on which he had been employing an industrious file and listened to Tucson's request. The order was quickly filled and paid for and Tucson again started out of the shop. Near the doorway was a showcase containing second-hand revolvers, and Tucson, from sheer force of habit, stopped a moment to look them over. The proprietor of the shop, a gray-haired, nearsighted man with glasses, was quick to take advantage of the cowboy's hesitation. "Can I sell you a good six-shooter—cheap?" he asked.

"I reckon not—thanks. Just lookin' 'em over. I'm pretty well fitted out—" Tucson stopped suddenly, gazing at one weapon in particular. He pointed with a forefinger against the glass of the showcase. "Damn if that don't look like a blood brother to my guns."

The next instant the six-shooter in question was out of the case and in Tucson's hand. Tucson hefted it, tried it for balance. "A dang sweet weapon," he murmured.

"I'll let it go cheap," hopefully.

"Nope," shaking his head. "I don't aim to be a walkin' arsenal." Tucson looked at the gun, turned it over, noting the initials P.E.L. stamped in small letters on the butt. "Somebody in town sell this to you?" he asked.

The proprietor shook his head. "I got it from some stranger who was just drifting through—or so he said. Needed money. I didn't exactly want to buy it, but—" with an apologetic smile, "—I just couldn't resist. I've had no time to try it yet, but I'll bet a cookie she shoots truer'n true."

"I'll bet—" Tucson commenced agreement, then stopped with an exclamation of surprise, "By gosh! This *is* a twin to my guns—a triplet rather. Look—" pointing out the factory number on the bottom of the butt, "—this gun was made right after my two was turned out. See—the number, here?" He produced his own guns, held them up for inspection. "See, the same numbers, exceptin' for the last figure? My guns end in 6 and 7. The number of this one finishes with an 8. Well, that's a queer one to beat."

"You really ought to have it," the shopkeeper urged. "Show me eight dollars and the gun is yours. That's exactly what I paid too. But it's a nice gun. I'd like to see you have it."

Tucson grinned. "I reckon you're right, brother. Darned if I know what I'll do with three guns, though. Oh, well, a fool and his money, as the sayin' goes. . . . Here you are."

"Thank you. I hope it gives good service."

"Ain't no doubt of that." Tucson slid his regular guns into holsters, and stuck the new purchase into the waistband of his overalls. "So long."

He closed the door behind him, and stood on the sidewalk under the wooden awning of the shop, glancing along the street in search of Lullaby and Stony. Neither was in sight, though a short distance down the block he noted their horses standing before a saloon. His fingers strayed to the Durham tag dangling from a vest pocket. He waited while he rolled a cigarette, then touched a match to the tobacco. As he was about to toss the match away, a man jogged his elbow.

31

"Sorry," Tucson said automatically.

The man didn't reply, but brushed brusquely past Tucson to enter the gunshop. The door banged behind him.

"Polite cuss," Tucson said ironically to himself. "Looked like he was plumb worried and in a hurry to get some place. Sort of a mean-lookin' hombre too. . . . Guess I'll go get Stony and Lullaby."

Still he didn't move, he couldn't quite decide why. Something in the man's manner had aroused Tucson's interest. Again Tucson started to leave and again he halted, curling spirals of cigarette smoke drifting from his nostrils. Behind him the door to the gunshop suddenly opened. The man who had entered again appeared followed by the proprietor of the shop.

"You're lucky," Tucson heard the proprietor say, "there's the man who bought your gun."

Tucson half turned to face the big man bearing down on him.

The big man said abruptly, "I'm after my gun. You just bought it. I want it."

Tucson smiled, leaned one shoulder carelessly against an upright supporting the wooden awning overhead. He drew deeply on his cigarette, exhaled slowly and said with some interest, "Is that so?"

"Ain't I just told you?" the big man said harshly.

"I just paid for a gun in there—" and Tucson gestured toward the door, "—I reckon it's my gun. Unless you got some good reason for wantin' the gun—"

"I just told you it was my gun," the other growled.

"So you did, so you did," Tucson said softly. He was disliking the big man more every minute.

"Well, by God—!"

"Take it easy, brother," Tucson advised calmly. "No use gettin' riled. If I got anythin' of yours, you'll get it, but there's no use you flyin' off'n the handle—"

"Well, I'm in a hurry—"

"I ain't. So long as you're so plumb insistent, I got a hunch mebbe we better move slow. Cripes! I never saw you before—"

"I don't see what difference that makes—" The big man stopped, controlled his temper with an effort, attempted a new tack, "Look here, pardner, I didn't mean to get proddy. My name's Crawford—Tench Crawford. You see—"

"Wait a minute." Tucson turned to the proprietor to ask, "Is this the man who peddled you the gun I just bought?"

The proprietor shook his head. "I never seen him before. He come rushin' in, described the gun and offered double what I'd paid for it."

Tucson's eyes twinkled. "Without bargainin' none?" incredulously.

Crawford scowled. "Cut out the palaverin'. I want my gun."

33

"I ain't got your gun," Tucson said.

"You're a liar!" Crawford started to reach for the gun in Tucson's waistband.

Tucson's eyes narrowed. "For the minute we'll let that pass," he said, and his voice was dangerously quiet. "Your name's Crawford, you state—"

"Dammit, yes!"

"The initials on the gun I bought are P.E.L."

Crawford flamed out, "Take warnin', hombre. I'm losin' patience—"

"You're li'ble to lose more than that—"

"I won't be put off no longer," Crawford's voice seethed with baffled rage. "Regardless of the initials on that gun, I want it and I'm goin' to have it. Either that or—"

"Or what?" Tucson snapped. "Talk quick or back up your bluff!"

# 3

# Powder Smoke

Crawford swore at Tucson and reached for the gun. Tucson pushed his hands away. Crawford's face flamed scarlet. He pushed in a second time, reaching for the weapon. Tucson laughed and shoved him back.

"Quit pawing me," Tucson said.

"You thievin' son!" Crawford snarled.

He rushed at Tucson, one clenched fist swinging

at the cowboy's head. Tucson's eyes narrowed. He shifted swiftly to one side. Crawford's flailing fist struck the upright against which Tucson had been leaning. Staggered by the impact, Crawford half whirled around. Tucson drew the gun in question and rapped Crawford smartly across the side of the head as the man passed him.

"You wanted the gun," Tucson stated grimly. "I hope you're satisfied."

Somewhere down the street a man yelled. Two more men came running. A crowd commenced to collect. Crawford was down now, sprawling on hands and knees, shaking his head like an angry bull in an effort to clear his senses.

Somebody in the crowd laughed. Crawford stumbled to his feet, stood swaying on uncertain legs before Tucson. Tucson leaned against the supporting upright, his bronzed features creased in a grim smile. The gun had been replaced in his waistband.

Again Crawford shook his head, peering beneath lowered brows at Tucson, his eyes bloodshot. "I'm comin' for that gun, hombre," he stated, and the tones were ugly. He added a word that Tucson didn't like. Tucson took one quick step, hit Crawford in the face. Following up, he struck him a second time.

Blood spurted from Crawford's nose before he struck the ground. This time he bounced right up, clawing at the gun in his holster. Tucson swayed to one side, his right hand jerking down. The hand jerked back, stopped in a burst of smoke and white flame. Two reports sounded almost simultaneously.

A leaden slug thudded into the upright at Tucson's back. Crawford was whirled half around by the impact of Tucson's shot. His gun clattered from his hand. One arm hung limply at his side— the one on which a spreading stain of crimson was seeping through the sleeve.

"Don't shoot—don't shoot again!" Sheer terror shook Crawford's voice. He swayed and nearly fell.

Tucson eyed the man contemptuously a moment, then plugged out his empty shell and reloaded. Next he shoved his gun back in holster, and approached Crawford. Crawford shrank back. Tucson laughed softly, examining the injured arm.

"You're yellow, feller," Tucson said quietly. "You ain't even hurt bad. My lead didn't even stay with you. Just a flesh wound. You still want that gun?"

Crawford gulped and shook his head. A deputy sheriff pushed through the crowd, asking questions.

"Nothin' much," Tucson said, "this Crawford hombre wanted my gun and kicked like a steer when I gave it to him."

The proprietor of the gunshop expanded on the story, told what had happened. Tucson looked over the heads of the crowd, saw Lullaby and Stony standing near, ready to take a hand if trouble increased. The deputy turned to Crawford, "You think this man's got your gun? Can you prove it?"

Crawford shook his head. "Reckon I must have been mistaken," he mumbled.

"I don't know what to say," the deputy said doubtfully. "Mebbe I should take you up, Crawford." He turned to Tucson, "What do you think?"

Tucson shrugged broad shoulders. "Suit yourself," he said, "but I don't see any sense puttin' more burden on your taxpayers. I'm satisfied. Reckon Crawford is too."

The deputy turned sternly back to Crawford. "If you got business in Lobo Tanks, get it finished and ride out. D'you hear?"

Crawford nodded and commenced to push through the crowd. He found someone to tie a bandanna around the wounded arm, then headed toward the bar in the Lobo Tanks Hotel.

"If he kicks up any more trouble, let me know," the deputy said to Tucson.

"I'll do that."

The deputy turned away and headed down the street. The crowd commenced to break up. Lullaby and Stony approached Tucson, asking questions. Tucson talked while the trio made its way along the sidewalk. His two companions examined the gun of contention, handed it back.

"What was wrong with that galoot?" Stony asked. "Drunk?"

Tucson shook his head thoughtfully. "I don't think so. There's somethin' dang queer about it. He acted so sort of excited, when he saw I wasn't goin' to hand the gun over. Cripes! He could have had the gun if he'd gone at it decent like." He turned suddenly, "C'mon."

"Where you goin'?" from Lullaby.

"Hotel bar. Mebbe I'll talk to Crawford some more."

The three headed for the bar and entered by the front door just in time to see Crawford leaving by another door which led through the hotel office. From his position at the bar, Tucson could see through the office to the stairway which Crawford was ascending.

The three cowboys ordered small beers. After the first sip, Tucson set down his glass and saying, "I'll be back in a second," entered the hotel office. The clerk behind the desk looked up as Tucson approached him.

"Looking for a room?"

Tucson shook his head. "That feller, Crawford, that just went up. Is he stayin' here?"

The clerk shook his head. "He came here on business, a short time back, to see one of our guests. He's a stock raiser, I guess."

"Who—your guest?"

"No, Crawford. The guest's name is Gage—"

consulting the register, "—J. Gage. Works for the Speede Packing Company. Cattle buyer. Gage has been here a week but he's hardly moved outside his room. But he told me, just before Crawford arrived, that the man was calling to see him about some stock. Say, what was the trouble between you and Crawford?"

Tucson grinned, "You see the ruckus?"

"Just part of it—from the front door there. I couldn't leave the office."

"It didn't amount to much," Tucson said easily. "Crawford just made a mistake. He thought I had somethin' belongin' to him. I proved I didn't. By the way, does Crawford own a ranch hereabouts?"

The clerk replied in the negative. "I never saw him before."

"Uh-huh. Thanks. By the way, I reckon I will want a room here for the night. My two pards—they're in the bar—will be stayin' too. Three rooms."

The clerk swung the register around. Tucson paid for the three rooms and received an equal number of keys with tags, bearing the room numbers, attached.

"We won't sign right now," Tucson said. "Crawford might see the register and learn we're stayin' the night. Can't tell—he might get proddy again and start more trouble. I'd like a peaceful night's sleep. We'll sign before we go up to our rooms. My name's Smith. And I'd just as soon Crawford didn't know I was inquirin' about him."

Tucson added mysteriously, "Official business, see?"

The clerk blinked. "Oh, certainly. Official business? Just as you say, Mr. Smith. You working for the Cattlemen's Association?"

"I've done a mite of work for 'em in my time," Tucson evaded.

He nodded to the clerk and rejoined his companions in the bar. Here he presented each with a key to a hotel room.

"What the hell?" Lullaby asked puzzledly.

"We're stayin' the night in Lobo Tanks," Tucson went on.

Stony's eyes lighted up. "You smell somethin', pard?"

"I ain't sure," Tucson frowned. "Just actin' on a hunch. Mebbe we'll just be wastin' time—"

Stony gave a whoop of delight. "Barkeep, set 'em up again!"

The bartender filled the orders and again retired to the far end of the bar. Cowpunch conversation was nothing in his young life and he went on polishing glasses.

Stony jabbed Lullaby in the middle. "Hear that, Pickle Face? The old warhawss is smellin' gunpowder smoke again."

"I suppose, I suppose," Lullaby said dolefully. "Just my luck. More trouble I suppose. I never saw nobody for smellin' out trouble like Tucson Smith."

"Listen, you sour-lookin' bluffer," Tucson grinned. "You're just as bad as Stony—"

"I couldn't be—"

"—only you won't admit it," Tucson finished.

"All right, all right," Lullaby growled. "I give up. What's yore hunch this time?"

Tucson shook his head gravely, repeated his conversation with the hotel clerk in lowered tones. "I dunno, mebbe I'm all wrong, but somethin' in this whole business seems queer. In the first place, I've met, I reckon, every damn one of Speede's cattle buyers. I never yet heard of one named Gage."

"Mebbe he's a new man," Stony put in.

"True enough," Tucson nodded. "The fact remains that he ain't been on the job—like a new man would be doin'. Stickin' close to his room for a week. Doesn't appear to be doin' a tap of business, until today this Crawford hombre shows up—and there's no Crawford runnin' cows in this neck of the range. How does it look to you? On top of it all, this business about that gun I bought."

"I wonder if the whole thing is tied in together," Stony speculated. "What do you think, Lullaby?"

Lullaby yawned widely. "What I think don't make no damn difference, only I got one of them premynishuns that tells me I better lay in a pronto supply of ca'tridges. Beyond that, I ain't thinkin'. My stomach feels like my throat is cut, and—"

"Did you two locate a place to grab a bait?" Tucson asked.

41

Stony pretended extreme disgust. "No, we didn't. We dropped into that saloon down the street first. In there, along with the pretzels, they had some little dried salty fish. To make a long story short, the barkeep finally asked Lullaby if he didn't think all them fish should have another drink to swim in. 'Bout that time, we heard the excitement and went out to see your ruckus—"

"Anyway, they was right good fish," Lullaby defended his appetite. "T'ain't often we hit a town big enough to have a saloon with a free lunch—"

"It's a damn good thing for the saloon keepers *you* don't," Stony cut in, "or you'd bankrupt the liquor business. That appetite of yours was never meant to be fed any place but a zoo—say in the elephant cage."

"What do you know about elephants?" Lullaby growled.

"They never forget and they like peanuts," Stony said promptly. "Which they're great travelers too. I never yet saw one that didn't pack a trunk with him."

Lullaby said disgustedly, "My God, the first time I heard that one, I nigh rolled out of my cradle, laughin'."

"Cripes," Stony said, "you never enjoyed a good laugh in your life."

"Where you're concerned," Lullaby drawled, "I find it plumb difficult to do anythin' else." He added plaintively to Tucson, "Hey, ain't we ever goin' to eat?"

"C'mon," Tucson laughed, "this town is full of restaurants."

Stony sneered genially, "There'll be one less when Lullaby gets through stowin' chuck. Nobody can do business and feed him." He drained his glass and hurried after the other two who were already headed outside.

# 4

# The Scorpion Plans

Gage Janisary was waiting for Crawford when the man shoved his battered countenance into the hotel room. He didn't meet Janisary's angry eyes. Janisary left off his ceaseless humming to sneer, "You don't need to tell me you failed. I saw you through my window. What in hell did you think you were doing- ?"

"Tryin' to get that gun. He wouldn't give it up." Crawford dropped on a chair and gingerly felt his wound, which had stopped bleeding. "I started to take it away from him. Somethin' went wrong."

"That something being named Crawford," Janisary said icily. He waited a moment, then said, "Well, go on."

Crawford supplied limping details, ending, "Just as soon as my wing quits throbbin', I'll go lookin' for that cowpoke. He can't gun Tench Crawford and get away with it—"

"It appears to me he's already done just that. Crawford, you acted like a fool—"

"I don't see what else—"

"You made your first mistake in offering double price for that weapon. That was bound to arouse their suspicions. And you shouldn't have lost your temper. If you'd approached that long-legged cowpunch quietly, he'd probably given you the gun for just what it cost him. He give you the gun, all right, but—" Janisary broke off to swear disgustedly.

Crawford admitted reluctantly, "He was plumb fast gettin' his own gun into action. I sure thought I had him covered in time, but—"

"I couldn't see that part because of the crowd around—just heard the shots. Then that deputy sheriff butted in. I moved away from the window then." Janisary frowned. "He must have been pretty fast at that, Tench, beatin' you to the shot that way. I reckon that wallop on the head must have slowed you up."

"Exactly the way I figure it," Crawford assented eagerly. "That's why I aim to try again—"

Janisary shook his head with some disgust. "He never would let you have that gun now. Crawford, you leave this to me. I'll get the gun—"

"You think you'll have better luck than I did, or you plannin' to rub him out?"

"Nothing so rough as that. He's just another fool cowpuncher with a strong back and a weak head. Probably got a few dollars and come to Lobo Tanks on a drunk. Well, I'll talk to him. I'll pay for that gun, probably a good deal more than it's worth, but I'll get it. When I talk, money talks."

"When you goin' to do all this?"

Janisary didn't reply at once. Finally he said, "I figure that puncher will be staying in town overnight. His horse is still standing in front of that gunshop. I'll watch the horse. If I see him start to leave I'll go out and talk to him. Meanwhile, you get out and keep on his trail. Don't go near him. If you do come in contact with him, act as humble as God'll let you. But let me know what he does, where he goes, and, if he stays in town tonight, where he rolls in."

"You figurin' to see him tonight?"

Janisary nodded. "If he don't leave before then. I'm not anxious to go out in broad daylight. After I've seen him, we'll be pulling out. I'll leave word to have my horse saddled, so we can pull out on a minute's notice, if we have to. Keep your own horse ready, down in front, too."

"It may go that far, eh?"

Janisary's features set determinedly. "I'm going to have that gun—one way or the other. Say, you didn't get that puncher's name, did you?"

"I heard him tell that deputy it was Smith."

"All right. Mr. Smith is due to give up that gun.

45

Better get going, now, Tench. If anything unusual breaks, report to me pronto."

"I got you, Gage."

Crawford left the room. Janisary heard his footsteps die out on the stairway. An hour passed, then two. Crawford didn't return. After a time, Janisary rose from the bed where he'd been stretched out and poured himself a small drink from the bottle on the dresser. The room was filled with the smoke of many cigarettes. From time to time, Janisary got up to look out of the window. Once he saw Tucson come after his horse. Janisary prepared to go downstairs, but Tucson didn't head out of town when he climbed in the saddle. Not many yards away Janisary saw Tench Crawford watching Smith.

By this time, Tucson had directed his pony along the cross street that passed the side entrance of the hotel, the movement taking him out of Janisary's line of vision. Janisary reached for his high-peaked sombrero, buckled on a six-shooter and left the room.

He was halfway to the staircase when he met Tench Crawford. Crawford said, low-voiced, "No need you goin' out, chief. Smith is just taking his horse to the hotel stables."

Janisary's face lighted up. "That means he's stayin' here tonight, then." He turned back into the room, followed by Crawford, closed the door and said, "Learn anything?"

Crawford shook his head. "Not much. Smith has got in with a couple of other cowpokes. Them and some other fellers have been playin' stud all afternoon in the Oasis Saloon. I heard Smith tell 'em he was goin' to quit playin' for a spell. Said he'd put his pony away and join the game after supper. The cards was sure runnin' against him."

"Smith see you?"

Crawford nodded. "Didn't start anythin', though. Sort of laughed. I spoke to him as pleasant as I could, told him I was sorry it happened and that I should have knowed better than to lose my temper when I wa'n't certain it was my gun or not."

"Good. Don't hang around him too much, or he may notice he's bein' tailed."

Crawford laughed. "If he don't notice things any better than he plays stud, he won't even see me. Them two cowpokes he picked up with were sure takin' him down the line for his roll."

Janisary nodded. "He'll sell me that gun all right."

Crawford started for the bottle on the dresser, but Janisary shook his head. "No more drinking, Tench. Get out now and keep an eye on Smith. On your way through the hotel office, tell the clerk I'd like to have my horse saddled right after supper."

Crawford nodded and left the room, closing the door behind him. Janisary removed his hat and gun and picked up a newspaper to pass the time.

When next he looked out the window, he saw the sun was setting. Long shadows stretched across the street. Window panes on the opposite side reflected red in the dying light. Here and there along the street, oil lamps commenced to shine from buildings. Dusk settled like a mauve mist over Lobo Tanks, stayed but a few minutes and gave way before the enfolding darkness.

Janisary descended to the hotel dining room, ate supper and returned to his room to await Crawford's return. He sat in darkness for a time, then lighted the lamp on the dresser. When next he glanced at his watch, the hands pointed to nine-fifteen. Three-quarters of an hour passed. Now and then one of the hotel guests walked along the hall to his room. A door banged shut; then, except for the usual noises from the street, all was silent again.

Janisary's impatient humming droned like an angry hornet, filling his room with sound. He smoked cigarette after cigarette. In the hallway, outside his door, someone stumbled along the passage, singing drunkenly in an off-key baritone. Janisary swore softly under his breath and was relieved when the singing ended with the slamming of a door.

At each step he heard, Janisary expected to see Crawford, but it was after eleven o'clock before the door opened and Crawford appeared. He closed the door carefully behind him.

Janisary's gun was at his right hip, ready for action if need be. He said shortly to Crawford, "Well?"

Crawford said, "Smith's in his room."

"What's he been doin' the last few hours?"

"After he stabled the pony he walked around town for a spell, then ate his supper at a joint down the line a ways. From there he headed straight back to the Oasis. The poker game was still on. One of them punchers Smith had picked up in the afternoon kept bellyachin' about bein' hungry. While he went to get his supper, Smith took his place at the table. By the time he got back, the other puncher was ready to eat—"

"What is this," Janisary cut in impatiently, "a description of a diet kitchen—?"

"You ask me what happened," Crawford said doggedly.

"All right, get on with your story. Smith been playin' poker all evening?"

"All evening. And them two punchers besides, though they pulled out of the game about an hour before Smith. I heard 'em say somethin' about going down to that gamblin' house and tryin' their luck at faro for a spell. They was plumb disgusted. Smith had won back the money he'd lost to 'em durin' the afternoon and was goin' strong. They left and Smith went on playin' with four other fellows, until just a short spell ago. He had a bunch of jack when he left."

"Smith see you hangin' around?"

"Just once, I reckon. Most of the time I was watchin' him through a window in the Oasis."

"Smith is in his room now, eh?"

Crawford nodded. "I saw him come upstairs just a few minutes back. I don't know what room he's got, but before I come here I saw a light shinin' under No. 18. That's on that hallway that runs crosswise to the one you're on."

Janisary nodded. "Nice work, Tench. All right, I'll go see him before he crawls in the hay."

"Want me to go with you?"

Janisary shook his head. "No, I ain't expecting any trouble. If he sees you, he might get on the prod. I'll handle it. If he's had a winnin' streak it may cost more than I figured, but—hell! I'll be back with that gun, plumb pronto, Tench. You've never seen the Scorpion fail yet, have you?"

Crawford matched his chief's smile with a nasty grin. "And I ain't expectin' to, neither," he said.

# 5

# "You're Cornered, Smith!"

Tucson had removed his boots and was stretched, hands clasped behind his head, on the bed, a cigarette dangling from one corner of his mouth. Excepting his hat, he hadn't removed his other clothing. Thought, speculation, was as responsible as the curling cigarette smoke for his narrowed eyes.

To the left of the bed was a straight-backed chair on the back of which his guns and belts were hung. Near the chair was a dresser on which an oil lamp burned. To Tucson's right, the shade was drawn to the bottom of the window. Tucson lay facing the door when the knock came.

A strange expression flitted across Tucson's bronzed features, but he said, easily enough, "Come in."

The door swung open. Janisary entered, closed it quietly behind him. His eyes darted at Tucson, shifted swiftly to the guns beyond Tucson's reach, noted the weapon for which he had come near the lamp on the dresser. Something of satisfaction crossed Janisary's face. Tucson wasn't missing this. He looked at Janisary, level-eyed, across the foot of the bed, deciding the man appeared thoroughly capable.

Janisary said, "Your name is Smith, isn't it?"

Tucson smiled thinly. "That's what my Dad told me a long spell back, I had a habit of taking his word."

Janisary nodded curtly. "You're the man I want to see—on business."

Tucson yawned. "I don't have any regular business hours, so go ahead. What's on your mind?"

"I've come to buy a gun from you."

"My guns aren't for sale."

"This particular gun is."

51

Tucson raised himself to a sitting position. "I take it you're a friend of Crawford's."

"You take it correct, Smith. My name's Lockhart. That gun was stolen from me—"

"Those your initials on the weapon?"

Janisary nodded. "I sent Crawford to get it. The damn fool lost his head. I reckon you're due an apology—"

"Forget it." Tucson waved one careless hand. "Y'know," he continued carelessly, "at one time or another I think I've met most of the Speede Packing Company's cattle buyers. I never heard of one named Gage."

Janisary laughed mirthlessly. "I see you've been looking at the hotel register, asking questions."

Tucson smiled. "I guess I'm a curious sort of a cuss. But, you were speaking about a gun, Gage. . . ."

"Lockhart's the name."

Tucson yawned. "All right, suit yourself."

"I always do. I'm here on business—private business."

"Why don't you say 'official business' and be done with it?" Tucson grinned.

Janisary's features tightened. He wasn't at all sure but what this lean, red-headed cowboy was making fun of him. "Look here," he said at last, "there's no need of us fencing around this way. You've got my gun. I want it. What's your price?"

Tucson said quietly, "Proof of ownership. Give me that and you can have the gun."

Janisary stiffened. This cowboy was proving stubborn. "I haven't got time to go into that," he said shortly. "What's your price—in cash?"

"I told you the gun wasn't for sale."

"A hundred dollars gold says it is."

Tucson laughed. "A hundred dollars gold is a blame liar, Gage or Lockhart, or whatever your name is. I don't need your money."

Janisary commenced to believe that fact. He whipped out his right-hand gun, covered Tucson. "I hate to do this, cowboy," and there was a certain amount of genuine regret in the tones, "but you force me to it. I've got my reasons for wanting that gun. It doesn't concern you at all. I'll raise my offer to one hundred fifty. That's the last word. Take the money or—"

The gun tilted slightly, Janisary's voice went hard, "—or the consequences," he finished. "I'm goin' to have that gun. I won't shoot unless you force me to it. I don't want a ruckus." He repeated, "I'm goin' to have that gun."

Tucson rose quickly, swung his feet off the bed and stood up—on the side away from his own guns.

Janisary went on, "Be sensible. You're cornered, Smith. It's all my own way. You wouldn't have a chance. Do you want the money or don't you?"

Tucson took one step forward. Janisary's gun tilted.

Janisary said, hard-voiced, "Stand over near that

window. I want you as far from your hardware as possible. You'll think clearer, that way."

"The gun isn't for sale," Tucson said, as he backed toward the window.

Janisary moved farther into the room, following Tucson as if suspecting some trick on the part of the cowboy. Only two yards separated them now.

"Keep your hands high," Janisary continued grimly, "that'll help your thought processes too. If I have to I'll shoot and take that gun anyway. But I'm offering money—good money—for the gun. What's it to be, yellow gold or hot lead? I'll give you half a minute to make up your mind."

Tucson remained silent. A queer humming sound arose from Janisary's lips while he waited. The two men eyed each other steadily. Tucson said finally, "Quit that damn humming. How do you expect a man to think?"

Janisary smiled thinly. "Your time's just about up, anyway. Talk fast or—" He allowed the words to remain unfinished.

And then from behind him came a new voice, "Shall I let him have it, Tucson? Don't move, you coyote!"

Janisary's face tightened. His dark eyes above the high cheekbones moved swiftly to the corners, then as though following the eyes he lowered his gun and turned slowly around to locate the voice.

There, protruding from beneath the bed was

Lullaby Joslin's head and a gun in Lullaby's fist. "Get his gun, Tucson!"

Again Janisary smiled thinly. He handed over the gun without a protest. His voice was admirably steady as he said, "I reckon I'll have to pay a higher price than I figured on, Smith."

"I wouldn't be surprised," Tucson said dryly, "if you had to pay a damn high price."

"Anything you say," Janisary offered.

Lullaby scrambled up from under the bed, holding his gun. "You keep him covered, Tucson. I'll run through his pockets and see if he's got any right to the name of Gage or Lockhart, either one—"

"Now look here—" Janisary commenced protest.

"Shut your trap," Lullaby growled. He holstered his gun and standing behind Janisary, reached for the man's hip pocket. Before he could touch it, the door had swung back and Crawford stood there, a gun in each hand.

"Up with 'em—stick 'em up!" Crawford rasped.

Janisary stepped quickly to one side. "Good work, Tench," he said earnestly, reaching for the gun in Tucson's hand. Tucson stepped back. For some reason he was laughing. Janisary stopped short. Something was wrong.

"—and I thought I better come and see what was taking you so long, Gage," Crawford was saying triumphantly. "Reckon I just got here in time and—"

He gulped suddenly as something round and hard was jabbed with no small force against the small of his back.

"Drop them guns, you measly scut. Quick!"

Crawford's guns clattered to the floor. His face went ashen. Stony's voice continued, "Now move into that room, quick!"

Crawford stumbled into the room, followed by Stony, who closed and locked the door. Then he grinned, "The damn fool was so busy sneaking up here that he didn't hear me right behind."

Janisary laughed contemptuously. "You've bulled it again, Tench."

Crawford said sullenly, "How about yourself?"

"I'll get what I'm after," Janisary snapped angrily. He turned to Tucson, "Look here, Smith, I don't know what your game is—"

"That makes it unanimous," Tucson grinned.

"—but I've got money. I'll pay what you ask for that gun. We seem to have got off on the wrong foot, all around—"

"Chop it," Tucson said, suddenly stern. "Gage, you and your coyote friend get over against that wall—no, not near my guns. I'm not that easy. Stay near the door."

Tucson plucked the shells from Janisary's gun, dropped them on the floor and passed the gun to Janisary. "I'm weary holdin' that weapon. I reckon my pards can cover you two." He sat down on the bed.

Janisary and Crawford backed angrily toward the door. Stony stood grinning with leveled gun at one side, Lullaby at the other. Tucson continued, "Lullaby, go through Gage's pockets."

Lullaby complied. The pockets revealed, in addition to a considerable sum of money, very little else of interest. Lullaby placed the money and other contents back in Janisary's pockets. "No letters addressed to a Gage or a Lockhart—no papers of any kind to tell us if he's a liar or not."

Tucson nodded, somewhat disappointedly. "Gage," he said, "you better get somebody else to do your trackin' from now on. Your man, Crawford, is plumb clumsy. Good Cripes! It seemed like I saw him every time I turned around. Sort of expected one of you might come after that gun tonight, so we laid a little trap for you. You walked right into it."

Janisary laughed easily. "All right, it's a horse on me. Now you got us, what you going to do about it?"

Tucson was forced to smile at the coolness of the man. The fellow had nerve, no doubt about that. He said bluntly, "Gage—or Lockhart, if you want it that way—what's your game?"

Janisary frowned, then said with an appearance of frankness, "I'll come clean, Smith. The name really is Lockhart. I'm gambling to make a pile of money, but I'm not saying how. It's a straight deal, though; I'd just as soon tell you, only if I did there's a gang that would spoil things for me."

"I'm not asking for details of your business affairs," Tucson said. "But there's something about this gun business I don't understand. You offered plenty more than it's worth—"

"Oh, that—" Janisary laughed carelessly. "I was in the wrong there. It made me mad when Crawford didn't get it. After all, I always thought a heap of that gun. You know how it is, when you get in the habit of carrying a gun you like particularly?"

Tucson was forced to acknowledge the truth of that argument.

Janisary continued. "I'll raise my price to anything within reason."

"Proof of ownership is all I'm askin'," Tucson repeated once more.

Janisary smiled. "You don't trust me, do you?"

"Would you trust me after what's happened?" Tucson countered.

"I guess maybe not," Janisary conceded, then, as though struck with a sudden thought, he said, "Look here, Smith, I haven't had a good look at that gun. I just heard that a gun with my initials was on sale and I jumped to conclusions. Would you let me look at it?"

Tucson was about to refuse, then reconsidered. He crossed over, got the gun, slipped out the loaded cylinder and handed the useless weapon to Janisary. He didn't miss the look of disappointment that crept into Janisary's eyes when he lifted out the cylinder.

Janisary took the gun, cocked it, squinted through the barrel against the light, turned it over and over, scanning every inch of its steel and walnut surface. Finally, he handed it back to Tucson.

Tucson said, "Satisfied?"

Janisary shook his head. "I'd like to see that cylinder, if you don't mind."

"What you lookin' for?" Tucson asked curiously.

Janisary considered, then said slowly, "You'll have to take me on faith, Smith. Let me see that cylinder. Maybe—just maybe—I may be able to cut you in on something. I can't tell you anything now, though—not until I've had a look at that cylinder."

Tucson frowned, pondered the question. He could think of no particular reason for refusing. Yet he didn't quite trust the man. Janisary met his gaze steadily; he hadn't quite planned what he would do if the contents of the cylinder proved important to him. Perhaps, make a rush for it, strive to escape; either that or make some sort of deal with Smith and the other two. The main thing, right now, was to get his hands on the cylinder.

"Go ahead," Tucson conceded with a short laugh, passing the bit of gun mechanism to Janisary. Janisary's eyes lighted eagerly as he examined the cylinder, turning it over and over. It contained five full loads and one empty shell upon which the hammer had rested.

Coolly, Janisary plucked out the loads and the empty shell, dropped them on the bed. The cylinder followed them. Tucson, watching closely for any sort of hostile move, started to protest when Janisary reached to a hip pocket, but Janisary produced only a small clasp knife and opened it.

Lullaby growled, "Don't let that knife slip, hombre. Somebody might be hurt—and I know it won't be me."

Janisary's dark eyes slipped sidewise to glance at Lullaby. He smiled contemptuously, knowing he was safe from attack, "Go ahead and shoot—and be damned to you," he invited carelessly.

Tucson, Lullaby and Stony were watching closely. Crawford was fully as curious, interested, as the three. He craned his neck to watch Janisary's movements. Janisary examined the empty shell, tossed it back on the bed. Then, one by one, he employed his knife blade to remove the leaden slugs from the ends of the cartridges. Tucson noticed that the man was breathing a trifle faster now; the humming that left his lips spoke of suppressed excitement.

One by one, Janisary emptied the shells of their tiny grains of black powder into his hand, squinted into the shells. As he worked, despite his effort to maintain a "poker face", Tucson could see that the man was experiencing disappointment—or was it relief? Tucson couldn't be certain. He said,

"They look like ordinary forty-five ca'tridges to me, Gage—or Lockhart."

Janisary's reply was sarcastic, "You don't say so." He tossed the last shell on the bed, shrugged his shoulders and forced a smile, "I reckon, Smith, I better tell you what I was looking for. You see, I've been working on a new formula for an explosive. Been trying it in my own shells. If the secret got out, somebody else would reap the result of my work. As it is—" he shrugged his shoulders, gesturing toward the gun and empty shells, "—I made a mistake. The gun isn't even mine—"

Tucson eyed the man steadily. Janisary met that doubting gaze and laughed. "I don't want your gun, Smith. I wouldn't give you a plugged peso for it now. Sorry I put you to all this trouble."

"Are you?" Tucson's voice was cold, unbelieving.

"You don't believe me, do you?" Janisary laughed easily.

"Not none," Tucson said flatly.

Janisary smiled, "All right, let's hear your version. What do you think I had in mind?"

"You were looking for something—something you didn't find."

"I told you about my new formula for an explosive powder. I thought at first this was my gun, but I'm sure now—"

"That the gun didn't contain what you were looking for?"

"That it's not even my gun."

"Anyway," Tucson smiled coldly, "that's your story—"

"And he's stuck with it," Stony put in. "I'd say, offhand, somebody was a first-rate liar. How do you feel, pard?"

Tucson nodded shortly.

Janisary cast an amused glance at the Three Mesquiteers. "All right, don't believe me, then. I don't give a damn one way or the other. Smith, the next move is up to you."

Tucson couldn't help but admire the man's nonchalance. He scratched his head, pondering, "Damn it, Gage," he confessed at last, "I don't see what I'm goin' to do with you—and your friend, Crawford."

Janisary laughed softly. "It's up to you. I can't see where we have any real fight. You won the last hand." He repeated, "It's up to you. If you have any doubts as to my honesty, you might send for the deputy sheriff. However, I'll tell you frankly, there's very little he could hold me on. You can't place a charge against me for entering. I knocked and came in here with your permission. True, we had a slight difficulty, but what of that? I haven't stolen anything of yours. I even offered to pay a good price for a gun I wanted. If you think you have a grievance against me, we can come to any sort of settlement you suggest. I'll be forced to stay in Lobo Tanks a week or more, until my present business is finished, and if you can't decide now what you want to do—"

Tucson raised one hand for silence. The brazen assurance of the man was disarming. Tucson was really puzzled to determine what to do with him and Crawford. He disliked the idea of calling in the law to settle his arguments. Besides, there didn't seem to be any particular argument. Gage— or Lockhart—whatever his name was—had admitted being mistaken, had apologized for the trouble he had caused. The man *might* be speaking truth, though some extra sense of Tucson's insisted on denying that. Tucson scowled.

Janisary continued again, impatiently, "If you don't mind, Smith, I'd like to get to bed—either here, in my room, or—if you insist on calling a law officer, at the jail—"

Tucson smiled, waved a careless hand, "Get out," he said shortly. "I ain't got any more business with you. Only remember, next time go slow before you try sticking me up—"

Janisary lifted a deprecating hand. "Sorry it turned out that way. Maybe if we have a drink all around we'll feel better. I've a bottle in my room—"

"We're not drinking with you," Tucson said flatly.

Janisary shrugged his lean shoulders. "Suit yourself. I can see you don't trust to my word. Well, we all make mistakes—"

Lullaby cut in, "You and Crawford made enough for a dozen men tonight."

Janisary's dark eyes held mocking lights. "Judge not lest ye be judged," he quoted. "Perhaps we'll be better friends before I leave Lobo Tanks. *Quien sabe?* And *adios*."

He turned leisurely and, followed by a much relieved Crawford, opened the door and sauntered out to the hall. The door closed behind them. Janisary heard it open slightly immediately, judged that Smith or one of his friends was watching him.

He didn't speak to Crawford as the two made the turn in the hall, their steps unhurried—though it required Janisary's hand on his companion's arm to prevent Crawford from breaking into a run. They entered Janisary's room, quietly closed and locked the door. Crawford's heavy features were bathed in nervous perspiration.

"That," Janisary announced with a slow breath of relief, "was a damn close squeak, Tench."

"You ain't tellin' me a thing I don't know." Crawford looked limp and drawn. "What now?"

"We're moving out of here just as fast as we can go. My horse is waiting, saddled, at the back of the hotel, isn't it?"

Crawford nodded, adding, "Mine's at the hitch-rack near the side entrance. You didn't find anything in that gun—?"

"You saw for yourself. Nothing there. My mind's relieved on that point. I didn't get the gun, Tench, but I got the information I wanted."

"You think fast, chief."

"The Scorpion has to think fast. I bluffed those cowpokes, and got away with it, but I don't know how long the bluff will hold. That redhead, Smith, is too damn shrewd. He didn't believe me. Before long, he'll be wanting to talk to me again. We're drifting. We'll meet Porky. I'll tell him to stick around Lobo Tanks a spell and get a line on Smith and the other two."

While he talked, Janisary was buckling on his other gun. Swiftly he tightened his belt, donned his steeple-crowned sombrero.

"Ready?" he asked.

Crawford answered nervously that he'd been ready for a long time. "Ain't you afraid they might hear us go out?"

Janisary smiled confidently, with one breath extinguished the flame in the chimney of the oil lamp, then crossed to the window and put up the shade. A second later he was raising the sash, swearing under his breath when it stuck a trifle. He glanced in both directions along the darkened street. A soft, almost noiseless song formed on his lips. There wasn't a soul in sight. He thrust his feet through the opening, dropped lightly to the wooden awning just below his window, then turned and cautioned Crawford to move quietly.

A moment later, Crawford stood at his side, shivering a trifle with nervous strain.

Janisary quietly closed the window from the outside. A moment later the two had dropped to the street and were climbing into saddles. There wasn't anyone but themselves in the vicinity of the hotel. The horses' walking hoofs made not a sound in the dust of the road as the Scorpion and his henchman melted into darkness.

# 6

## Tucson Draws a Stiff Gun

Stony quietly came back into the room, closed the door. "I heard 'em enter Gage's room," he stated, "so I reckon they're in for the night."

Tucson frowned. "That doesn't prove anythin', Stony. If Gage wanted to, he could get away—"

Lullaby said, "You didn't feel right about lettin' 'em go, did you, Tucson?"

Tucson shook his head. "Not none. I had a hunch to hold 'em—but what in time could I hold him on? He might have been speaking the truth. We turned the tables on 'em neat. If he had been on the square and had just lost his head temporarily, it would just have been rubbin' it in, if I'd had him arrested. I really couldn't prove nothin' important against him. He'd have provided bail and left anyway, when he was ready.

I couldn't have had him held indefinitely—"

"You believe what he told us about that secret formula for a new powder?" Lullaby asked.

Tucson shook his head. "Not none. I wish I could dope it out, though. He was plumb interested in gettin' hold of that gun. Once he'd looked at it and examined the shells, he sort of lost interest. Why?"

"You tell me and I'll tell you," Stony grinned. "Damn if he wasn't a cool customer. We didn't shake his nerve none. Dang it, and I was hopin' for some *real* excitement too."

Tucson picked up the empty shells on the bed, looked them over closely and sighed when he put them down. "Now, what in time was that feller lookin' for?"

Lullaby said slowly, "Once I heard of a feller smugglin' diamonds inside his shells."

Tucson nodded. "I thought of somethin' like that, but it's a cinch Gage didn't find any diamonds. I was watchin' close every move he made. Dammit, I still feel like I'd let somethin' important slip through my fingers—"

"And I," Lullaby stated grouchily, "felt he was laughin' at me when I started ribbin' him about makin' mistakes. What was that line he threw at me?"

"Sounded like 'lusty be judge'," Stony supplied.

"It don't make sense," Lullaby shook his head.

"Where you're concerned," Stony grinned, "nothin' does."

Tucson wasn't paying any particular attention to the pair. He reached over on the bed, picked up the empty cylinder and base pin, placed the cylinder in the gun and clicked the pin into place. Idly, frowning, he crossed one thumb over the hammer, drew it back, let it down easily again. Two or three times he did this. His frown deepened. "Somethin'," he muttered, "is tryin' to dovetail. What the devil—"

Stony cut in, "You say somethin', Tucson?"

Tucson grinned. "Just talkin' to myself."

"What's the matter?"

"That's what I want to know," Tucson answered. Again he drew the hammer back, let it down, then hefted the gun in his hand. "Damn if this don't feel like my own forty-five single-actions," he said, half absent-mindedly. "Same balance, same grip. 'Bout the only thing, the hammer pulls back a mite stiffer'n my guns. Reckon it ain't been used as much as mine, or mebbe the spring was stiffer in the first place—"

He broke off suddenly, eyes narrowing in speculation. "S'help me, I'll betcha that—" Again he stopped.

"What?" Lullaby demanded. "You got somethin'?"

Tucson laughed. "Just maybe, cowboy. I think —I *think* I have. Somethin' that Gage missed. Uh-huh, I don't feel quite so dumb now. I'd like to put somethin' over on that smooth hombre. He was too satisfied, too self-contented. I felt I was missin' somethin'—somethin' that he *did* miss—"

"What the devil?" Stony crowded close, Lullaby at his shoulder.

"Knew that spring was too stiff," Tucson laughed softly. His clasp knife was out now, one blade opened and working at the small screws that secured the walnut stock in place—one at the bottom of the butt, two more back of and below the hammer. The screws came out in swift turns, dropped, one by one, into Tucson's hand. A moment later, the walnut grip was slipped off, dropped on the bed at Tucson's side.

Lullaby swore. Stony's voice shook with excitement: "What is it?"

There, folded in beneath the exposed mainspring of the gun, was a bit of paper!

Tucson laughed triumphantly. "You see—" starting to remove the paper, "—it's a plumb snug fit. This folded paper offered just enough resistance to make that hammer pull stiff. I'm sure glad that Gage hombre didn't notice this. I'd feel cheap as thunder if I thought I'd lost my feel for a gun—"

He dropped the folded length of paper on the bed, leaped to his feet, snapped orders at the other two, "Slope down to the street as fast as you can! As you go through the office, send the clerk up with the key to Gage's room. Maybe he's still here, but I sort of doubt it—got a hunch thataway. Cut Gage and Crawford off if you see them—"

"But—but," Stony stammered, "what's the idea? What's that paper—"

"Probably some writin' on that paper," Tucson jerked out. "We can't take time to look now. Gage was plumb interested in findin' it. I want to find him. He was too damn ready to let me have the gun, when he didn't find what he was lookin' for. Somethin's wrong. If he's still in his room, so much the better, but if he isn't—"

He didn't take time to say more, but seized one of his forty-fives and whirled out of the room, Stony and Lullaby close at his heels. They parted in the hallway, Tucson to look for Gage's room, Lullaby and Stony to go clattering down the stairs.

Tucson dashed around the corner in the hall, then realized he knew only approximately where Gage's room was located. He stopped short. No light showed beneath any of the doors. Tucson raised his voice reluctantly to call, "Gage! I say, Gage!"

Receiving no answer, he repeated the call. A sleepy voice from one of the rooms, grumblingly consigned him to a warmer climate. There came the sound of running footsteps on the stairway. A second later the hotel clerk bore into sight carrying a large brass key.

"What is it, Mr. Smith? What's the matter—"

"What number?" Tucson jerked out.

"Number Five—"

Tucson grabbed the key from the clerk's hand.

In the dim light of a lamp burning at the far end of the hall, he saw that No. 5 was next to the door before which he stood. Thrusting the key into No. 5 he turned it, shot back the snap lock. Holding his gun at ready, Tucson kicked open the door and leaped to one side.

All was dark and silent inside. Tucson said rather sheepishly, "I didn't exactly expect any shots, but I wasn't taking chances."

"But what—what—what—?" the clerk stammered.

Tucson brushed past, scratched a match, lighted the lamp on the dresser. The window shade was up, the window catch unlocked. Tucson flung up the window. Below in the street he saw Lullaby. Tucson called down, "See anythin' of him?"

"Not a sign," came Lullaby's reply.

At that moment Stony appeared below. "He's plumb gone, Tucson. The stable man says his horse has been saddled, waiting, since supper time."

"I ain't surprised," Tucson replied. "Come on up again."

He withdrew from the window. The clerk said dumbly, "Mr. Gage is gone. He didn't pay his bill. I might have known when he left word to have his horse saddled—say! what's the trouble anyway?"

"No trouble, I reckon," Tucson said easily. "I had somethin'. Gage wanted it. I just found it. I guess he must have thought it wa'n't any use waitin' for it any longer."

"I don't understand."

"It ain't clear in my mind yet, either," Tucson smiled grimly.

"But what about the hotel bill Gage owes?"

"That," Tucson said, "is your problem. You don't know any more about him than you told me?"

"Not a thing," the clerk said angrily. "It's a dirty trick, him running off this way and owing for a week—"

Tucson pushed past and started for his room. Several lodgers had emerged from rooms now and were questioning the clerk. Tucson reached his own room at the same time Lullaby and Stony appeared around the corner of the hall. The three entered the room, closed the door. Tucson waited a moment, then, suddenly, his jaw dropped.

Stony said, "What's wrong?"

Tucson pointed to the dismantled gun. "That paper that was hid in the gun—it's gone! I left it here on the bed—"

"Take it easy, pard," Lullaby chuckled. "I got it. You pulled out in such a hurry and—well, figurin' that paper might be important I slipped it into my pocket before I left. Not taking a chance of somebody grabbing it while we were out of the room."

Tucson laughed and reached for the paper which Lullaby produced. "Damn if you didn't give me a bad minute. Let's give a look at this paper."

The commotion in the hall had died away by this time. The clerk's footsteps were heard descending the stairs. The paper Tucson held was approximately 2¼ x 5 inches in size—probably a trifle less—and had been folded lengthwise to fit snugly beneath the flat, tapering mainspring in the butt of the gun. The paper was soiled and oil-stained but Tucson had no difficulty in deciphering the written words when he unfolded it. The writing had been done in lead pencil and read as follows:

*Twenty miles southwest of Malpaisaño, Roca Catedral. Tunnel to Valley of the Singing Scorpion at point where Catedral corners into San Federico Range, north side. Janisary holding us prisoner. Position desperate. Bring large armed force. Use utmost caution. Tunnel entrance guarded, well hidden by rocks and tall plant growth.*

*Pete*

With the other two crowding close, Tucson reread the message aloud, then looked up at Lullaby and Stony. Stony gave a low whoop of delight, "We're headed for some *real* excitement, Lullaby!"

Lullaby said sourly, "I suppose so. But, shucks, we don't know—"

"I know where the San Federicos are," Tucson cut in. "They're part of the Sierra Madres—across the border in Old Mexico. That Roca Catedral—Spanish for Cathedral Rock—is strange to me. 'Course, there's a hundred Cathedral Rocks scattered around—both sides of the border. They're all about the same—big, queer-shaped rock formations that look like churches—"

"Who's Janisary?" Stony put in.

Tucson shook his head. "What's more important is—who's Pete?" He frowned, "Seems to me like I've heard of a Valley of the Singing Scorpion, some place. Never reckoned it was anythin' else but Injun legend—"

"Say," Lullaby interrupted, "Didn't we hear some place about a Mex bandit called the Singin' Scorpion?"

Tucson nodded. "I was just thinking about that. Both governments have been tryin' to capture him for some time—"

"Tucson—" Stony again, "—you and me rode through a Mex town called Malpaisaño one time —quite a few years back—"

"I remember it," Tucson said. "Heap bad town —tough."

Stony grinned widely. "And we're goin' back and see just how tough it is, ain't we?" eagerly.

"Pull up, cowboy, pull up," Tucson laughed softly. "This isn't any of our business."

Surprisingly Lullaby put in, "I ain't so sure of that. I keep thinkin' of this Pete that wrote that note. Sounds like he needs help bad—"

Stony gave a howl of delight. "Ol', peaceful-hate-to-fight Joslin. You're a lousy bluff, Lullaby.

You're just as anxious as me to look into this."

Lullaby Joslin looked sheepish and said, "I keep thinkin' of this Pete hombre. And why was Gage—or Lockhart—so interested in this gun. Damn his hide, he knew somethin' was up. He wanted to prevent word gettin' through to Pete's friends, but he wa'n't shrewd enough to look in the gun butt—"

"I," Tucson suddenly broke in disgustedly, "am one simple, mule-headed, dumb rannie!"

"How come the outburst?" Stony asked curiously.

Tucson said, grim-voiced, "'Member how that Gage hombre had a sort of habit of singin' to himself all the time?" At the others' affirmative nods he continued, "I've got a hunch we let the Singin' Scorpion slip through our fingers."

Stony whistled softly. Lullaby groaned, "And I thought I was smart tryin' to rib him about makin' mistakes. Tucson! Stony! That slippery cuss was laughin' at us every minute."

"You're right," Tucson nodded ruefully.

"Think we better take his trail?" eagerly from Stony.

Tucson shook his head. "He and Crawford are too far away by this time. But we'll catch up with him, we'll catch up with him eventual." Tucson swore softly under his breath, "Oh, hell, we may be shootin' a mile wide of the mark. The fact remains though that the gun reached this town.

75

Gage—or Lockhart—say, mebbe his name is Janisary—good Cripes! how can you keep up with a hombre like that?"

"Ask a coupla governments and a heap of law officers, if what we've heard about the Singin' Scorpion is correct," Stony advised, sober-faced.

Tucson, from his sitting position on the bed, leaned over and drew his boots on. "You two wait here," he said, standing up, "I'll be right back."

A minute later he had entered the office of the hotel. The clerk was propped on a stool behind his desk, eyes closed in slumber. It was after midnight. Looking through, into the bar, Tucson saw only a few men standing there. The bartender was starting to close up.

Tucson spoke to the clerk. The man awoke with a jerk, gazed sleepily at Tucson. Tucson said, "Did your man Gage come back and pay his bill yet?"

The clerk yawned, the question penetrating slowly his slumber-beclouded senses. Finally a light of anger shone dully in his blinking eyes. "Say, did you wake me up just to ask that?"

Tucson laughed. "No, but I wanted to see you fully awake. Now listen close. Do you know a man named Pete around here?"

The clerk laughed sarcastically. "I know of a dozen in Lobo Tanks—a dozen anyway. Which one do you want?"

Tucson said patiently, "I'm not sure yet. The last two initials of the man I want are E. L.— Pete E. L. Think hard."

The clerk growled something unintelligible and shook his head. "I don't know—let me see, there's Pete Lewis—he runs the general store—and Pete Lazare—owns the saddle shop. There's a Pete Ligget works for the Oasis Saloon—swamper, old man, crippled with rheumatics—"

"I don't guess you know the one I mean. Think hard."

The clerk rubbed his bloodshot eyes. "I am thinkin' hard. Hell! This is a good-sized town. Lord knows how many Petes there are with initial L's—say, wait a minute—" his sleepy eyes widened, "you're here on official business, aren't you? Might you be meanin' Pete Lockhart?"

Tucson's heart gave a leap. His voice was steady, "This man, Gage, you had stayin' here, told me his name was Lockhart."

"T'hell he did!" unbelievingly. "Well, he's a liar. Leastwise, he ain't the Lockhart I'm thinkin' of—"

"What one you thinkin' of?"

"Young Pete Lockhart. I heard he was in some sort of trouble down in Mexico. Ever hear of the Singin' Scorpion?"

Tucson nodded. "Mex bandit by that name, ain't there? Yes."

"The Scorpion nearly killed Pete Lockhart's

77

father a week back. We was real excited about that for a couple of days, but you know, those things die down. I'd almost forgotten—"

"Where's this Lockhart man to be found?"

"Why, out to his ranch—the R-Cross-L."

Something else clicked in Tucson's mind, then dovetailed with his memory. "I knew a feller used to rod a R-Cross-L outfit in this neck of the range—name of Buck Patton."

"Sure, he still works for Rufus Lockhart. Say what were you—?"

Here a new voice broke in at Tucson's back: "Tucson Smith! Why, you ornery, slab-sided, cow-hocked imp of the devil! Where did you come from?"

Tucson whirled around, his face lighting with pleasure, "Buck Patton! Give me your hand. Damn my eyes it's good to see you again. Where did *you* come from?"

The two men were laughing, gripping hands. Buck Patton was a leathery-faced individual with a close-cropped grayish mustache. "—and I'd just dropped into the hotel bar for a drink before it closed up," he was explaining. "Happened to look into the office and saw you standing here. What you doin'?"

"Ramblin'—"

"As usual, eh?"

"You have to come to town for your nightcaps?"

Patton explained, his face falling a trifle, "I

been ridin' on Rufe Lockhart's business. He was hurt, you know. Damn nigh murdered."

"I heard somethin' about it."

"Just gettin' back. Lobo Tanks was right on my trail. . . . Say, Stony Brooke still with you? I suppose he is, from what I've been readin' in the papers. You boys sure turned into outlaw busters. Got a new man ridin' at your side, ain't you? Feller name of Joslin—"

"And a hell-bent lead slinger if there ever was one—"

"If what I been readin' is true, you need him. You did a nice job over Arapahoe City way. That Whistlin' Skull business—"

"Say, Mr. Patton," the hotel clerk broke in, "Mr. Smith was asking about young Pete."

Patton's features tightened. "What do you know about Pete, Tucson?"

"Maybe nothing," Tucson said promptly. "Maybe plenty. Come up to my room where we can talk. Stony's up there. You can meet Lullaby Joslin too."

Much to the clerk's disappointment, Patton accepted the invitation. "I'll betcha," the clerk mused, as the two men disappeared up the stairway, "that the official business Smith mentioned today, has got somethin' to do with young Pete Lockhart."

# 7

# Headed for Trouble!

Morning sunlight streamed through the windows of the big dining room at the R-Cross-L ranch house. Rufus Lockhart sat impatiently waiting at the oak dining table on which were the remnants of breakfast. Lockhart looked pale and drawn, his face was thin and white and creased with deep lines of worry. Even his huge frame, propped with pillows in his chair, seemed wasted and bony.

While he waited, a Mexican boy with a healing wound at one side of his head, entered and removed the breakfast dishes, set out a box of cigars, glasses and a bottle of whisky. "The Señor Buck an' his frien's is wait'," the Mexican boy said.

"You tell Buck," Rufus Lockhart growled, "that that idea ain't original with him. I been waitin' too—a damn long time. Him and his doctor's orders. Bah!"

The Mexican boy hurried out. An instant later Buck Patton entered, followed by Tucson, Stony and Lullaby, and introduced the three. Lockhart surveyed the trio from beneath his shaggy eyebrows and liked what he saw.

"So you're the Three Mesquiteers I been hearin'

about, eh? You've done some nice work in the Southwest country. Buck tells me you got a good piece of reward money for recoverin' that Government gold. Seems like I read in the paper where you three was going to get an outfit and settle down. There was a fourth feller, too— Guadalupe Kid, he was called. . . . Hell's bells! Sit down, grab a chair, a drink and a smoke. Get comfortable. We got talkin' to do."

The invitation was accepted. Tucson said laughingly as he found a seat at the table, "Guadalupe's lookin' up an outfit for us. He thought he knew of a spread that could be bought reasonable over in east Arizona. He was headin' that way, anyway, to visit a sister of his. We'll know later if the place is worth lookin' at. Meanwhile, I reckon it was just luck brought us down this way, Mr. Lockhart, to stumble into your troubles."

Lockhart flashed a look of gratitude at Tucson for coming so quickly to the business of the visit. "I'm beginning to think," he said earnestly, "that God himself brought you ramblin' this way. If Buck had been on his job he'd brought you here last night—"

"The doctor said you was to take it easy—" Patton began.

"Rot!" Lockhart growled, "You and your doctor's orders. You'd think I was a yearlin' the way I been nursed along. Nothin's wrong."

"You lost a heap of blood and had a narrow escape," Patton said.

"The blood's buildin' up fast. The wound's nigh healed. I'll be ridin' before long," Lockhart snapped. "For once, Janisary failed. Meanwhile—" He broke off, then, "Tucson, Buck has told me about you getting Pete's gun and what happened after, but I'd like to hear it from your own lips."

Tucson repeated the story in brief detail, ending, "I sure feel foolish lettin' the Scorpion slip through my fingers thataway."

Lockhart nodded. "He's fooled plenty of good men in his time. Slippery as an eel, Janisary is. It must have been him, all right. Your description of the man tallies—especially that humming of his. It's an old habit. You see, he was a decent hombre once. I called him friend. I knew he had a wild streak, but didn't think it was anythin' more. He was quite a bit younger than me. It just happened we fell in love with the same girl—my boy Pete's mother. I married her. Janisary never got over that. In those days I owned an outfit in west New Mexico, before Pete's mother died. I thought—" and Lockhart's voice broke a trifle, "that Janisary would forget the old grudge, then, but he didn't—"

"I reckon he's plumb bad," Stony put in.

Lockhart cleared his throat and nodded. "You don't realize how bad. He's raided all along the border, stole cows and horses right and left.

Buck and I caught him red-handed stealing stock on my old spread once. I could have put him in the penitentiary then. Like a damn fool I didn't. I wanted him to have another chance. We let him go. That's over five years ago."

Lockhart broke off to ask Patton to pour "a neat two fingers of bourbon." Patton obeyed instructions, filled the others' glasses. Lockhart continued.

"I never realized until the night Janisary came here and tried to kill me that he and the Scorpion were the same. He admitted it then."

"We've heard of the Scorpion, of course," Tucson said, "but just what is his game?"

Lockhart said, "He's got a bad crew of outlaws following him. He pretends to be a Mexican revolutionist, but he's a bandit, pure and simple—"

"Not so pure and not so simple, if you ask me," Patton put in. "Law officers on both sides of the border have tried to get him. Somehow, just about the time they think they have him trapped, he disappears—just like he'd vanished into thin air. He's a ghost!"

"He's a fiend," Lockhart said, cold-voiced. "I've talked to Mexicans who've seen him, or claimed to. They say he's a devil with the voice of an angel. Probably that's a lot of talk, but that's what I hear. I knew years ago he was smart— more than average intelligence. A brain that's like the crack of a whip. Even in his younger days he was greased lightning with his guns—six-shooter or rifle—and plumb accurate. Lord knows, he must have improved since then—"

"Smart," Patton growled, "look how he fooled me, imitatin' Rufe's voice that night he was here. I'd seen him, years ago of course, but I never thought he'd have the nerve to come right to the R-Cross-L, even if he had sent word to Rufe once, that eventually he'd kill him."

"Janisary outguessed me," Lockhart confessed reluctantly. "I never dreamed he'd come here to carry out his plans. Then, that night he entered the room, behind me, it flashed on me all of a sudden, who it was. But that's the way he works. Plumb sudden and slippery."

"We trailed him," Patton said, "but he slipped away. We caught up with his Yaquis, just across the border." His face darkened. "It was a finish fight. I lost two men. Two more were wounded. My worst disappointment was to learn that Janisary wasn't in the fight. He'd been miles away at the time. But that's how he is. It's like fightin' the air to put a hand on him. He's a ghost, I tell you."

"I reckon," and Tucson smiled wryly, "it's a good thing I didn't have to cross guns with Mister Janisary. Well, mebbe he'll have another chance."

Lockhart said eagerly, "You going to try and rescue Pete?"

Tucson laughed. "I'm plumb curious to try, Mr. Lockhart. I can see that all this talk about how bad Janisary is, is more or less of a challenge to get me started."

Lockhart's pale features showed a sudden flush of warm color. He nodded slowly. "So help me, Tucson," he confessed, "I admit it. I need a man like you—men like you three. I can't go myself. I can't appeal to you with money. But make no mistake, Janisary's just as bad, worse, than Buck and I have said he is. Buck will go with you, or anybody else you need. Just say the word. When I first heard about this, I planned to send a small army down to rescue Pete. But that won't do—"

"I understand what you mean," Tucson nodded. "One or two men may be able to get into the Valley of the Singing Scorpion—where an army would fail of its purpose."

Lockhart nodded. "At the first sign of an army, Janisary would kill Pete. Good God! He may have done that already—but somehow, I can't believe it. I wish we could learn how that gun got into Lobo Tanks, who brought it here."

"Suppose we leave it to Buck to work on that end," Tucson suggested quietly. "In case we fail, Buck may be able to trace that weapon in some way."

"I doubt it," Lockhart said hopelessly. The strain was commencing to tell on him. "Good Lord! In another week I'll be able to ride, but— well, Pete may be dead in another week. I'm going to owe you men a lot, Tucson Smith—"

"Better withhold your thanks," Tucson said awkwardly. "We—"

"Whether you succeed or not." Lockhart's voice was firm.

Lullaby put in a question, "Does anybody know anythin' about this Valley of the Singing Scorpion?"

"Down in Old Mexico," Lockhart said slowly, "I've heard it mentioned, now and then, but nobody ever seemed to know where it was. I've always sort of felt that it had to do with some old Indian myth. Then Pete got interested—"

"I was just going to ask about your son," Tucson put in. "I've wondered what he went to Mexico for. So that's what he—"

"That's it." Lockhart sighed heavily. "Dammit, I wish he'd never left me. I should have kept him by my side, but I thought—well it seemed reasonable to suppose, and Pete agreed with me, that a university education might be a good thing in these days when beef stock is producing new strains and scientific methods of fighting disease have become necessary. Anyway, I sent him east for his schoolin'. He was away from me, with two exceptions when he came back for brief visits, over seven years."

Lullaby put in his slow drawl, "A little learnin' prove to be a dangerous weapon?"

"It's not that," Lockhart shook his head. "Pete came back with all the stock raisin' knowledge I'd sent him to get and a lot of other things besides. He panned out one hundred percent. The fact that he'd been east to school, didn't necessitate the buyin' of a larger size Stetson, like it does in a heap of cases. Nope, Pete's turned out fine. Trouble is, he got interested in ruins."

"Ruins?" from Tucson.

Lockhart nodded. "He got acquainted with a professor of archaeology—"

"You have to be interested," Stony grinned, "just to learn a word that long. Don't try to explain it to Lullaby. He wouldn't understand."

Lullaby told Stony to shut his bread-trap. Lockhart smiled slightly and went on, "This Professor Norquist had done a heap of exploring both in North and South America—you know, digging up old ruins, remains of ancient Indian villages, pueblos—that sort of thing. He could even read some of those old writings, accordin' to Pete. Some place in his searchin's, he found an old writin' with a reference to a place called the Valley of the Singing Scorpion—"

"And Pete," Tucson interrupted, "right away told this Norquist that he'd heard of such a place?"

Lockhart shook his head. "Pete had never heard of it, but last spring when he come home, after gettin' his diploma, he was telling me about Norquist's explorin'. He mentioned the Valley of the Singing Scorpion. I told Pete I had heard of such a place, damn fool that I was. Anyway, the next thing I knew Pete was packed up and headed for Old Mexico to see if he could locate the valley—"

"Him and this Norquist?" Tucson asked.

"No, he didn't tell Norquist anything about it. Said he wanted to see if he could locate the place and then surprise Norquist. Pete was workin' alone. Cripes! He didn't even have the least idea what way to head. He's been gone two months—"

"You haven't heard from him at all?" Tucson asked.

"Not a word—until that message in the gun came through. Some place down there he ran into Janisary. He'd never seen Janisary, but he'd heard of the devil from me. Now, God only knows what's—"

Lockhart broke off, his eyes misting. He gulped heavily, tried to go on, finally set his mouth tightly and remained silent, his blue eyes under the shaggy eyebrows pleading with Tucson.

Tucson stood up. "I guess that's all," he said a trifle awkwardly. "We've got a startin' point anyway: we know where Malpaisaño is. The sooner we get goin' the better."

Lockhart couldn't speak for a few minutes. "You're—you're going down there," he said slowly, "going to bring my boy back to me?"

"We're goin' to do our dam'dest," Tucson replied.

"But—but suppose," Lockhart faltered, "he's—he's—well, Janisary—" Again his voice broke.

Tucson assumed a light tone he didn't at all feel: "Don't you worry none, Mr. Lockhart. You stay here and get healed up. Mebbe we'll bring Janisary back to you, too. But the main point is, Pete hasn't got his gun. I've got to return it to him."

Lockhart staggered to his feet, hands outstretched. "You're *men,* Tucson Smith—you and your pards. I feel stronger already."

Buck Patton hastily pressed Lockhart back to his chair, uttering worried little clucking sounds that had to do with "the doctor's orders."

Lockhart went on, "I said before that money wouldn't bring you into this trouble of mine, but it will help in other ways. Call on me for anything you need. If you get Janisary cornered—"

"*When* we get Janisary cornered," Tucson corrected.

"When you get Janisary cornered," and Lockhart's smile was stronger, "get word to me. I'll be ready to ride then. I'll be riding anyway in a week. I'll bc headin' for Malpaisaño—"

"Don't you!" Tucson cut in swiftly. "Until you hear from me, this is a three-man job—maybe less. You can't afford to let Janisary know you're coming—and that's exactly what would happen if you showed up in that country with an outfit of fightin' punchers."

"But can't I do anything to help?"

"Sit tight. Get well," Tucson said. "Oh, yes, we're not carryin' rifles, and I'd like—"

"Hell's bells!" Lockhart exclaimed. "There must be a dozen Winchesters, of various calibers, here at the ranch. All good guns. You can have your pick." He started again to thank Tucson.

Tucson brushed away Lockhart's thanks, said, "We'll be lookin' at those rifles and then startin' pronto."

"Take a day's rest first," Lockhart urged. "You may not get another for a long spell. You're headed for trouble."

Tucson shook his head slightly, eyes narrowed, thoughts concentrated on the future. "Headed for trouble," he repeated slowly, then with a short laugh, "Sufferin' rattlers! It won't be the first time."

# 8

# "Long Shootin'!"

Old Mexico. Where nothing ever happens—and where anything may and does happen, suddenly, violently. A land of peace and quiet and a land where the blood of millions has seeped into the sands, generation after generation. A country of spiny plant growth and blue skies and purple peaks. A nation of brave warriors and bandits and noblemen finally emerging, still fighting for the right, up through the sanguinary centuries of oppression. In short, a great people!

"Some day," Tucson was saying, his lean form jogging easily to the motion of his horse, "Mexico will come into its own. This country will be opened up, its resources developed. Lord! It's rich. But first some way will have to be found to prevent the so-called civilized other nations from plundering these people of their wealth."

The Three Mesquiteers were riding across a great sand and alkali sink, dotted sparsely here and there with stunted *mesquitl* and cacti. A mile to their right a long rocky ridge paralleled their course, the terrain sloping gently toward the ridge being covered with giant *pitahayas,* their great spiny arms uplifted to the cloudless, turquoise sky.

The faces and clothing of the three riders were coated with alkali dust. Now and then one of them reached to the canteen on his saddle and drank sparingly of its lukewarm, brackish contents. The sweat-streaked ponies plodded patiently on and on, their hoofs hock-deep in the loose sand.

Twenty minutes passed before Lullaby got around to answering Tucson's words. "Say what you want about Mexico bein' a great country," he grumbled. "I'm wishin' I was back in the States right now. I'll betcha the sun is twenty degrees cooler back there—"

Stony grinned, "You better get used to heat, Lullaby. You'll be dyin' sometime, and where you're goin' they don't know the meanin' of that word 'cooler' you just mentioned."

91

"The hell you say," Lullaby retorted.

"That's the place I'm speakin' about," Stony shot back. "Ain't you havin' a good time?"

A long sinuous brown form rippled out of the paths of the approaching horses, disappeared beneath a low clump of prickly pear. A harsh dry rattling reached the riders' ears. Lullaby's right hand dipped down, his gun exploded. Automatically he plunged out the empty shell, reloaded, without looking back.

Tucson glanced past Lullaby's back, on his right. "Got him," he commented shortly, eyeing the writhing form whipping up small dust clouds from the sand.

"Afraid he might strike my pony," Lullaby said shortly. He continued the conversation with Stony, who rode on Tucson's left, "Do you call this havin' a good time? Me, I crave to be peaceful. This day after day ridin' through a furnace with a grinnin' idjit—"

"Hear what he called you, Tucson?" Stony chuckled. "Hell, Lullaby, you were as keen as any of us to be headin' for Malpaisaño. Fact is, if it wasn't for you, me'n' Tucson wouldn't thought of startin' this rescue party to bring Pete Lockhart out of Mexico—"

"Me?" Lullaby exclaimed indignantly. "Me! I was the one that was all for stayin' home peaceful and gettin' that outfit and raisin' cattle. But no, you two has to go ridin' off, curious to see what's on the other side of the mountains all the time. I never in all my life see such a pair of long noses for smellin' trouble. If trouble was perfume, you two would be scented up like a Garden of Paradise."

"Speakin' of dice," Stony said, "reminds me of the time I took that pair of dice off'n that crooked tin-horn in Juarez—"

"Oh, Gawd," Lullaby groaned. "Ain't you ever heard of the Garden of Paradise?"

"Certain I have," Stony grunted good-humoredly, "it's where I'll be if Tucson and me can ever persuade you to stay behind when we start a trip. It's where eatin' apples gets you a plumb bad bellyache, too."

"Apples," Lullaby sighed blissfully, "what I wouldn't give to sink my teeth into a nice juicy Baldwin, right now. We ain't had a downright good meal since we crossed the line. Days we sweat under the sun, nights we nigh freeze to death, 'cause we don't dare build up a good fire. On top of that, a coyote throwin' lead at us all day yesterday—"

"That's why we don't want a fire at night," Tucson said. "That feller doin' that long-range shootin' yesterday was pro'bly some goat-herder lookin' to steal a few bucks. He didn't dare come nigh enough to get our range. But supposin' we lit a big fire to show where we was sleepin' nights—"

"You tellin' me why we don't have a fire?" Lullaby laughed sarcastically.

Stony sneered genially, "You never would learn anythin' if we didn't tell you—"

"Cut it out, Stony," Tucson said gravely. "No use rubbin' it in on Lullaby. After all, he's right. I been thinkin' things over. The best way is to let Lullaby go back to the States. This is a two-man job and there's no use him riskin' his hide. I don't blame him for growling—"

"Huh, me?" Lullaby's voice shook with indignation. "You heard us wrong, Tucson. It was me, tryin' to make Stony quit crabbin'. Me, I like it hot this way. Sure, that's the idea, let Stony go back across the line. He ain't ever satisfied. I get plumb weary nursin' him along all the time. My Gosh! What ever give you the idea I was complainin'? I thought it was all settled. Young Pete Lockhart is interested in ruins, so we're bringin' 'em to him—"

Stony asked suspiciously, "What do you mean?"

Lullaby drawled, "You. If you ain't a ruin I never saw one."

Tucson laughed. The other two followed suit. The horses were much nearer the long rocky ridge now. Tucson motioned to the hundreds of *sahuaros* covering the slope. "We might head over there and get some shade from those giant cactus—"

"I'd sooner keep on the way we're goin'," Lullaby said. "We'll make better time travelin' in a straight line, than we would dodgin' those things every few feet—"

He stopped short, as a spurt of dust spouted up

from the sand a few feet ahead of his horse. To their ears came the crack of a rifle from someplace among the cluttered rocks on top of the ridge.

Lullaby reached for the Winchester in its rifle boot under his left leg, then changed his mind. "No use wastin' more lead on that hombre. He keeps too well covered. There's your goat-herder friend again, Tucson."

Tucson didn't reply. His eyes were scanning the top of the ridge, but failed to note any movement.

Stony growled, "My gosh! Have we got to put up with that hombre again, all afternoon? I don't mind bein sniped at if the feller comes close enough to make it interestin', but that hombre's like a hornet. He buzzes around and never does do any real harm, but it's plumb annoyin' when a feller wants to think or carry on a quiet conversation. I'd like to—"

*Crack!* Stony swore, removed his Stetson and surveyed ruefully the spot where a bullet had ripped away an inch of hat-brim.

Lullaby laughed shortly. "Is that close enough to make it interestin'?"

Stony swore again and reached for his rifle. The three riders had come to a halt. Tucson's rifle was at shoulder, his finger tightening around trigger. The Winchester barked. High up, near the top of the slope, fragments of rock spurted into the air.

Tucson said quietly, "Missed him. We better spread out—"

A slug whined close to his body, followed by the gun report of the hidden rifleman. Stony's Winchester spurted white flame, twice in quick succession. He grunted disgustedly,

"Chalk up two more misses."

Lullaby's rifle was out now, but he held his fire, scanning the ridge for movement. The three backed their horses slowly, guns at ready. No more shots came.

Five minutes later, Lullaby growled, "If I ever lay hands on that blasted goat-herder—"

"I'm thinkin' I'm mistaken, after all," Tucson said quietly. "That was damn good shootin'. He had our range. That's not a goat-herder. I'm guessin' maybe Janisary left Crawford to watch us—or say, that might be Janisary himself!"

"Better shootin' than yesterday's," Lullaby conceded. "Mebbe it's a different man—"

"Sounded like the same gun," Stony pointed out.

"He didn't dare come so close, yesterday," Tucson said. "The country was more open. Here, he knows damn well there's plenty of rock to hide behind. By the time we pushed up to the top of that slope, he could be clean out of sight."

There were no more shots. The three wheeled their ponies abreast and continued on their way. An hour passed. From time to time Tucson glanced toward the top of the ridge their path was paralleling, but could see nothing.

"You think we ought to hit Malpaisaño tomorrow?" Lullaby asked after a time.

Tucson nodded. Lullaby said, "Unless that hidden rifle shot finds our range again. He was doin' better every minute. It was dang long shootin' too—"

Tucson's horse reared and snorted violently as a small bloody smear replaced the tip of its right ear. From the top of the slope came the vicious crack of the unseen rifle. Again the three backed their ponies, and went through the motions of getting guns into readiness. Three times more the hidden gunman fired from three different points. Tucson and his two companions replied with quick shots, but were forced to admit the impossibility of scoring a bull's-eye on a target they couldn't see.

Five minutes slipped past with no further firing. Tucson wheeled his horse, "C'mon," he said, again striking out on the path they'd been following. The other two reined their ponies on either side.

Tucson said, "This has got to stop. That coyote is comin' too close for comfort. Eventually, he'll get one of us. We got a job to do."

"So what?" Stony said.

"I figure he'll be at it again before long. He's gettin' more nerve the farther we go. Next time he shoots, the feller that's nearest to his bullet— if it doesn't get him—drops off his horse."

"I don't see," Lullaby commenced, "what you expect—"

*Crack!* A leaden slug whined viciously past Tucson's head. He uttered a sharp cry, flung his arms in the air, and slipped from the saddle.

Stony and Lullaby swore violent oaths, unleashed a flaming stream of lead at the ridge top. Tucson said quietly, from his sprawled position on the hot sand, "He didn't hit me."

A moment later, Lullaby and Stony crouched at Tucson's side as though examining a wound. Lullaby went through the motions of tearing up a bandanna. Stony rose once, shook a clenched fist at the top of the ridge and again dropped at Tucson's side. The two turned him over. Tucson was talking all the time:

"Now you two take your horses—and mine—and head back the way we come from. There's a slight roll of land a mile back. Go on farther, as though you were headin' back to the nearest town for help—"

"And leave you here?" Stony cut in.

"That's the idea—"

"We won't do it."

"Listen, Stony, don't argue," Tucson pleaded from his facedown, motionless position on the earth. "We've got to trick that hombre some way—"

"But Tucson—" Lullaby started protest.

"Dammit, Lullaby, do as I ask, will you? You'll have to go well back. Remember that hombre can see farther from the top of the ridge than we can from here—"

"But supposin' he shoots you when we leave—?" from Stony.

"I'll have to chance that. I don't think he will—"

"Look, Tucson, we can't do—"

*Spat!* A slug buried itself in the sand at Lullaby's side. Lullaby rose, shook his fist.

"You see," Tucson spoke earnestly, his face cradled on one arm, against the sand, "he'll keep on until he gets one of you. Go on now. Drift pronto. Wait—you better pretend to examine me some more, so you can leave me in a position to watch that slope."

The two "examined" Tucson again, leaving him on his left side, knees drawn up slightly, head resting on arm, his face toward the ridge. Reluctantly, Stony and Lullaby mounted. Lullaby reached for the reins of Tucson's mount, saying in a flat, strained voice, "S'long, you addle-pated rannie. I hope you have a heap of luck."

"Get movin'," Tucson said anxiously, not daring to look at them.

"S'help me," Stony's tones sounded choked, "if this stunt—"

*"Will you get goin'?"* Tucson snapped. "I'll see you later."

The horses were passing to his rear now. He could hear their hoofs moving through the sand. Finally those sounds died away. . . .

# 9

# Gun-Quick Action

The sun beat down with a fierce intensity on Tucson's motionless form. Once a horned toad scurried near, then, sensing that the big man-animal wasn't dead, darted off like a gray-brown flash. Insects inspected Tucson's bare flesh. At times it was torture not to be able to brush them away. Luckily, his sombrero hadn't fallen off when he dropped from his horse. The wide brim shaded his eyes and he could see all that moved, in a wide range, before him.

Overhead a *zopilote* floated on motionless wings, dipped and wheeled, coming closer and ever closer to the man on the earth. Finally it sailed down cautiously, struck the earth with a stumbling awkward hop, then moved a few feet nearer to make a cautious inspection of its prey. A few minutes later, two more arrived.

"Damn buzzards," Tucson mused, eyeing the birds steadily from a distance of seven or eight yards, "I hope I can fool 'em. They pro'bly figure I ain't dead yet. Which same is true. If they ever realize just how lively I am, they'll leave pronto, and warn that coyote up on the ridge. Wonder what he's doin'. Pro'bly hit out for a higher point where he could watch Lullaby and Stony. I sure hope they go far enough so's to be out of sight."

A fourth buzzard traced a slow, lazy path down the turquoise sky to join his three waiting companions. Tucson wanted to stretch, move, scratch numerous insect bites. "Dang it," he muttered, "I'm thinkin' I bit off a big job. I wish that hombre would put in an appearance. He's pro'bly plumb cautious. Betcha he can't quite figure out why my pards should go 'way and leave me. If I'm dead I should be buried. If I ain't, one should have stayed while the other went for help. Shucks! I'm commencin' to think this idea wa'n't so bright."

The sun was swinging far to the west now, toward the distant greenish-opal peaks of the Sierra Madres. Tucson grew more uncomfortable. "I wonder if that hombre is drawin' a bead on me, right this minute. He's watchin', that's certain. Any minute now he may score a bull's-eye on my worthless carcass. S'help me, if somethin' don't happen right soon I'm goin' to get up."

The strain of waiting dotted Tucson's forehead with drops of perspiration. Despite the sun's warmth, a shiver coursed Tucson's spine. Since his two pardners had turned him over, he hadn't, seemingly, moved a muscle. His limbs grew cramped. The sun dropped lower, touching the western horizon with waning light.

There were five *zopilotes* now, arranged in a waiting half-circle ten yards from Tucson's place on the sand. Their wings rustled with harsh impatience from time to time, as they stretched out scaly red necks inquiringly. Now and then one of them would hop awkwardly nearer the body of the prone man, then retreat with the same clumsy motion. A vagrant breeze lifted a sickening stench to Tucson's nostrils.

Tucson's nose wrinkled disgustedly despite himself. "Damn stink birds," he mused. "Sittin' around waitin' for me to die. Like doctors attendin' a dyin' bedside. Dirty doctors. No, they're surgeons, in a hurry to get at the autopsy. And they don't intend to make such a neat job of it either."

It grew cooler. The *pitahayas* on the slope were casting long shadows. Tucson wondered how long he had been waiting in that position. Two hours? Three? It seemed like a hundred. "Damn buzzards," he grumbled, "they know I ain't dead. If that hombre on the slope knows anythin' he'll take a cue from them. I'm surprised he ain't sent some more lead my way. Pro'bly scared Lullaby and Stony would hear it and be drawn back."

The day was dying in varying shades of gray and black and red and gold. Over all hung a misty lavender haze. A cool breeze lifted momentarily to disturb the dust in fine flying particles. The buzzards cocked inquiring, dubious heads.

Abruptly, a leaden slug whined over Tucson's body clipping a tiny bit of sleeve on his right shoulder, but leaving the skin unscathed. The start

Tucson gave was involuntary, very similar to that made by a lifeless body when struck a violent impact with flying lead.

"It's startin'," Tucson thought grimly. "I hope he don't sling another shot without comin' within my range."

The *zopilotes* had lifted themselves on heavy reluctant wings and were wheeling toward the dying light in the sky now. Far above they dipped and soared and zoomed like black pieces of paper flung helter-skelter by the wind. Five minutes dragged past on leaden feet. Tucson hadn't moved.

His eyes were alive, scanning the side of the slope. Slowly a horse's head edged into view from behind a giant cactus. The horse and rider appeared cautiously, viewing the plain and the silent form sprawled on the sands. A few seconds later the desert growth blotted out the rider.

Tucson waited, patiently, his heart thumping under his ribs. When next the rider appeared he was nearer, coming out in the more open stretch of country. He walked the horse slowly, now and then lifting his head to gaze around, as though suspecting some trick, then again dropping his glance to Tucson's motionless body. It required nerve, iron nerve, to lie there like that. Tucson knew he couldn't hold out much longer.

Step by step the horse approached nearer. Tucson through narrowed eyes could see the man plainly now. He was a chunkily built man in sloppy clothing with a face the color of a fish's belly. A round, unhealthily-fat face with muddy eyes.

Now he wasn't more than ten yards away. The rifle in his hand was lifted to shoulder for a final, self-assuring shot. And then Tucson moved, an instant before the explosion came:

Catlike, he threw his body to one side, rolled over, came up with one hand drawing his six-shooter. The gun roared once, twice, three times, the reports apparently blending into one continuous sound.

Through the drifting powder smoke that mushroomed from the gun, Tucson saw the man's jaw drop, his eyes widen with surprise. A look of fright and shock paralyzed the slack features in set lines. For a moment he sat, slumped sidewise in the saddle, the rifle dropping from his fingers. Then he toppled from the saddle, as the frightened horse reared frantically and started away at a swift terror-urged gallop.

"Curiosity," Tucson said flatly, "killed more'n a cat."

His voice sounded strangely toneless in the silence following the echoes of the shooting. He approached the man on the sand at a swift walk. The man lay face down, his open mouth pressed against the sun-baked earth. He whimpered a little when Tucson stooped and turned him over. Three wounds, any one of them mortal, within a space the size of a man's hand.

Fear died out of the man's muddy eyes, some-what, when he saw Tucson slip the six-shooter back into holster. He asked weakly, "Am I finished?"

Tucson nodded. "If you got anything to say you better talk fast."

The dying man said bitterly, "Not a thing— 'ceptin' I wish you hadn't outguessed me. It all looked—funny as hell—but I bit."

"What you been shooting at us for?"

"Orders."

"Whose orders?"

The man forced a feeble laugh. "T'hell with you. Give me a drink."

Tucson glanced around the horizon. The man's horse was some distance away, still running. "No can do, hombre," Tucson said, not unkindly. "Your canteen has went ridin'. Mine ain't here. It's tough."

An expression of pain crossed the man's white features, but he didn't say anything. His eyes closed slowly. It was almost dark now.

Tucson said, "Janisary back of this—the Scorpion?"

The eyes opened. "You know—about him, eh?"

"I learned a heap after I bought a gun."

The man cursed weakly. "Dammit—I sold that— hawg-laig. Hoped to get it. Picked up—your trail—near the R-Cross-L. Been followin' you—"

"Where'd you get the gun?"

"Took it off a Mex that young Lockhart sent—" He stopped suddenly.

"It's all right, hombre," Tucson said, "we know about—"

"Muh name's McReich—Porky McReich." A ghost of a smile flitted across the pallid lips. "Just so you—get the right—moniker on my—tombstone."

"All right, Porky," Tucson said quietly. "You didn't spill anything. We know about Pete Lockhart being held prisoner. Is he still alive?"

"So far as I know. What about it? Janisary will finish him when he gets back."

"Janisary left you to keep an eye on us, eh?"

Porky cursed Tucson in feeble accents. "None of your business."

"What's Janisary's game?"

This time McReich refused to reply. He closed his eyes, his breath coming in quick gasps.

Tucson said, "Suit yourself. I'm just giving you a chance to come clean. I'll make Janisary tell me—"

Porky's weak laugh was scornful. "You'll never—get close—enough to him—for that. Or mebbe—you'll be too—close, and—he'll do the talkin' in a way you won't like. The Scorpion'll—outsmart—all of you." The eyes closed again, opened, "Wish I had a drink."

"My pards will be back pretty quick."

"How—about—a smoke?"

Tucson could just hear the words. It didn't seem any use, but he brought out his sack of Durham and brown papers, deftly rolled a cigarette and reached for a match. He looked at Porky again, noted the muddy eyes that had suddenly gone glassy. Then he placed the cigarette between his own lips and scratched a light.

Tucson thought of the *zopilotes*—how they'd be wheeling overhead again tomorrow—and cast around for a flat piece of rock with which to dig a shallow grave. It was night now, the silvery stars commencing to wink through the indigo east. . . .

Tucson had just finished kicking earth back into the opening when he heard swift hoofbeats. Lullaby and Stony took form in the gloom, their voices showing relief when they caught Tucson's hail.

"Thought we never would get here," Lullaby growled, when Tucson had concluded a relation of the events transpiring during their absence. "I'm sure glad it turned out right."

"We could just hear the shots," from Stony. "We found an old stream bed, washed deep by last season's rains. It's dry as a bone now though. We waited down in there. That first shot sure had us on edge. Then, three more, comin' fast, made us feel better. . . . Here, you lucky stiff," handing over the reins of Tucson's horse, "I'm plumb sick of leadin' this crowbait for a dang fool that will run risks like you do. Or do you figure to camp here?"

Tucson shook his head, climbed into the saddle, took a long drink from his canteen. "We're ridin'. Got to make up the time lost today."

Two hours later, when the moon edged above the eastern horizon, the three men were still traveling steadily, relentlessly, onward.

# 10

# Tucson Goes Down!

It was night—the following night—when the Three Mesquiteers walked their weary ponies into Malpaisaño. The day's travel had carried them through a weird land of sand and manzanita and cactus—a veritable Devil's Garden where the huge agave, or century plants, towered in places above the heads of the riders. No human beings had been sighted all day, though rattlers, tarantulas, horned toads and other forms of life had been numerous.

Malpaisaño wasn't, by any stretch of the imagination, a typical Mexican town, though it was larger than the average settlement found in this section of mañana land. There was one winding main thoroughfare and three or four cross streets. The buildings were of adobe, sun-baked and whitewashed. A few of the structures, among the smaller dwellings, were tinted pink. There were any number of *cantinas,* their open doorways throwing off a strong odor of liquor and the sour-smelling *pulque.* The main street was ablaze with lights streaming from shop windows and cafés. Near the center of the town was a larger building which served as the *fonda,* or inn. Its windows were fly-specked, its once-white wall surfaces dingy.

There were any number of waiting horses along both sides of the roadway, but few pedestrians on the footpaths. The fact that struck Tucson as most important was found in the large number of men from the United States side of the line noticed on all sides. Their heavy voices resounded from the *cantinas* and other buildings and along the streets, now and then punctuated by shriller feminine sounds. Cheap phonographs rasped out tinny music in a dance hall and two or three other ill- lighted places, competing with the softer twanging of guitars in the quieter buildings.

Mexicans and Indians in thin cotton garments that flapped loosely about their bodies were to be seen, but it was plain they were in the minority. To Tucson and his companions, Malpaisaño appeared to be a tough town transported from north of the international boundary line and dropped down helter-skelter to concoct a devil's brew in a peaceful land.

Stony reined his horse close to Tucson's. "What do you think?"

Tucson shook his head. "It's one tough town if you ask me, a headquarters for all the down-at-

the-heel scum that's been kicked off the border
—and I'm talkin' about our side of the border."

"I'll bet the Mexes don't like it," Lullaby said, shifting in his saddle.

"I ain't seen very many," from Tucson. "Those that didn't have property or businesses here have pro'bly left. This town ain't got anythin' but dregs. I been thinkin'—"

"Make your head ache?" Stony asked quickly.

"That's somethin' you never had, Stony," Lullaby said, "solid bone can't ache—"

"Shut up, you two," Tucson interrupted. "I been thinkin' we better scatter. Janisary may have left word to be on the lookout for three punchers, travelin' together. It's a cinch we don't want to sleep at that lousy *fonda* we passed. We'll have to bed out in the brush tonight—outside of town. I'll meet you rannies southwest of Malpaisaño inside three hours. You two split up, too."

"Good idea," Lullaby nodded. "Then what?"

"We'll all three circulate around town, see what we can pick up. No—don't ask me what to look for. I don't know. There's guards at the entrance to that valley we're headin' for. We've got to work out some way to get past 'em. Go on now, split. We'll compare notes later."

He wheeled his own horse down a side street, and pulled it to a halt beneath the drooping feathery leaves of a large pepper tree that had survived through many seasons of drought and hot sun. Five minutes later, he headed back toward the main street, taking a roundabout course. When he had returned to the lighted district, nothing of Stony or Lullaby was to be seen.

Someplace, a block away, a revolver barked suddenly. Tucson's eyes narrowed. "If that dang Stony—" he commenced, and then fell silent, urging his pony toward the sound as fast as he could without arousing notice.

A crowd had swarmed from buildings and formed a ragged circle of curious onlookers in the street when Tucson arrived. His sharp glance brought no sign of Stony or Lullaby. A man was down in the dust of the road; another man in the togs of an American puncher stood over him with a raised six-shooter in one hand while he weaved drunkenly on very uncertain legs, cursing fluently. A woman crouched over the wounded man in the roadway, trying to do something about a dark crimson stain on one arm. The woman was a Mexican as was her wounded companion.

Evidently little damage had been done. The Mexican girl swore in quick, crackling Spanish. The drunken puncher laughed, a trifle sheepishly, and staggered away through the crowd. After a moment, the Mexican girl rose and ran after the puncher. Tucson caught the sharp flash of a thin-bladed knife. The puncher swore viciously, caught the girl's wrist. Tucson heard the tinkle of steel as the knife fell to the roadway.

The girl came back, sobbing, to her wounded companion. The onlookers commenced to scatter, two of them staying to help the woman with her wounded mate. The quartette stumbled off to the nearest *cantina*. Someone laughed. Two more cursed in bitter Spanish. Tucson gathered that this was only one more of many such brawls. In a few minutes the street was as clear as before.

Tucson touched spurs to his pony, continued at a walk along the street. "Sweet town," he murmured ironically.

The blare of music and voices from open doorways swelled in volume the later it grew. Twice, Tucson saw Lullaby and Stony, on foot, sauntering about the town. They passed with no apparent recognition.

Finally Tucson reined his pony toward a hitchrack fronting, according to a sun-faded sign in washy blue, the Cantina of Singing Birds. Here he dismounted and entered the building, finding himself in a long, low-roofed room along one side of which was a long counter, liquor-ringed and damp, presided over by a round-faced, greasy bartender with beady black eyes.

The bar was lined with men most of which, in Tucson's estimation, were badmen from the States. A sprinkling of Mexicans stood among them. The loud voices at the bar tapered off to silence as Tucson entered. Several men casually, all too casually, left the bar and crossed to the opposite wall.

Tucson didn't like the looks of the place. He approached the bar at a point not far from the doorway and ordered a bottle of beer. A bottle was set out before him. No glass. Tucson spun a silver half-dollar on the bar and lifted the bottle to his lips. It was lukewarm and tasted bitter, flat.

"You like *tortillas, señor,*" the bartender offered, "ver' good *tortillas?*"

Tucson remembered now that he hadn't had any supper. "It might help this beer some," he nodded.

A greasy hand slapped half a dozen of the pancakelike *tortillas* on the bar, using a torn sheet of paper for a plate. Along with the *tortillas* was a handful of small pickled chili peppers and a chunk of cheese made from goat's milk.

"Without the ice," the bartender was saying, "theese beer no so good. Eet is better eef you take of the *tequila* for the thirst."

Tucson thanked him and said no. He swallowed some more of the beer, made a wry face and munched on the cheap food. Once he glanced about the room. Everyone seemed to be watching him. There was little talk. Tucson shrugged contemptuous shoulders and returned to his apology for a supper. The beer was half gone now, helped down by bites of the tough, stringy *tortillas.*

Quite suddenly Tucson became aware of certain pertinent facts: he was strangely weary, his eyes heavy; all talk about him had ceased. The men in the room seemed to be waiting for something.

Tucson remembered now that he hadn't seen the bartender uncap his bottle of beer.

"I reckon, *amigo*," Tucson said quietly to the barkeep, "that I'll have another bottle of beer—and I'll watch you open this one."

"No beer, *señor,* no more of beer. Ver' fine *tequila*." The man was grinning insolently. A dawning suspicion was crystallized in Tucson's mind.

"T'hell with your *tequila*," Tucson said, steady-voiced. "I don't trust your drinks."

A jeering laugh arose at Tucson's rear. Tucson swung around, one thumb hooked in his right gun belt, near the weapon's walnut butt, to see a hard-bitten man surveying him with some amusement.

The man said, "Plumb suspicious, ain't you, pardner?"

Tucson nodded. "I ain't your pardner, but I am suspicious—"

"Cripes, feller, you don't need to be afeared of knock-out drops here. This is the cleanest place in town."

"That," Tucson stated a bit thickly, "don't say much for the town." That was the game, make 'em believe the drug hadn't taken hold, until he could get out of the Cantina of Singing Birds. He simply *had* to get out of here. Luckily he hadn't finished all of the drugged beer.

The bartender was protesting about something,

the words not registering on Tucson's dulling senses. It required every ounce of his will power now, just to maintain a steady front.

Tucson laughed silently. "The joke's on me," he half mumbled, "but you got a long way to go yet, *amigos*."

The men were laughing openly now, two or three of them watching Tucson through narrowed lids, wondering how much longer he could last. Tucson was wondering the same thing. He should be on his way now, but he was reluctant to move for fear of showing how unmanageable he feared his legs had become.

The man who had spoken first said, "Take it easy, pardner—"

"I ain't your pardner." Tucson forced his voice to be steady. Dammit, why didn't he start? Things were getting sort of blurred now.

"All right, no need to get huffy. But you needn't be so damn suspicious. You got a touch of desert sun mebbe. Let's you and me have a nice shot of *tequila*. That'll clear your brain plumb pronto."

Tucson smiled thinly and said, "This beer will serve my purpose." He reached to the bar, got a firm grip on the neck of the bottle and flung it, with considerable effort it seemed, at the man who had spoken.

Something queer about this: there were three bottles flying through the air; rather, they seemed to be floating lazily through space. Queerer still, the three bottles contacted three separate heads, and bounced, apparently with no force, against the back wall with a thin shattering of broken glass. Tucson had the satisfaction of seeing three men double up and pitch to the floor.

The room was swimming in a thick, blurry haze now. A hundred faces seemed to be looking at him. Funny thing, Tucson thought dumbly, I didn't think that bottle hit so high up. He could see the splash—several splashes—on the opposite wall. Up high. The ceiling seemed higher too.

The man he had struck with the bottle—no, the three men downed with three bottles—was still on the floor. He and Tucson seemed to be on nearly the same level. Tucson shook his head doggedly. Cripes! What a dumb business this was. He realized quite suddenly he was down on the floor, in a sitting position. Now when in hell did that happen? Tucson laughed rather foolishly. Shucks! It would be dang nice to curl up right here and go to sleep. His eyes were pretty dang heavy. Mebbe forty winks of shut-eye would chase that heavy feeling away too.

There seemed to be several men laughing at him now. It was all a dense blur. The Cantina of the Singing Birds. Tucson waved one drunken arm in a careless gesture. "Yep," he stated, "they're singin' plumb sweet in my head right this minute. Yep, Singin' Birds. Singin'— Singin'—what was it? Oh, yeah, Singin'

Scorpions." He pronounced the words, rather tried to, aloud. Cripes! What was wrong with his tongue? It felt like a thick piece of flannel.

The other men in the room laughed harder than ever. The man who had been downed with the beer bottle was sitting up now, scowling at Tucson. No, three scowling men, with three hands held to three battered heads.

"I'll betcha," and Tucson giggled foolishly, "you can hear them singin' birds too—all three of you. Three cheers for th' singin' triplets. No—" trying to get a hold on himself, "—that don't make sense. Oh, hell!"

What difference did it make? Let 'em laugh. He was goin' to have his sleep out. Nice soft floor. Sure he was drugged. What of it? Knockout drops didn't kill a man. Just made him sleepy and—and—Besides, Stony and Lullaby would come after him. They'd clean out this nest of singin' rattlers. Forty winks, that was all he needed, forty winks. Lullaby and Stony would—

But wait! Mebbe Lullaby and Stony had picked up knockout drops too! Cripes! Hell of a note! He'd have to go find 'em.

Tucson was leaning back, resting on one elbow now. With an effort he raised his head, his glance meeting the beady black eyes of the bartender who was leaning, grinning, over the counter.

Tucson gained a momentary command of himself. "You," he said clearly to the bartender, "I never did like your face." His voice sounded thin and far away to Tucson.

The bartender laughed until tears rolled down his cheeks. Everybody else laughed, including Tucson. Damn if it wasn't funny. Yep, the joke was on him. Fallin' for an old stunt like—like three singin' birds? What kind of birds? *Zopilotes?* Nope, they didn't laugh like this. Cuckoos, that was it, cuckoos! Three of 'em—Tucson, Lullaby and Stony.

Abruptly, Tucson grunted, "Goin' to get up. Laughed enough."

The rest of the room laughed louder. Somebody closed the entrance doors. A voice reached Tucson's dim consciousness: "I'm damned if he ain't a tough bird to knock out."

Another voice answered, "He's slippin' fast. He'll go out like a lamp in a wind in another minute."

"T'hell you say," Tucson said thickly. "I'm gettin' up." He renewed his efforts.

After a minute a man said in an awed voice, "By God! He *is* gettin' up!"

"It won't last—it can't."

"He'll go down again. Watch and see."

Valiantly, inch by inch, Tucson fought his way up on leaden limbs. Perspiration stood out on his forehead, he gasped for air like a dying man. Sheer will power, this business of climbing erect.

"By God! He's one tough buzzard!"

"Hell, he's nearly finished right this minute."

Tucson swore and said, "Betcha ten dollars I make it." And wished immediately he hadn't wasted his strength. There, there, his hand had clutched the bar now. Thank God, his arms still had strength in 'em. For a moment Tucson swayed at the bar, one hand keeping him from falling. He surveyed the room with something akin to triumph. The men had fallen silent again. The room swirled madly about in a sea of faces and mist and broken bottles.

For a moment Tucson's head cleared. He saw the bartender was scowling now, watching closely. Tucson said, "Your face looks better with a smile on it, but even if you was handsome I wouldn't like it."

The bartender said something low and vicious in Spanish. Tucson laughed lightheadedly. "Through playin' now," he stated, the tones somewhat drunken in sound. "How do you like this?"

More will power: his right hand let go the bar, plucked a gun out of his right holster, raised it and batted the bartender over the head. The arm completed the circle it had started. Tucson was thumbing the hammer now. Sharp flashes of scarlet flame spurted from the forty-five's barrel.

Now his other gun was out. It wasn't held steadily but weaved about just enough to cover the crowd. Tucson didn't realize it, but he was backing toward the entrance. His legs seemed made of stone, but somehow, step by step, he made progress.

He laughed grimly. "You and your singin' birds."

*Wham!* The light back of the bar went out in a shattering of glass and splashing of oil. Two men were down, writhing on the floor. The rest were huddled in one corner, arms raised, eyes wide with terror.

A man gasped frantically, "Lemme out, lemme out. He's gone crazy!"

"Cuckoo," Tucson corrected gravely. "Three cuckoos. Three singin' cuckoos!"

*Wham!* The suspended oil lamp above the center of the room rocked drunkenly and left a jagged rim of chimney fragments around the smoking flame.

Tucson was at the entrance now. He kicked backward to force the door open, nearly lost his balance. His arm jerked. The lamp flame was extinguished as the oil bowl crashed down.

The Cantina of Singing Birds was in darkness now. Sharp flashes of light crossed the pitch-black room. Tucson was framed a moment against the lighted street seen through the open doorway. A slug whined viciously between one arm and his body. His own forty-five thundered a swift reply, rocking the building with the savage detonation.

Then he was outside, slamming the entrance door shut. "I'll be pluggin' the first skunk that sticks a head out," he called.

Turning, he rocked drunkenly toward his horse. My gosh, what a job it was to get into the saddle. There, his feet were settling into stirrups. He breathed a long sigh of relief.

The *cantina* door banged open. A streak of flame split the night. Tucson's gun hand jerked. He laughed savagely, plunged in his spurs. The horse snorted and wheeled away from the hitch-rack, front hoofs pawing at the air. It came down, running—running madly.

Men were sprinting up now. Guns roared at Tucson's ears in a steady, drum-shattering violence. He clung drunkenly to the saddle-horn and reins, swaying perilously with the swift motions of the horse.

Far back a voice penetrated his slipping consciousness: "Get horses. He can't last much longer."

Tucson mumbled, "T'hell you say," and pitched forward on the horse's neck, his last conscious effort that of putting his guns back in holsters. Hell! They were empty anyway.

Grimly, automatically, he held on without knowing it. The sounds were farther to his rear now, but he could hear the drumming of pursuing hoofs. The buildings grew more scattered. Open country ahead. Cactus, giant cactus, prickly pear, rugged upthrusts of rock. The moon shone palely on a man hunched in his saddle, a man who was sound asleep. The horse had slowed to a walk. Behind, the staccato pounding of hoofs drew nearer.

Tucson didn't know it when he fell off, though the habit of years loosened his feet from the stirrups. He struck the sand, one arm and shoulder partly breaking the fall. Dimly he heard the sounds of approaching horses. He didn't hear them stop, but felt somebody tugging at his shoulders after a time. His consciousness faded into oblivion like night blotting out a dying light in the west. . . .

# 11

## "You Will Meet Death!"

Tucson awoke to find the sunlight of midday streaming through a window on his right. There wasn't any window-pane in the opening, just wooden bars. Other things were impressed on him after a moment: he was stretched out on an old wooden bed in a strange room. Directly opposite the bed was a closed door. The four walls were whitewashed, the dirt floor swept clean. Two goatskin rugs were spread on the floor. An oaken chest of drawers stood against one wall, flanked by two straight-backed chairs with woven rawhide seats. In a niche on the opposite wall was a tiny statue of the Virgin Mary. Below it on a shelf a tiny candle burned with steady flame in a small red glass receptacle.

A calendar with a lurid colored landscape adorned one side of the room. At another spot a portrait of the President of Mexico, torn from a newspaper, had been tacked up. It was a bare room, in a way, but peaceful and clean. A few articles of apparel, masculine and feminine, hung on a series of wooden pegs driven into the wall at the foot of the bed. Tucson, after a moment, saw his own clothing was there, his guns and belts hanging on still another peg.

Tucson felt better on seeing his weapons. "Reckon I ain't a prisoner then," he mused, "but where in time am I? Some Mexican's house, but what—"

His mind strayed to other things, the happenings of last night—or was it last night? His head felt clear now. He stretched lazily in the bed, then stiffened. Where were Lullaby and Stony? Just what had happened?

"But how in time did I get here? Must be Lullaby and Stony found me. Last I remember was gettin' on my hawss. My gosh! I'm shore lucky. And all them coyotes laughin' at me. Seems like I laughed some myself. Plumb light in the head I reckon—"

The door pushed open slowly and a small Mexican boy-child stood there. Tucson raised up on his elbows, grinned at the youngster. The child surveyed the man with owlish eyes.

"Hai, Sober-sides," Tucson chuckled, "can't you speak?"

There came a quick step from the outer room

and a comely Mexican woman pushed past the child, her large, dark eyes inquiring.

Tucson said, "*Como 'stá, señora.* Where am I?"

"*Como 'stá,* Señor Smith," the woman replied in Spanish. "We are pleased to have you in your house."

"My house—" Tucson stopped and remembered. Pure Mexican courtesy dictated those words. It was a Mexican habit. He continued, using her language, "But who lives here? How did I get here? Where are Lullaby and Stony?"

"You ask many of the questions, *señor,*" with a smile. "Of this Lullaby and Stony you mention I know nothing. You came here of yourself. It is more correct to say that your *caballo* brought you to the *rancho* of Esteban Mercado."

"Horse brought me here, eh? Esteban Mercado?" Was the name familiar? Tucson searched his memory.

Hoofbeats were heard outside. The girl turned swiftly from the doorway, saying, "That is my husband now. Come, Antonio—" taking the child by the hand. Her voice raised from the outer room, "Esteban? Esteban, hurry? The Señor Smith is awake at last."

"At last?" Tucson echoed in a mutter. "I wonder how long I been out."

Quick footsteps were heard at the door; a good-looking young Mexican entered. He stopped short, just inside the room, "Ha! The

Señor Tucson is awake with the clear head at last. That is good!" He rushed across the room, seized Tucson's hand, shook it warmly, white teeth flashing in a pleased smile.

Tucson smiled back, trying to remember. The man looked familiar, no doubt of that. He wore a huge straw sombrero, dark tight-fitting trousers, riding boots. His shirt was white, mended and clean.

"You do not remember your friend, Esteban Mercado?" inquiringly.

"Your face is familiar—but, say, how did I get here?"

"Your *caballo* stops at my corral. I hear him. Then I look around. I find you near—sound asleep on the earth. I hear many men riding. I call to Benita. Together we carry you into the house and hide you under this bed. I do not know what is happening, but always when I hear many riders coming from Malpaisaño, I act first and think later."

"Sensible Esteban—"

"The riders stop here, push into my house—your house—and ask if I have seen a tall redhead who went insane on one drink of beer, and killed two men, wounding three others. I reply that a horse passed at a mad gallop sometime before, but I do not know if he has an insane redhead in his saddle or not. It is fortunate, they do not think to search the house, or look about for your horse. At once, they rush out and go in pursuit of you. They do not return."

"And then—"

"Benita and I see that much is wrong. Many bullets have torn your clothing, but your body is untouched. I put you to bed. It is a drugged sleep, that is plain. Then trouble begins."

"Trouble?"

"You refuse to sleep. You keep waking up, talking of one stony lullaby and three singing birds and scorpions. All night you fight to get from the bed. It is better if you relax and sleep off the poison, but you will not hear sense. All the time is a strain on your heart I think. Benita gives you hot coffee, but you think it is drugged. You will not drink."

Tucson said, "I must have been a nuisance."

"You were the devil for fighting. Together, Benita and I fail to hold you in the bed. It happens several times. Always, just as we fail, you fall off into sleep for five minutes—maybe a half hour. You talk much of a man named Lockhart and a gun to be given him. Ah, I tell you, you were a mad one, stark raving mad—*demente!* In time, your struggles grow more weak. Finally, you go to sleep. Now you are awake. *Por dios!* You will not refuse coffee and food now."

Tucson was suddenly aware of the keen pangs of hunger. "You're right, *amigo.*"

Esteban leaped for the door. "Benita!" Other

words followed that had to do with food. Then he returned, drew a chair up to the bed.

"It is good to see you again, Señor Tucson."

Tucson laughed. "It was damn good you saw me. You have my thanks. But I do not see why—"

Esteban's eyes widened. "Even now you do not remember? Look you, think back to Agua Prieta of five years ago. You do not remember Esteban Mercado, the *Mejicano* boy whom you say speaks always the 'fonny Anglish' like that?" He dropped Spanish completely, "You remember, you say I am the foolish for rideeng? No, that ees not eet. So long I no spik Anglish, I forget, no? I was the rideeng fool, that ees eet. I'm break a *caballo* you are purchas' for a frien'. I'm come weeth my family weeth horses to sell. In Agua Prieta. Think, *amigo.* When my Antonio ees made—"

"Something to do with a doctor, wa'n't it?" Tucson frowned, also dropping into his own tongue, while memory's fingers commenced to trace past events on his brain.

"*Sí, sí,*" excitedly, "that ees eet. My Benita and my little 'Tony get seek with the long disease. They can not make the breath. Not yet have I the money for the doctair. There ees no doctair een Agua Prieta. You pay for the horse you buy, cross the line to Douglas, rouse out of a bed a doctair who does not weesh to come, but you make heem. *Socorro!* At once my Benita gets well. Two days later little 'Tony he show sign of life. Only for you, my so good frien', my 'Tony be *poco angelito* now—"

"That's good." Tucson was remembering the incident at last.

"Is better than that. That doctair he charge high price to stay so long. I have not the money for my *caballos*. Eet ees you, my so good frien' that leave money when you ride away. Always I am look for you to pay." His face fell. "Now eet cannot do. I am what you call broke again."

"Forget it," Tucson said awkwardly, brushing away the man's thanks. "Judgin' what you've done for me, that was dough well-spent."

Esteban smiled widely, "Dough cast on the water comes back bread, no, Señor Tucson?"

Tucson laughed. "You're a long way from Agua Prieta now."

"*Sí,*" and Mercado's face fell. "I come here to raise the cattle. I have, look you, a good bull and twenty cows. Now is left only the bull and eight cows."

"Rustlers?"

"Thieves from Malpaisaño," bitterly. "They take my stock and I dare say nozzing. Eet's bad town."

"Not all bad Mexicans, either, eh?"

"Only Mexicans what is lef' ees bad, but not so many. Some few, like myself would like to leave, but we do not wish to give up our property. Mostly is bad *Americanos*. All the time is raise hell. The *jefe* is pay money not to ask the Government for help. I do not like eet, no."

"They sure tried to raise hell last night."

"Las' night," looking up in surprise, "you mean your trouble?"

"Uh-huh—"

"But Señor Tucson, that is night before las'."

"What!" Tucson fairly shouted the word.

"*Seguro.* You have been sleep—"

"Yes, like a damn fool," Tucson said bitterly. "I've been here damn nigh two days. And I should have met Stony and Lullaby southwest of Malpaisaño two nights ago. They'll be plumb crazy—"

He swung his long legs out of bed and commenced to dress hurriedly.

Benita appeared with plates of food and a steaming coffee pot which she set on the chest of drawers. Esteban was sputtering swift Spanish protests, to which Tucson paid little heed. The woman joined in, pleading with Tucson to eat. The small boy started to weep noisily.

Mercado finally made himself heard. "You mus' eat," he said firmly, "an' get the strength back. While you eat I'll talk."

"About what?" Tucson snapped. "I've wasted too much talk already."

"It will not be wasted—what I say now. I'm come to my senses and think a leetle."

"Shoot," Tucson said impatiently.

A chair was drawn up to the bed. Tucson seated himself on the blankets and commenced to eat from the chair that served as a table. Benita had departed with the small boy.

"Look you," Esteban said, "I'm go to town theese morning to see what I can hear. Rumors I listen for. One hears much but puts the finger on so little. But of this I am certain. It was known that you were coming to Malpaisaño. The word was out you were to be captured."

"That explains the knockout drops—"

"But this Lullaby and Stony you speak of. They are names, no?"

Tucson nodded. "My pardners."

Mercado nodded sadly. "In town I hear much of two *Americanos* who go on the—how you say heem, the prod?—go on the prod. They ask for one who is known as *El Escorpión*—"

"Cripes!" Tucson started to his feet, then again sat down.

"I am afraid they weel find this scorpion. When I was riding from the town, I'm see two *Americanos* tied in their saddles being taken away—"

"Good God!" Tucson quickly gave a description of his two pardners.

Mercado nodded. "Those are the men."

A wave of pain swept across Tucson's face. "They pro'bly got tired waitin' for me to show up. Mebbe they heard those shots. Anyway, when

130

they can't find me, like a coupla of loyal rannies they go gunnin' around, askin' for the Scorpion, thinkin' I been captured. This is a hell of a note!"

"Is so," Esteban agreed sadly. "What can I do to help?"

Tucson pondered, his features screwed into furrows of thought. Finally, "Listen, Steve, did you ever hear of the Valley of the Singing Scorpion?"

Esteban shrugged his shoulders. "One hears many rumors. If such a place exists, I do not know where."

"You've heard of a man calling himself *El Escorpión?*"

"*Seguro!* Who has not? He is a *bandido,* a revolutionist, a devil to some, a saviour to others. He claims he will bring great changes to Mexico. I only know he is not good for my people. The government would pay highly for his head. In Malpaisaño, those bad ones call him a great man. But, *por Dios!* those *Americanos* make up his following."

"If you know this, why don't you report it to the Government?"

"Because I do not wish terrible things to happen to my family. I would not dare hint it outside. The Scorpion has spies everywhere. Many think he has men of the Government behind his actions."

Tucson shook his head. "I reckon that's bluff, but it keeps folks hereabouts from talking. . . . You ever seen the Scorpion?"

"If so, I did not know him. There are many *Americanos* come to Malpaisaño—"

"Do you know where his hideout is?"

"Someplace, it is rumored, in the San Federico Mountains, south of town."

"Listen, Steve, I know about where it is. I've got to get in there. Lullaby and Stony are waiting—"

*"Madre de Dios!"* and Mercado's face went ashen with fright. "You will meet only death, Tucson *amigo.*"

"It's a chance I've got to run," grimly. "Where's my horse?" Tucson drained his coffee cup and rose, buckling on his gun belts.

"The *caballo* is well taken care of, out back. Your saddle and saddle roll are there—"

Tucson strode swiftly out of the room, through the kitchen, thanking Benita briefly as he passed by, and stepped into the ranch yard. There was a corral several yards away, a rickety barn, and a *ramada* in the shade of which stood his horse.

"No, you'll stay here," Tucson was answering Esteban's suggestion. "You stay here and take care of your family. I'll be back. I just want to look over the ground today, unless—"

"Unless what, *amigo?*"

"I can tell you better later," Tucson said grimly. "What direction is Malpaisaño from here?"

"Three miles to the northeast—"

"Good, I'm headed in the right direction anyway." The bridle and saddle blanket were on the horse now. Tucson lifted the saddle. A few moments later he had tightened the cinch, put foot into stirrup and swung up.

His hand went down to grip Mercado's. "I'll see you later, *amigo.*"

"*Que vuelva pronto,*" Esteban said anxiously.

"Sure, Steve, I'll be back as soon as I can."

"But if I could be of help—"

"Maybe you can later. *Quien sabe?*"

"*Quien sabe?*" Mercado nodded. "*Adios.*"

"*Adios, amigo.*"

Tucson turned the horse's head, touched its ribs lightly with spurs and rode out of the tiny ranch yard. A hoof-marked and rutted trail was found a quarter of a mile from the house. It led southwest.

Tucson rode steadily for an hour. Once when he looked back, the Mercado house had been blotted out with the tall cactus growth. "Good Mex," Tucson mused once. "Good luck he found me."

He kept going. Tall century plants, giant cacti, prickly pear and other forms of growth barred his way, but always before him he had the rutted trail to show the way. Once he passed the ruins of an old adobe house. The walls were down and overgrown with stunted *mesquitl.* Tall agave towered on all sides.

Tucson said to himself, "Looks like there might have been a *pulque* plantation here twenty-five years or so ago. Reckon that helps to account for so many of these big century plants."

He was passing through a regular forest of the huge spear-pointed agaves. Beyond, above their tips, he could see the purple rugged line of the San Federico Mountains. Within another fifteen minutes, the trail broke up: hoof marks and wagon ruts ran off in all directions.

"Just in case," Tucson said, "anybody gets to followin' this trail they won't know what way to head. Seems like I should be seein' that Cathedral Rock before long."

Now the horse was commencing to climb. The way grew more rocky. Great slabs of granite and huge boulders barred the way. The agaves were giving way to twisted yuccas. There was more rock and less plant growth encountered. Suddenly, swinging from around a gigantic upthrust of pinkish granite, Tucson saw Cathedral Rock.

It towered up and up, a great fantastically formed mass of red sandstone, jutting out from a long rocky ridge, against the blue sky. On a bare, level plain it would have been visible for fifty miles or more, but Tucson had been traveling through high plant growth or huge heaps of broken rock.

Tucson drew rein a moment to look around. Cathedral Rock must have reached, straight up, for three hundred feet. The wind and sand erosion of centuries had formed those high, fluted spires, carved those lacy-looking filigreed walls of crimson rock. Grotesque figures lined its terraced walls—men and queer animals and ships, huge beyond comparison. Apertures like great windows showed blue sky here and there. At one point a large flowerlike formation balanced precariously on a long tapering stem—the stem in reality probably thirty feet in diameter. No doubt in Tucson's mind now why it was known as Cathedral Rock. The three towering spires, themselves cut in thousands of fantastic designs, at the front end of the massive bulk of red sandstone, were strangely like the spires seen on famous churches.

"She's somethin' to look at all right," Tucson mused, "but I got business."

He walked the horse from now on. Twenty-five minutes passed, before he stopped and dismounted, weighting the dragging reins with a chunk of loose rock. From this point on he went forward on foot. Ticklish business this. It seemed almost impossible to approach quietly.

Now sheer cliffs rose hundreds of feet above Tucson's head. Cluttered bits of rock barred Tucson's progress. He twisted and turned and doubled back more than once, vaguely sensing, at last, that he was following a dim trail that had been coursed a thousand times before. Here and there, queer carvings, almost obliterated by sand-blasting winds, caught his eye, as he passed flat, upstanding rocks.

With huge boulders towering all around him, he felt like an ant crawling for endless miles through a gravel pit. Suddenly, he heard voices.

He slowed pace and approached more cautiously. Past a great gray slab of stone he proceeded, then rounding an eighteen-foot high granite boulder, he suddenly dropped on his stomach and peered around an edge of rock.

The earth sloped steeply to his right and below. For a moment he couldn't see anything except a twisted mass of *mesquitl,* yucca and prickly pear. Then, far down the slope, he made out a huge dark opening in the rock. He couldn't see light beyond, though he knew it for the tunnel entrance.

Voices again. He was too far away to distinguish the words, but he made out through the spiny growth the forms of two men, seated on low boulders, at either side of the tunnel entrance. Both men were armed with six-shooters and held rifles across knees. Tucson recognized the men as having been in the Cantina of Singing Birds the night he got the drugged drink. He drew back a trifle, settled to a more comfortable position to consider matters. It would be impossible to approach the tunnel entrance without being seen. That would mean shots. Even if Tucson downed both men the shots would probably raise an alarm for those at the other end of the tunnel.

The tunnel entrance was high and wide enough to admit a horse and rider. Did that size continue for its length, and how long was it? Were there other guards, farther on? It would be impossible to drop down on the guards, at the entrance, from above. The tunnel opening was cut in a flat rock wall that stretched up and up for hundreds of feet. No shelves nor ledges there on which to gain a foothold. Tucson frowned.

Somehow he'd have to get into the tunnel without the guards knowing it. But how? He might try slipping past at night, but that appeared almost impossible. They might have lanterns. Nope, it couldn't be done that way.

And then, quite suddenly, Tucson caught the glimmering of an idea. But would it work? Mebbe yes, mebbe no. Anyway, it was worth trying. If it didn't work. . . . Hell! He simply had to get into that tunnel. This was no time to consider risks. Tucson cast a last glance at the tunnel entrance. Somehow it didn't look like a work of nature. It had more the appearance of a man-made job. The top of the tunnel entrance was a straight, horizontal line. The sides were just as straight but slanted slightly outward. It all looked too perfect. Tucson laughed as he edged back.

"I'm sure goin' cuckoo, I reckon, if I figure Janisary and his gang of coyotes tunneled straight through that ridge. It'd take years and years. It's sure a neat job, at that, judgin' from that entrance with its slanting sides. Sort of reminds me of pictures of these old Aztec buildings I've seen. Come to think of it, those carvin's I noted on those flat rocks a spell back, looked like ancient Injun work too. Howsomever, the thing to do is get into the tunnel, not stay here figurin' who built it."

Quietly he retreated back through the cactus and rock, the way he had come. A short time later he was on his horse, heading back toward the Mercado *rancho.*

"It'll need Esteban's help, but mebbe it can be worked," Tucson mused, as he pushed the horse along at a fast gait. . . .

# 12

# Into the Scorpion's Nest

It was night when Tucson arrived back at the Mercado establishment. Esteban met him in the ranch yard, relief showing plainly in his words of welcome. The Mexican called to Benita to prepare food, then unsaddled and rubbed down Tucson's horse while the cowboy talked:

"To begin with, Steve," Tucson said, "I found an entrance into the Valley of the Scorpion. It's guarded—"

"*Por Dios!* It really exists such a place then—?"

"What I'm up against now, is to find a way to draw those two guards away from the entrance long enough to allow me to get in. I can't think of any way to steal up on 'em and silence 'em. When they come to, they'd realize somebody had slipped into the Valley—"

"You cannot shoot them—?"

"That won't do either. They'd be found in time. Probably when the guards change. It's a cinch those two don't spend all their time guarding that entrance. Besides it goes against the grain to shoot a man down without a chance."

"Would they give you a similar chance?" Esteban asked quickly.

"Pro'bly not," Tucson conceded. "That's not the point. Any shooting would raise an alarm. I've got to get into that valley without anyone knowing there's been a stranger even near the place. Once inside I can—"

"You can what?" Esteban asked eagerly.

"Dam'd if I know," Tucson laughed. "I'll start makin' plans for that end of it, when I'm in the Valley—"

"Look you," Esteban said, his eyes wide with the idea. "It might be done this way. Together, you and I will go to this *Roca Catedral*—to think, so many times I have seen that huge rock, but never did I think of a tunnel—but I waste time in the talk. Look, you and I will go there, very quietly. You will creep up, close to the tunnel. A short distance away I make the groan like a sick man. The guards come to see what is wrong. You steal inside—"

"And what happens to you?" Tucson asked curiously.

"I'm lay on the groun', like ver' sick man. Make the heart-rendering groan while I tell those guards

I'm lose my way while I have the illness of the stomach from drink too much of *tequila.* They weel get ver' angree, call me lous-ee bum, because they hav' waste time on such a low one as me."

"So what?"

"So then, they tell me to get the hell from out theese place. I get on my *caballo* and ride away. Meanwhile, you are go like the flash of lightneeng through theese tunnel." He paused, teeth flashing white in the starlight, then added, *"Muy bueno,* eh?"

Tucson shook his head. *"Muy malo, amigo."*

The Mexican's eyes widened in surprise. *"Por qué así?"*

"Why not?" Tucson countered. He explained his objections to the Mexican's plan: "It's a good idea, Steve, except that they wouldn't take a chance on letting you go. They'd probably fill your carcass with lead. At best they'd take you prisoner."

"On that I would take the chance—"

"Not on my account you won't. You've got Benita and little Tony to think of—"

"Once you gave them their lives—"

"I told you to forget that once—"

"But, Tucson *amigo,* it is my wish to help."

"You'll get your chance. You come along with me and it'll be your job to bring my horse back here—"

"You will not require the *caballo?*"

"It's a cinch I can't sneak a horse into that tunnel.

Even if I could get him in, the tunnel might narrow down a heap after I've left the entrance. Then what would I do with a horse? Turn him loose?"

Esteban nodded comprehension. "Eet ees one problem."

Benita's voice called from the doorway of the kitchen. Esteban finished with the horse and the two men made their way to the house. Benita was all smiles as she placed food on the table before Tucson. There were *frijoles, tortillas,* a sweetish preserve, coffee and a bottle of native *vino.*

After a time the smiles left the brown features of the Mexican woman as she listened to the talk of this tall, red-haired *Americano.* She stifled little Tony's childish prattle and listened intently to every word spoken. Now and then she placed a stick of wood in the small iron stove, or fumbled busily with the wick in the lamp.

Tucson finally noticed her look of apprehension. "There is no need for you to fear, *señora,*" he said. "Esteban will have no risks to take. He accompanies me only to have charge of returning with my *caballo.*"

"I fear also for our good friend," the woman said quietly. "This is not the United States—"

"But I go to deal with bad ones from the States," Tucson cut in. "It's not an unfamiliar job."

"That's as it may be. For anything we can give to help, you are gladly welcome. We already owe much."

*"Muchas gracias,"* Tucson thanked her.

Finishing his supper, he went on talking to Esteban: "First," he said, "will you sell me a goat?"

"A goat?" the Mexican asked blankly.

*"Sí"* Tucson grinned, "I noticed you have a half dozen or so. They were straying about your barn today. Were they not yours?"

"Oh, *sí,* the goat. But for what?"

Tucson switched back to his own tongue, "Mebbe this plan sounds crazy, but I want to take a goat out to that tunnel, get it to make some sort of noise. Anything to draw those guards away long enough to see what is happening. I'm figurin' on their curiosity doin' the work. A man would arouse their suspicions as well as their curiosity. They'll think nothing of finding a goat. If a goat is shot, there is little lost."

"I don't know," the Mexican said slowly. "It might do; again it might not. But I can furnish the goat surely."

"I'll pay you a good price—"

*"Socorro!* Would you insult me?"

"Listen, Steve, when—if—I ever get back to the States I'm aimin' to pay for all this, enough to set you back in cattle."

There were further protestations. Benita broke in to say swiftly, "Let him have Maria—"

Esteban's face lighted up. "Maria! The very animal. For a year now I have been urged to dispose of that fiend in a goat's likeness. A very devil of sin, that Maria. A nuisance that devours fine clothing and digests rubbish with equal ease. A very imp of perversity, with the long whiskers of a grandfather, who attacks, with stealth, from the rear. A being of skin and bones and hair with the soul of the Evil One himself and with horns that—"

"Did you say the name was Maria?" Tucson chuckled.

Benita blushed. Esteban coughed apologetically, and tried to explain in English. "Theese Maria, he is not of the female species. Some one, when he is a ver' small goat, hav' make the slight error in naming heem. In all probability eet ees because he ees stubborn like a woman even in those days."

Benita cast a reproachful glance at Esteban who laughed heartily. He stopped suddenly, "But, see, I talk foolishness when we should be on our way."

"No particular hurry, now," Tucson said. "I don't want to get there until after the moon has gone down. Too much light before. I'm not even sure the idea will work, but if those guards do bite they won't think anything of a goat straying over their way. There's plenty goats in this country and they stray around pretty much like the mind of the man must have done that named Maria."

Three hours later the two men were mounted and started on their way. Across the saddle, in front of Tucson, rode a very ancient and intractable goat which uttered from time to time plaintive bleats, through the burlap that covered its head, in protest regarding the indignity of having its feet bound and its head muffled in an old sack.

Tucson said, "Seems like Maria don't like this night ridin'."

"Since I have heem," the Mexican replied with some warmth, "that Maria hav' not like *anyzing.*"

"I sure hope he shuts up his bellyachin' before we get there," Tucson said seriously. "Dumb fool that I am, I never thought of his bleatin'."

"Pairhaps he weel make the stop before long."

Tucson wasn't so sure of that. He commenced to feel that Maria was very likely to upset all his plans.

The two men rode on in silence. The moon had crossed its peak now and was on the decline. The tall *agave* branches threw barred shadows across the riders as they traveled through the night, only the soft thudding of the horses' hoofs breaking the silence.

Mile after mile slipped past. Once, looking at Esteban's face in the light of the dying moon, Tucson could see the Mexican was worried about the outcome of all this. The horses were reaching higher ground now, the rock becoming more scattered, the plant growth less. A wisp of cloud floated across the face of the moon, followed by a deeper darkness. The horses were forced to proceed more slowly.

At last they arrived at approximately the spot where Tucson had left his horse earlier in the day. He climbed down, stretched his legs. Esteban stepped down at his side.

"It is bes', *amigo,*" the Mexican faltered, "if I go with you. I do not like to see—"

"Look here, Steve," Tucson said warmly, "that means a lot, but my plans are all made. I'm goin' through with 'em."

By this time, Maria's pitiful protests had been succeeded by a philosophical, sullen silence. Tucson expected the goat to break out in a renewed clamor when it was lifted down, but, apparently, Maria was reconciled to his fate. He didn't utter a sound.

Tucson set the trussed-up animal on the earth, fumbled at the roll back of his saddle a moment. A second later Esteban saw he held a forty-five six-shooter, very similar to the ones he wore at his thighs.

"Just somethin' I figure to deliver to a friend," Tucson said lightly. He thrust the gun inside his shirt.

Esteban's voice wasn't steady when he said good-bye. He gripped Tucson's hand hard, swung up to his saddle and took the reins of Tucson's horse.

"I am wish," he said seriously, "I could wait here—"

"I may not come out for some time, Steve—"

"Or at leas', leave the *caballo*. You may need heem—"

"Wouldn't do to leave a horse tied out here," Tucson shook his head. "Somebody might find him and then realize that somethin' was wrong— but, shucks, I'm not in the valley yet. You run along back to Benita and the kid. I'll have a good time with Maria."

"That goat," the Mexican tried to be humorous, "if anyzing should happen to heem, I'm hope it ees nozzing simple."

Tucson grinned in the darkness. *"Adios, paisano."*
*"Vaya con Dios, amigo."*

Slumped dejectedly in the saddle, Esteban turned the horses and started back over the course they had come. Tucson looked after him through the darkness, until the gloom swallowed up horses and man.

"Go with God yourself, you game little Mex," he said softly. "You ain't expectin' to see me again, I reckon. Well, maybe you won't. *Quien sabe?* Who knows?"

Tucson reached down, got a grip on Maria and slung the old goat over his shoulders, then started off on foot, toward Cathedral Rock.

It grew darker as he threaded his way as softly as possible over the rock-cluttered way. The moon was dropping fast now. Another hour and a half and dawn would be near. Tucson commenced to breathe a trifle harder.

"Maria," he said softly, "you sure ain't no feather-weight on a hike. Me, I can feel blisters formin'. How do you like that?"

The goat struggled a trifle but remained silent.

"Esteban certain slandered you proper," Tucson mused. "He said you wa'n't nothin' but skin and bones and horns and whiskers. If you wa'n't a goat I'd say you was plumb hawg-fat."

He set the goat down on the earth to rest, after a bit. Maria struggled violently for a time, let out a frightened bleat. Tucson swore softly in the darkness. "Hope that sound didn't carry, Maria. I don't want those yeggs to suspect you're only a old bachelor goat, until they've had time to get a good look at you."

He picked up the goat again and trudged on, swinging farther to the south than he had done earlier that day in making this journey. For a time the stars showed brighter with the moon gone. Tucson was grateful for their pale light. The way was difficult to negotiate in silence through the gloom. Remembered landmarks had, somehow, disappeared.

He had put down the goat to rest himself three times, before he sighted dimly the huge dark mass that was Cathedral Rock. Now he moved more cautiously than ever when he again picked up his hairy burden.

"And you don't smell like no lady either, Maria," Tucson cogitated. "I'll sure be glad when the time comes for you to justify your fragrant existence. Whether this stunt works or not, Steve ought to be plumb pleased that I took you away."

Before long Tucson spied a light through the tangled thicket of cacti and chaparral. He bore farther to his left and made out, peering around an edge of upstanding granite, the gleaming flames of a small fire before the entrance to the tunnel. Two guards were seated there, as before, but at this distance Tucson couldn't decide whether or not they were the same guards he had seen previously.

Now came the ticklish part of the business: to approach close enough to dash into the tunnel entrance at the first opportunity, and yet stay far enough away so as not to be heard moving about. Stealthily, step by step, Tucson proceeded nearer —no easy task loaded with Maria as he was. Maria struggled from time to time, but in his gratitude at the goat's continued silence, Tucson almost became fond of the animal.

"Mebbe it's just your personality that's against you, Maria," Tucson said to himself, and added, "A dang good scrubbin' with soap and water might remove some of that personality, at that."

Now he wasn't more than twelve yards away from the tunnel entrance. Shielded by a low row of tumbled boulders and broken sandstone fragments, he set down the goat and peered at the guards. No, they weren't the same fellows he had seen earlier that day, but evidently they had been in the Cantina of the Singing Birds the night Tucson made his escape:

Tucson heard one of them say, "I tell you, Bart, I'd like to draw a bead on that long-legged redhead. One thousand bucks would look good to me—dead or alive, the chief said. I reckon he'd sooner get him alive though."

"If you didn't have no more luck downin' him with your gun than you did that night they slugged his beer, you wouldn't get far—"

"J'ever see a feller fight off the dope the way that Smith hombre did?"

"It was plumb miraculous, Rube. I never see the like."

The guard called Bart bent over and tossed a fresh length of wood on the fire. For a few moments the flames brightened in the chill night air, then the fire died down again. Tucson crouched close to the top of his rock shelter. So Janisary was offering a reward for him, eh? Dead or alive, but preferably alive.

The guard named Rube rose from his seat, commenced to pace back and forth, stretching and yawning. "Sure seems a long time until dawn, Bart."

Maria suddenly struggled and made faint sounds. Rube stopped and listened, looking straight at the point at which Tucson was hidden. Luckily the fire was small, too small to throw a reflecting light of any consequence. Maria quieted after a moment.

Bart said, "What's the matter?"

"Thought I heard somethin'," from Rube. "Reckon I was mistaken." He resumed his seat.

Tucson knelt at the old goat's side, gently removed the burlap sacking. Maria rolled his eyes as Tucson laid the sacking on the ground and commenced to untie the rawhide thongs that bound the animal's feet. There was an evil light in Maria's eyes that Tucson couldn't see. Maria was willing to be peaceful for a few minutes longer, while his pent-up emotions contemplated revenge.

The rawhide thongs were off now. Marie rose stiffly to his feet, wagging his long beard. He shook himself a trifle and stood stiff-legged watching Tucson with belligerent gaze.

Tucson gave the animal a push, hoping to send it running past the fire, but at a distance which would prevent its form being distinguished between the rocks and cacti. Lord! If Maria could only draw the guards away from the tunnel entrance for half a second, he'd make a dash for it.

Maria sidled, crabwise, a few feet away, still eyeing Tucson, but moving peacefully enough. Tucson swore under his breath. Dang it! he wanted that blasted goat to make some noise. He'd probably have to urge it on its way. The billy-be-damned-goat was altogether too peaceful and forgiving. Tucson thought, mebbe it's taken a liking to me. Well, I was pretty gentle with him.

The goat had stopped. Tucson thought of the

burlap sacking and rawhide thongs. It would never do to leave "sign" like that where it might be found. He stooped lower, reached the articles, tucked them into his belt and started to rise.

*Crash!* Something struck Tucson on the shoulder with terrific force: Maria! Maria had started, and concluded, one of his head-down charges. From the standpoint of accuracy and devastating results it constituted a score that Maria could well be proud of. Tucson was bowled over as though struck with a battering ram, which in reality he had been!

He went down with a clatter against the loose rock, kept his head, swore to himself and scrambled to his knees. Maria was backing off, horned head lowered, preparing for a second charge.

By this time the guards were on their feet, eyes peering into the darkness beyond the firelight.

"Who's there?" Rube called sharply.

Bart snarled. "Come in slow, with your hands up. I'll be shootin' if you—"

Rube's gun cracked sharply. A splinter of rock chipped off near Tucson's head, the leaden slug ricochetted with an angry whine off through the darkness. Bart's rifle sounded now, the slug coming perilously close to Tucson.

But Tucson had his hands too full with Maria to think about flying bullets for a moment. Maria had started another charge. Tucson drew one gun, jerked aside as Maria came in, full of battle.

As the goat neared him, Tucson rapped it sharply on the head with his gun barrel.

Maria stoppped short, whirled half around, shaking his head. His legs commenced to quiver, then he opened his mouth and emitted a loud bleat.

Tucson groaned, "Oh, cripes!" under his breath. And in the next instant had an inspiration: he raised his head and a long, blood-curdling scream left his lips in a very excellent imitation of an American cougar's cry. The sound echoed and re-echoed through the night.

"By God! It's a puma cat!" he heard Bart exclaim.

Tucson waited with beating heart for the next move. He was trying to watch Maria and at the same moment keep an eye on the guards. Maria looked undecided. Suddenly, as though realizing he'd better not chance another blow from that gun barrel he went bounding away over the rocks, his hoofs making a clatter as he moved.

Tucson watched him disappear, saw him a few moments later, a ghostly gray form in the darkness, moving swiftly through the screening growth directly opposite the tunnel mouth.

"There he goes!" Bart yelled.

Rube levered in another cartridge, jerked the rifle to shoulder. An orange lance of fire left the long barrel. An instant later there came a frantic thrashing at the point where Tucson had last seen Maria.

Bart exclaimed, "You got him!"

"Fast shootin', eh?" exultantly from Rube. "C'mon!"

The two men left the tunnel entrance and ran toward the spot where Maria had vanished. Forgotten for the moment were their duties as guards.

Tucson rose, slipped through the rock shadows like an Apache Indian with scarcely a sound. Once inside the tunnel he breathed a long sigh of relief. It was dark as pitch a few feet back in the long opening. Another long sigh. He was past the first guards anyway. Would there be more?

"I reckon," he mused, "it don't make no difference what your sex is now, Maria."

Listening, he heard the two guards coming back. "Dammit," he heard Rube say, "I wish I'd got that damn cat, 'stead of a stinkin' ol' goat. I thought I heard a goat, once—"

"Can you imagine that damn cat comin' that close to us?" Bart said. "I never do like to hear them things howl. Always reminds me of a woman screamin'—"

"They do when you hit 'em hard," Rube laughed.

"But you know what I mean."

"Sure. Reckon it's a good thing for us that was a goat. Pro'bly got away from some Mex headin' him to market. I suppose that cat was stalkin' it an' the goat headed our way. Regardless if it was only a goat, you got to admit that was straight shootin'—right through the heart—"

"Say," Bart put in, "you better drift back and tell the boys not to get excited about those shots. They'll be comin' out hell-bent for election and will be sore as hell havin' their sleep broke off just for a little goat huntin'—"

"*I* better go back?" Rube said indignantly. "You got a broken laig?" He added, "Hell! I don't think them shots would carry that far. These cliffs is pretty high you know—"

"High or not high," Bart said stubbornly, "if the boys is waked up without good reason, Gage will be plumb peeved."

Finally they tossed a coin to see who would go. Bart lost, and after accusing Rube of cheating, headed for the tunnel mouth.

Tucson crouched back against one wall in the darkness. He could have reached out and touched Bart when the man passed. Bart's steps died away after a time. The minutes slipped by. Rube, seated by the fire, rolled a cigarette, muttering over and over to himself, "Imagine that damn cat comin' that near. Must have been plumb hungry. Lucky he didn't jump us."

After a time, Tucson heard Bart's returning steps. Again the man walked close to him while Tucson held his breath. Then Bart was back talking to Rube. Tucson heard him say, "Nobody was awake. I guess they can't hear shots in there."

Tucson commenced to retreat from the tunnel mouth. Farther and farther he penetrated into the inky darkness. The tunnel seemed endless. Twice he made sharp turns. Finally, a spot of grayish light widened and widened before his eyes. A minute later he saw a few faint stars just fading from sight.

"Well," he told himself grimly, "so far so good. The show's about to begin."

As he stepped from the tunnel, he saw that dawn wasn't far distant.

# 13

# Dead Man's Chance

By the time Tucson emerged from the tunnel into open air he saw the reason for the sharp turns he had encountered in negotiating the long passage: the tunnel builders, whoever they were, had undoubtedly taken advantage of the most narrow places in cutting through the high rock wall, thus cleverly shortening to a minimum the work to be accomplished. Two long spurs of rock extended for a hundred yards on either side of the valley entrance to the tunnel.

It was still too dark to see much. Tucson knew little more than that he was in the Valley of the Singing Scorpion at last. The next thing was to see what could be done about getting in touch with Stony and Lullaby, see if he could locate young Pete Lockhart.

Tucson moved cautiously through the slightly

graying light. There didn't seem to be any guards at this end of the tunnel. Probably Janisary felt himself immune from discovery. Hugging the high wall of the spur of rock on his right, Tucson edged gingerly farther into the open, rounded the end of the spur and kept pushing along between tumbled heaps of rock and great clumps of prickly pear. Here and there he felt grass under his feet, and concluded that the valley must possess more fertile earth than was to be found outside.

A few minutes later, to his surprise, he passed a tree that gave off a dry rustling sound in the early dawn breeze—a cottonwood tree. There were other trees here and there, both cottonwoods and mesquites. Darkness was fading from the sky. Across the valley Tucson could see a high, dark mass where the opposite wall of the valley cut a sharp line across the swiftly fading stars. It was too dark yet in the valley itself to see a great deal, though Tucson managed to make out the outlines of several moundlike hills.

Looking back once, toward the southern end of the valley, Tucson caught the shine of a fire being lighted. Someone was astir. It would probably be best to find a hiding place until daylight pointed out a more exact procedure. Edging still further toward the north end of the valley, Tucson found a spot between two granite boulders, well screened by various growths from view of the rest of the valley. The earth sloped slightly upward here, until it reached the precipitous sheer rock wall that formed the north end of the valley, at Tucson's back.

Tucson sat down to wait, rolled and lighted a cigarette, shielding the flame of the match with his hands. Objects in the valley grew more distinct. The stars were gone now. Abruptly, it seemed, night was gone. A faint rose light was stealing into being, dispelling the gray curtain that had obscured Tucson's vision.

Tucson's jaw dropped as he craned his neck to see over the stretch of land. He was in a long, platter-shaped valley, probably two miles long by half a mile wide, stretching north and south. The valley was enclosed by a steep rock wall, extending on all sides, that rose for hundreds of feet skyward. Not a chance of scaling those abrupt heights. There didn't seem any way for a man to get a toe- or hand-hold anywhere. Once a prisoner was held inside the valley, the guards at the tunnel were the only required precautions to prevent escape.

Tucson's eyes widened as he took in the sight. Less than half a mile away was a huge, four-sided mound of earth, slanting upward in the form of a pyramid. It was probably a hundred feet in height and three hundred feet square. Mostly it was covered with earth and cactus growth, but on one side, facing due east, this covering of centuries had been cleared away to disclose the broad flight of stone steps, apparently stretching the width of the pyramid's eastern side, which led to the flat surface at the summit of the huge stone structure. On this surface was a small building, similar in size to a small one-room house. The building was flat-roofed and surrounded by a low wall. The whole appeared to be constructed of well-fitted blocks of volcanic rock, probably held together with an adobe mortar.

"My gosh!" Tucson exclaimed with some awe. "Ancient Injun stuff—Aztec, maybe. I remember seeing a picture of a pyramid somethin' like this once. Lemme see, Pyramid of the Sun, it was called. Seems like it was down near Mexico City, though. Never heard of anything like this, this far north. If I remember, it wa'n't Aztecs built that sun pyramid, at that. What were they called? Toltec people? That was the word, Toltec. Wonder if this is the same sort of buildin'. I'll be damned!"

His eyes strayed farther through the valley. From his position on rising ground, he had a fairly good view of the whole valley. A hundred yards south of the pyramid was a flat-roofed, square building, about the size of a small house and built of the same material as the pyramid. A wall, with a break for a narrow entrance on the north side, surrounded the building. Apparently, this building had been recently excavated, as the heaps of rubble and earth about tended to show. On either side, also, was a smaller flat-topped mound with slanting sides of earth, overgrown with cacti. Picks and shovels lay about.

"This sure beats anything I ever saw," Tucson mused. "I'll bet there's a buried city hereabouts and that there buildin' is a temple of some sort. Those old Injuns was hell on religion. Probably two more temples under those other mounds."

Set perpendicularly into the earth, midway between the southern face of the pyramid and the three buildings Tucson had chosen to term temples, was a row of eight, oblong-shaped monument-like slabs of solid rock. Tucson judged each one to be a foot in thickness and two feet wide. He figured the height above the earth to be about six feet. These also had but recently been uncovered. Dirt, broken bits of masonry and uprooted plants were scattered everywhere about.

Farther up the valley a slight movement caught Tucson's attention. Now it was light enough to distinguish a good-sized corral containing horses, and at some distance from the stone buildings. A short way from the corral five tents were pitched, their flaps closed. Trees dotted the valley floor— big mesquites and cottonwoods. Grass grew thickly at spots. To Tucson it was strange to see so much verdure in a semi-arid country such as this was. There must be a quantity of water some place.

And then Tucson caught the glimmer of a small stream, emptying into a wide pool at the farther, southern, end of the valley. Cottonwoods lined its banks thickly. Tucson's gaze followed the line of trees and discovered that the stream coursed nearly the whole length of the valley, along the western wall. In fact, it appeared to disappear directly under the wall itself, up near the northern end.

"Reckon that explains the growth," Tucson thought. "Probably underground springs around through here. My gosh! What a sweet spot to hole up, when the law is ridin' your trail hard. Water and grass and a hidden entrance. No other way to get in. A handful of men could stand off an army here, providin' they had food. Food could be raised too. I wonder did Janisary follow Pete Lockhart here, or did Pete stumble on Janisary's hideout. I'll bet that's it! No wonder they ain't ever been able to capture the Scorpion."

Life was commencing to spring up in the valley now. At a fire near the horse corral, a cook was doing things with pots and pans. Several men had emerged from the tents. They wore loose-flapping white cotton garments. Tucson took them to be Mexicans when he saw their big straw sombreros. Other men, garbed in the togs of the range, wearing guns, were rolling blankets under trees, rising, stretching, yawning. There must have been some twenty-five of these last. Probably twenty Mexicans.

Tucson, in his hiding place, rolled another cigarette and considered. No sign of Lullaby and Stony anyplace. When next Tucson glanced toward the fire, the men were gathered around it, holding plates and cups. This much he could see, but the men were too far away for Tucson to recognize any of them. The sun was higher now, touching the topmost rim of the valley's western wall.

While he watched, a white-aproned cook detached himself from the group about the fire and approached carrying a large basket and a pot of coffee. Tucson wondered where he was headed, half wished the man would come near enough that he might get a bit of breakfast himself. On and on the man came until he had reached the middle one of the three buildings Tucson had designated as temples. Here he disappeared through the entrance in the surrounding wall. Two minutes later he reappeared, this time with empty hands, and headed back toward the cook fire where an assistant cook was still tending pots and pans.

"I wonder," Tucson mused, narrow-eyed, "if Lullaby and Stony are held prisoner in that middle temple. I reckon I'll stay right here and watch for a spell. It's a cinch someone's in there."

Impatiently, he waited. A half-hour passed, then three-quarters. No signs of life about the center temple yet. The white-cotton-garmented Mexicans had left the cook fire and were now approaching down the valley floor. In their midst walked a tall, slim man in overalls, woolen shirt and boots. A puncher's roll brim sombrero covered his head. Tucson noted that although he wore a cartridge belt, there was no gun in his holster. Something about the man's bearing reminded Tucson of Rufus Lockhart.

"I'll betcha," Tucson cogitated, "that's young Pete Lockhart. He sure don't look like much of a prisoner though. Wonder what the game is."

The white-clothed *peones* were nearer now. Tucson counted twenty of them in their loose-flapping garments. The man he had guessed to be Lockhart commenced giving directions. The *peones* scattered, most of them heading toward the pyramid, where they commenced clearing away the earth and loose rock that still partly covered the eastern sloping side of the massive structure. Four of the men went to the western-most of the three temples, picked up shovels and picks and started further excavating. The last two commenced digging about the bases of three of the monumentlike rock slabs that faced the pyramid. The young fellow in the overalls went from group to group, directing the work.

Tucson wished he'd come near enough to speak to, but didn't dare step into the open for fear of being seen by someone else.

A movement near the entrance in the center temple wall caught Tucson's eye. Tucson swore softly. Janisary appeared, laughing and talking to a small wisp of a man in riding clothes and flat-heeled boots. This newcomer was a stranger to Tucson. His build was slight, he was baldheaded

162

as the proverbial billiard ball with ragged tufts of gray hair jutting above his ears. As he moved his head from side to side in talking, Tucson caught the glint of light on the spectacles resting on the newcomer's nose. He carried a soft tan hat in one hand.

Janisary proffered cigars. The two lighted up, laughing and talking, and strolled toward the row of slablike monuments, where the little man appeared to be pointing out certain characteristics to Janisary, regarding one of the big stones.

And then, Tucson got the surprise of his life: two women had emerged from the wall surrounding the center temple.

"Well, I'll be everlastingly damned!" Tucson grunted. "What next? And where did they come from? Pete came down here alone, his father said. Friends of Janisary's? Shucks! I'd sort of hate to think so."

The foremost girl, so near as Tucson could judge, was young and pretty, with a piled-up mass of cornsilk hair. She wore white linen riding clothes, with a brilliant-colored neckerchief about her throat. The second woman was probably ten years older, taller than average, with dark chestnut hair. She was dressed in a mannish flannel shirt, high-laced boots, and a divided riding skirt of brown corduroy. In her right hand she carried a stiff-brimmed black Stetson.

Something about the woman caught and held

Tucson's attention. He didn't know exactly what it was, except that he liked her on sight. So greatly did she occupy his attention, that for a moment Tucson didn't notice that young Lockhart —if it was he—had come up to the pair and stood talking to the blond girl.

A moment later, Janisary noticed this, swung away from the little man standing near the monuments, and approached Pete and the two women. Janisary said something to Pete. Tucson couldn't hear the words, but even at that distance he saw Pete flush red, then turn away. Janisary remained talking to the two women.

In a few minutes the blond girl strolled over to join the man at the monuments. Janisary followed, leaving the other woman behind. Something about all this that the other woman didn't like: that much was plain to Tucson from her stiffened attitude.

The blond girl said something to Janisary, turned back toward the center temple. Together, the two women passed through the entrance in the wall. Janisary remained with the other man a few moments, then strode swiftly away, heading toward the southern end of the valley.

"And that's that," Tucson said, "but what does it mean? Where's my pards? S'help me, if the Scorpion has wiped 'em out—" He stopped, refusing to consider that thought. "I sure wish I could dope out a way to talk to Lockhart, if it is

164

Lockhart. Mebbe if I get a better look at him I can tell somethin'. . . ."

The thought remained unfinished as Tucson, crouching low among the rocks and brush, started to work his way around the northern end of the valley wall, that he might approach nearer the man he thought to be Lockhart who was at that time standing among the workmen engaged in digging away the earth that covered the mound to the right of the center temple.

Moving cautiously among the rocks and brush, Tucson finally worked his way around to a point where he wasn't ten yards from the man at whom he wanted a better look. Crouching behind a clump of prickly pear, Tucson could see his features when the man turned toward him two or three times. There was no doubt in Tucson's mind now: it was Pete Lockhart. He had the same bearing as his father, the same build, Rufus Lockhart's bulky shoulders, blue eyes, aquiline nose and straight, firm mouth and chin.

But how to get near him, that was the problem, without being seen by the others? Tucson finally decided the best way was to wait patiently in the brush. It might be that Lockhart would send the men away, or something of the kind. Fifteen minutes passed while Tucson sat motionless, waiting for a break of luck.

Once glancing up, he noticed a buzzard soaring overhead and to his rear a trifle. "Wonder what's back there?" he mused. "Dead rabbit, mebbe, or snake. Reckon I'll give a look-see."

He edged carefully back in the brush, back and back, until he had reached the foot of the western wall. The buzzard flew off as he approached. And then, Tucson realized what it was that had drawn the bird:

About a foot from the precipitous rock wall, sprawled face down on the ground, was a dead man, clothed in the white-cotton garments of a laborer.

"Hmm," Tucson muttered. "Shot, I wonder?"

He stooped by the body, turned it over, and discovered the *peon's* neck was broken. The man didn't appear to have been dead more than a few hours. Tucson looked around, saw nearby a pick lying on the ground, also a length of hempen rope with a loop at one end. Tucson examined the rope, found it to be a lariat.

"Now what in time was that feller tryin' to rope?" he wondered. "And what's the pick for? How'd he break his neck?"

In a few moments the picture was clear to Tucson: twenty feet up the side of the rock wall was a tiny projecting knob, and a short distance above it a second one. Tucson could visualize the dead man tossing the lariat over that small knob.

"That's what happened," Tucson exclaimed softly. "The poor cuss was trying to escape out of the valley. I reckon he figured he could pull himself up to that first knob, once he'd caught it. Then go on to the next. Pro'bly planned to use his pick and dig in to make further progress. Hell's bells! He couldn't make a dent, hardly, in that rock. And he might have known that knob was too small to support any weight on a rope. Nothin' for the rope to grip on. The knob looks too smooth."

He considered some more: "I reckon, at that, it held long enough for this dead hombre to climb part of the way. Then the rope slipped off the knob of rock, and he fell, breaking his neck. He was game to try it, at that. It was just a chance— a long chance. Shucks! If he'd only known it, he was as good as dead when he started. A dead man's chance, that's what it was. . . ."

He broke off, suddenly, eyes widening with a new idea. At last he said softly, "It might work at that. If it does, I can talk to Pete Lockhart. If it doesn't—oh, hell, I won't be any worse off than this dead *peon*. His dead man's chance didn't work; mine may."

# 14

# Pete Lockhart's Story

Fifteen minutes later, Tucson stood arrayed in the loose once-white cotton garments of the dead *peon,* his feet bare, and the big straw sombrero pulled low on his forehead. His own clothing and guns were hidden in the brush, under fragments of loose rock. At another spot he had hidden the corpse of the dead man in the same manner. He hadn't wanted to leave his guns behind, but deemed it best, inasmuch as it would be difficult to conceal three guns under the loose flapping clothing: he had already shoved Pete Lockhart's gun inside his trousers, the weapon being held in place by the strip of twisted rope that supported the pants.

Tucson stooped down and secured the pick, then straightened up. He glanced at his bare feet. "Not so good," he muttered ruefully, adding, "the same goes for red hair. Lookin' like this, it'll be a dead man's chance to pass for one of those *peon* laborers, all right."

His face and arms were well tanned a deep brown. That part was all right. But what to do about the feet and red hair? Finally Tucson had another idea.

He dropped the pick and, crouching low, crept cautiously along the western wall of the valley, until he had reached the stream that flowed there. Here the grass grew high, the brush was thick. The stream wasn't deep, but for several yards along either side the banks were wet and muddy.

Glancing back cautiously from time to time, Tucson rolled up his pants and thrust his legs deeply into the mud. He sank nearly to his thighs. When he stepped to firmer ground, his legs were coated thickly with the rich brown mud. The sun was higher now and he allowed the thick mire to bake on his limbs, while he proceeded to gather up handfuls of the wet earth and rub it well into his thick red hair. In a short time no trace of white skin appeared below the bottoms of his trousers. His red hair had been similarly changed until, while it wasn't the *peon's* black, it still would have more opportunity of going unnoticed beneath the big straw sombrero. More mud had been allowed to cake on arms, shoulders and chest, beneath the flapping white upper garment. After a time, Tucson returned to the spot where he had left the pick.

Picking up the tool, Tucson stood considering a moment. Two other facts bothered him a trifle: the first being the danger of his gray eyes being noticed beneath the sombrero brim; the second, that of being recognized as a stranger by the other *peones* and some sort of alarm being raised. Tucson shrugged his lean shoulders, "Reckon I'll just have to chance that."

For the moment, luck appeared to be with him. Lockhart had moved the laborers around to the opposite side of the temple. Tucson looked quickly about him, then, carrying the pick, he emerged boldly from the brush, strode across the intervening yards to the nearest, partly excavated temple, and commenced to swing the pick with lusty vigor into the sun-baked earth.

For five minutes he worked steadily. At last he

was rewarded by hearing the crunch of footsteps on the gravelly earth, then a voice, "Thought I heard somebody working around here. What you doing, Manuel? I've been wondering where—"

The voice stopped, footsteps crunched on the earth again as the speaker came nearer. Tucson, head bent, kept on working until the man had come close.

The man said suspiciously, "You're a little long-geared for those clothes, hombre."

Tucson replied, between strokes of the pick, "I thought of that, too."

"Look here," sharply, "you're no Mexican. What are you doing here? Where's Manuel? Who are you?"

Tucson kept up the pretense of working while he talked, "Your initials P. E. L.?"

"Yes, what about it?"

"Had 'em stamped on your gun butt once, didn't you?"

Lockhart stopped, his blue eyes narrowing on the working figure before him. He said slowly and suspiciously, "Yes, when I had a gun. Look here, hombre—"

Tucson stopped swinging the pick, looked quickly about him. No one was in sight on his side of the mound. He thrust his hand inside his shirt, produced Lockhart's gun, "Here, you better get this out of sight pronto. It's loaded. All chambers. Thought you might need 'em all—"

Lockhart uttered a quick exclamation, took the gun, glanced at his initials in the butt and quickly thrust the weapon out of sight under his own shirt. His face was ashen white. He said a trifle unsteadily, "Dad knew in time then—"

"I got the gun through sheer chance. Your dad told me—"

"When was this?" the question fairly hurled at Tucson.

Tucson told him.

Pete Lockhart said happily, "Janisary lied then. He said he killed Dad—"

"He damn nigh did." Tucson had resumed his picking. "I'm looking for two pals of mine—Lullaby Joslin and Stony Brooke. I'm Tucson Smith—"

"They're here—in the valley. Janisary captured them somehow. I don't know the details, but—"

"Lord, that's good news—"

"Janisary is holding them captive. Keeps them bound hand and foot most of the time. A heavy guard over 'em at others. I haven't been allowed to talk to them, but so far as I know they haven't been harmed. So you're the hombre who's made all the trouble for Janisary. He's offered a reward to any of his men who bring you in—you or your body—"

"You seem to have quite a bit of freedom," Tucson cut in to say. "Your note—"

"But how did you get that note—and the gun—where's Manuel? How did you get his clothing?"

"I got these clothes off a dead man, back by the wall. He'd tried to scale it. Fell and broke his neck—"

"That's mighty tough news," and Lockhart's face grew grim. "He was a good boy. He told me he'd try to get out. I didn't think he'd be able to do it. I'm wondering about that gun—"

Tucson laughed shortly. "We're sure shootin' questions back and forth. There's a heap I'm wonderin' about too. Your note said you were being held captive. You seem on fairly decent terms with Janisary."

"I have to be," bitterly, "on Norquist's account —and Frieda. Janisary has threatened—"

"I don't get it," Tucson frowned. "Is Norquist here? Your dad mentioned his name. But Frieda?"

"Norquist—Professor Jason Norquist. He holds the Seat of Archaeology at Illaconsin University— where I went to school. Frieda is his daughter—"

"Thought there must be a girl in it somewhere," Tucson grinned under the big straw sombrero.

Pete Lockhart blushed and hurried on, "Professor Norquist says he's on the trail of something big, in this uncovering of the Scorpion People—"

"I don't get that."

"These ruins," Lockhart waved one hand around, "may be the sole remnants of an ancient civilization—centuries before the white man ever set foot on the western continent."

"Injuns—?"

"Call it that if you wish. Aztec or Toltec, perhaps, but Norquist thinks something different. They had a high type of culture."

"Why Scorpion People?"

"They worshipped a god in the form of a scorpion. Where other ancient tribes in Mexico had a feathered serpent for their deity, here, a golden scorpion ruled. Most of it's Greek to me. The feathered serpent was known as Quetzalcoatl, the scorpion was called Zexonteotl—and Norquist isn't even sure of that last—"

"Don't bother to spell those names," Tucson said dryly. He was liking young Pete Lockhart more every minute, admiring the cool attitude with which he was meeting the situation.

"—and Norquist is having one tough time reading the stelae—"

"The which?"

"Have you noticed that row of stone slabs between the pyramid and the temples—this is a temple you're uncovering at present, by the way."

"I'd guessed that much. . . . You mean those sort of monuments?"

"That's it. They're known as stelae. Each one is called a stela. They're covered with glyphs," and at Tucson's look of consternation, Lockhart added, "hieroglyphics, pictographs—you know, ancient writings that can be read by men who study up on such things. Norquist is considered the greatest authority in America—"

"I get you now—"

"But even he is having a tough job. He can only get an idea here and there what it's all about, but he's enjoying himself plenty—"

"Enjoying? Is he working with Janisary?"

"Cripes, no!" Lockhart said. "But he doesn't realize he's a prisoner, either—Say, dig some place else for a while. You've been moving around on one spot—"

"You're right." Tucson shifted position, followed by Lockhart. Glancing around, he saw no one had approached. A group of *peones* labored some distance away. The little baldheaded man, Professor Norquist, was on his knees, intently gazing at one of the stones in the row of stelae. Janisary wasn't in sight; probably with the men gathered at the far end of the valley.

Tuscon said, "I'm gettin' a little more mixed up all the time. Suppose you tell me just what's happened, while I swing this pick?"

"I'm mighty interested to hear about Dad," Pete said wistfully, "and how you got that gun and all."

"All right," Tucson nodded. He related as briefly as possible all that had happened since he and his two pardners had arrived in Lobo Tanks and ended up with the finding of the man with the broken neck.

"My gosh!" Lockhart's eyes widened. "You

haven't had any time to stop and pick daisies, have you? I don't see how that Porky hombre got that gun. I sent a young Mex—"

"They got wise to that. Janisary had him followed by Porky—as I've told you. What I'm waitin' to hear is what happened here. How come you got mixed up with Janisary . . . ?"

Lockhart talked while Tucson pretended to excavate: "Dad has told you how I went to the university to learn something about raising beef. Well, I met Frieda there. Jason Norquist cares about only two things in the world, Frieda and archaeology—no, I reckon archaeology comes first. Norquist's wife is dead. Frieda has accompanied her father on his exploring trips for a number of years. He's afraid she'll meet some man while he's away. He's not keen on having Frieda meet too many men. Funny old codger, jealous as the devil."

Tucson said dryly, "And so, he brought the girl into Mexico."

Lockhart smiled, "Back at school they tell a story of how once Norquist left Frieda hanging by her fingernails on the side of a cliff while he was trying to bring down from an ancient cliff dwelling, without dropping it, an old piece of pottery. I don't say that story's true, but it shows how Norquist stands on archaeology. He's a fanatic on the subject, thinks of nothing else the greater part of the time. Nutty Norquist they called him at school—"

175

"We're not getting any place," Tucson hinted quietly.

"You're right. Anyway, me, I'm a cowman from start to finish—always will be. But I wanted Frieda—still do. Norquist wouldn't hear of me calling on her. Suddenly, I became interested in archaeology—"

"I can understand the sudden interest, Pete. It gave you a chance to see Frieda more often."

"You get the idea. But I did have to read up on the subject, call on Norquist a great deal to consult him. One day he mentioned having run across in ancient writings a reference to a tribe known as the Singing Scorpion people. Somehow, it stuck in my mind. After I returned home I happened to mention it to Dad. Dad remembered hearing some place about a Valley of the Singing Scorpion, supposed to be down in Mexico, though he considered such talk to be based merely on old myths or Indian legends. To cut a long story short, I decided to come down into Mexico and look around, see if I could locate the valley—"

"I get that idea, too. You figured if you could find the valley, you'd be strong enough with Norquist so you could see Frieda oftener. By the way, is she the blond girl?"

"Did you ever see such lovely hair—and eyes—and—did you ever see such a girl, in fact?" Lockhart said enthusiastically.

Tucson said dryly, "How did you say you found

this valley?" He wasn't swinging the pick quite so often now.

Lockhart flushed. "Just stumbled on it by accident. It was pure luck. I was all alone, prospectin' around through this section. My packhorse got away. I trailed him. As it happened he had strayed to the mouth of the tunnel. Naturally I was curious. I entered the tunnel and emerged in the valley, saw all these earth-covered mounds. Got busy with a shovel, here and there. Unearthed one of the stelae. It had a figure of a scorpion sculptured on it. I recognized one or two other signs from things Norquist had taught me. I knew then I had stumbled on the Valley of the Singing Scorpion."

"How did Janisary capture you? Did you lead him here?"

"He's known of this valley for a long time. Used it for a hideout. Some old Indian had showed it to him, told him it was called the Valley of the Singing Scorpion. Janisary adopted the name for himself. You've heard him sing?"

"I've heard that humming sound he makes."

"You should hear him sing Mexican love songs by firelight," Lockhart said bitterly. "I hate to admit it, but it's a grand voice the man has. I'll swear he's got Frieda bewitched—and her father as well—"

"Haven't you told them—?"

"Cripes! I don't dare—but I'm getting ahead of my story. You can imagine I was plumb excited when I found this valley. It happened Janisary was away on one of his raids at the time. I saw sign, showing several campfires had been built here, and so on, but thought it had been done by wandering Indians. Anyway, I saddled up right pronto, and headed for the nearest town with telegraph service. I wired Norquist I had found the valley and gave directions how to get here, told him what to look for, Cathedral Rock, and so on—"

"And the telegraph operator spilled your stuff to Janisary?"

Lockhart said scornfully, "You don't know that telegraph operator. Dumbest Mex I ever talked to. No, don't rush me, cowboy. Here's what happened. By the time I returned to the valley, Janisary and his gang had come back. I walked right into 'em, didn't know who Janisary was, until he gave me his name. Then, I realized. I'd heard Dad and Buck Patton talk about Janisary more than once. By that time, Janisary knew who I was. He laughed at me, made me prisoner, boasted that he was the *El Escorpión* who had been raiding along both sides of the border. Do you realize what a fix I was in?"

"Plenty fix, cowhand."

"Janisary wanted to know why I was interested in the valley. Like a damn fool I told him, mentioned that treasure had been found in some of these old ruins in other parts of Mexico. I think he would have killed me, at once, hating Dad like he does, but he got hipped on locating the treasure here. He figured I knew more about this sort of thing than I do. He kept me digging, day after day, on the pyramid. I didn't undeceive him. I wanted to keep alive as long as possible. I only hoped that Norquist wouldn't show up. I might have known better."

"A hound on a scent, eh?"

"You get the idea—yipping hard with his nose close to the trail. Hell! He'd dropped everything on the arrival of my wire. He has money, influence with Washington. In no time at all he had the proper permission wired him from Mexico City to explore any place in the country. The same night he was on his way, taking a train just as far into Mexico as he could go. From that point on, he made good time—he and Frieda. Picked up a couple of cooks, tools, *peon* laborers, tents, supplies—hell! in less than three weeks after I'd wired, he and his gang had run into Janisary's guards at the outside entrance to the tunnel." Lockhart broke off to say, pointing to a shovel on the ground nearby, "Better change tools, Tucson. That picking is getting sort of mechanical. We don't want to arouse any suspicions, if anyone should notice you."

"Figure to get some work out of me, anyway, eh?" Tucson laughed.

"We've both got plenty work cut out for us," Lockhart said soberly. "Anyway, Norquist didn't know what it was all about and the guards wouldn't talk. Just took the party at guns-points through the tunnel. I was working on the pyramid, excavating. Janisary and a guard stood near. Janisary saw them bringing the professor and his party into the valley. He asked me about it. I told him who they were. While they were still quite a distance off, Frieda and the professor waved to me. Frieda called to ask, in a joking way, if I had found any jewels, yet—"

Tucson interrupted to say ironically, "And I suppose Janisary lost all interest in the diggin', then, eh?"

"Just another hound on the trail," Lockhart said wearily. "Something about Frieda got to Janisary, even before she'd come up close, and he offered to make a bargain with me to the effect that if I didn't tell what I knew about him, he would let us all go after a time. Of course, I didn't trust to his word, but I didn't know of any other way of stalling for time. Besides, I saw no reason for frightening Frieda—and the professor."

"Does she frighten easy?"

"She's a gamester," Pete said earnestly. "Still I wanted things as smooth as possible. So I promised to keep my mouth shut. With that, Janisary goes ahead and introduces himself to the professor as Gage Janisary—the damn hypocrite! Tells Norquist that the Mexican Government sent him here to see that everything moved smoothly for the expedition, and to take charge of the government's share of any treasure that might be found."

"And Norquist believed that?"

Lockhart nodded. "Scarcely heard it, in fact, he was so tickled to learn the exploring wouldn't be held up. Right away, Norquist spotted three mounds, guesses there were temples under 'em, and started the *peones* excavating. By the time the center one was cleared out, Janisary suggested that he get some furniture from Malpaisaño and use it for living quarters. He even had the nerve to suggest bringing his sister here, so Frieda would be properly chaperoned and have company."

Tucson's eyes narrowed. "So he claims the dark-haired one is a sister, eh?" And added, "That's goin' to be damn hard for me to believe."

Lockhart swore. "You don't have to believe it. Her name's Zella Frost—at least it was a few years back when I saw her dealing faro in a house in Juarez. To account for the difference in names, Janisary tells a story of her being married one time, to a man named Frost. She lives up to her name—cold, hard, nervy. In some ways, though, level-headed as hell. I reckon she and Janisary have been pardners in crime for a long spell."

Tucson didn't relish that thought.

Lockhart went on, "Janisary's gone sweet on Frieda, now. Zella don't like that a bit, either. I haven't had much chance to talk to her, but that much is plain. I asked her to get my gun for me.

She did it. At first I had an idea of fighting my way out of here, but it was too big a job. I placed that message in the butt, hoping Dad would think to take the gun apart. Zella had a Mex boy working for her. I told him to get the gun to Dad. Somebody must have overheard me. Zella pretended to discharge the boy. I can see now Janisary only let him leave the valley, so he could have the boy trailed."

Tucson cut in, eyes narrowing in speculation, "Maybe Zella Frost can solve the problem for us. With an ally in the valley, maybe she could work things—"

"I'm afraid not. Getting that gun for me was her limit. She won't go farther, I'm thinking. . . . I'd given up hope of ever seeing that gun again, especially after Janisary went away, leaving us heavily guarded. When he returned, he said he'd killed Dad. The man's a cruel coyote. I've been nearly crazy at times. He's ordered me to keep away from Frieda. I don't dare refuse."

"How about putting the professor wise?"

Pete sadly shook his head. "He's too occupied to listen. I hinted that Janisary might be otherwise than he appeared. Norquist laughed at me, insisted I was just jealous—you know—Frieda and Janisary. That's true enough too. Cripes! All Norquist thinks of is getting these ruins uncovered. I don't think it makes any difference to Norquist who Janisary is, so long as his researches aren't disturbed."

Tucson said grimly, "He's li'ble to have a rude awakenin'."

"That thought's not original with you, Tucson," Pete said gloomily. "Meantime, he and Frieda don't realize they're prisoners. Oh, they've having quite a social time of it with Janisary and Zella Frost. I think Janisary hoped the professor might take to Zella and leave Frieda unwatched, but it hasn't come to that—yet. If I spill the beans, it would make things a great deal tougher for Norquist—and Frieda. Sometines I think Frieda smells a mouse at that. She thinks it queer Janisary has to have this crew of Yaqui Injuns and gunmen with him. Luckily, Janisary has kept those coyotes at the other end of the valley."

"That *is* a break of luck."

"That's the situation. Any minute it is likely to be reversed. If these *peon* laborers only had guns and would fight—but shucks! they won't. They're not being harmed. They get good food and are paid well, so it's no skin off their teeth. They probably suspect something is wrong though. Another thing, they've heard Janisary mention treasure. If anything is found, they likely think they'll get a share."

"Didn't find any treasure in that center temple you cleaned out, eh?"

"Not what Janisary calls treasure. Norquist is nearly wild with delight. We uncovered some sarcophagi, but—"

"Come again, Pete."

"Stone coffins," Pete explained, "old bones in 'em that crumbled to dust when the air struck 'em. Then there were a few other things—painted *tinajas*—pots—a few knives made of obsidian, a number of spearheads. Some objects in the shape of crosses and crescents, carved from stone. A few silver rings. There were several small models of scorpions, carved from jade, too. They'll have some value, but it's got the professor going: he doesn't understand jade being in this country. You can figure that out for yourself."

"Not me," Tucson shook his head, bearing down one foot on the shovel. He heaved out a clump of earth, tossed it to one side. "I got too many other things to think about. Any danger of these other laborin' *peones* recognizin' me as a stranger? I figure to Janisary, unless he comes close, and the professor, I'll just be another pick and shovel man among all these others. But the natives might notice Manuel missing and—"

"I don't think they'll say anything," Pete said slowly. "Manuel had come from a different part of the country. He didn't get along well with them, probably because he was a little higher type. Manuel was a darn good boy. These *peones* keep their own counsel pretty much. Even if you're noticed, I doubt anything will be said to Janisary. And Norquist wouldn't bother his head about it, so long as you did your work well—but hell's bells! Tucson, you can't get away with this laborer's disguise indefinitely."

"Don't expect to, but I want a chance to scout around a mite, see what I can do for Stony and Lullaby. Besides, we'll have to work out a plan of some sort. Even if we all had guns, we wouldn't be strong enough to buck Janisary's gang. We'll have to move plumb tricky—"

"Peter—I say, Peter," came the voice of Professor Norquist from the other side of the temple.

"Pete, you're wanted," Tucson said.

Pete swore. "What now?" irritatedly.

Norquist appeared around the corner of the partly excavated temple. He was a little birdlike individual with a long inquiring nose on which rested spectacles equipped with thick lenses. He had the absent-minded attitude of the true scholar as he peered at Pete, paying no attention at all to Tucson. His tones were heavy and rather deliberate.

"Yeah, what's up, professor?" Pete asked.

"Bring that man over to Stela No. 1. I want it removed and laid flat on the earth. I'd like to commence casting this afternoon."

Without waiting for Pete to reply, he turned and headed in the direction of the row of monuments. Pete swore wholeheartedly, "Dammit! I wanted to keep you working away from the rest of the gang. Tucson, old horse, the risk isn't getting any slimmer."

# 15

# Tucson Bluffs Through

"I'll have to chance it, Pete," Tucson said. "Maybe I can bluff my way through, by putting on a bold front. What's the job?"

"Clear away the earth from around that first stela this way. You'll probably find it's set about four feet down—you know the whole row of monuments was beneath the earth when we started. The one Norquist wants will have to be removed and laid flat."

"Who told you I was Hercules?" Tucson asked.

Pete smiled thinly. "I'll see that there's plenty help when the time comes. You'll have just to clear away the accumulated dirt and débris of centuries from the base of the stela. Pick and shovel job."

Tucson followed Pete, carrying his tools, to the first stone in the row, a short distance away. Norquist was now engaged in studying the next monument in line, some yards beyond.

"—and all you have to do," Pete was saying, low-voiced, "is clear away this earth so the stela can be lifted out. For the love of longhorns, though, don't strike the stone, or chip it, with your pick or shovel by accident. Norquist will go straight up for fear his beloved hieroglyphics will get damaged."

Tucson surveyed the stela from the top to the point where it entered the earth. It appeared to have been hewn from a kind of limestone. The surface of the stela, facing the pyramid, had been divided, by deep channels cut from the rock, into squares approximately six inches in size, leaving a raised series of figures arranged in straight lines, down and across the stone.

Each of the squares comprised, in clear-cut relief, several small pictographs sculptured in the limestone. Examining them, Tucson discovered birds, animals, faces, hands, reptiles, ovals and oblongs, all intertwined with certain other queer symbols which Tucson couldn't find a name for, many of these last having somewhat the appearance of letters of the alphabet in reversed positions. Bars and dots were arranged in rows, circles, or above one another. The likeness of the human eye appeared frequently. Most often, Tucson noticed the sculptured form of a scorpion. The figures were all a bit crudely done, but easily recognizable.

Tucson observed, where side views of faces appeared, that all had similar physical characteristics: hooked noses, receding foreheads, enormous lips with the lower lip full and pendulous. These weren't, he decided, unlike many of the faces of the natives seen throughout Mexico.

"Look here," Pete cut in low-voiced on Tucson's thoughts, "you better get to work. You can't read those hieroglyphics anyway."

"I'd like to see anybody that could," Tucson spoke from under the straw sombrero as he commenced to swing the pick about the base of the monument.

"Take a look at Norquist then. Anyway, he can make out a little of the stuff."

Thud! went the pick, and again thud! Four *peones* were engaged on the eastern side of the temple mound Tucson had just left, the rest still working on the steps of the pyramid, fifty yards away. Janisary wasn't in sight. He was probably with his men at the other end of the valley. Norquist was studying the next stela in the row.

Tucson said, after a time, "Am I li'ble to find a treasure under this stone?"

"If you do, I'll be surprised," Pete replied. He stood near, yet kept a watchful glance all around. "Keep on working, I've got to move around a bit, or it will look queer." He walked away in the direction of the temple being excavated, after first stopping for a few words with Norquist, who barely took time to answer and didn't even look up from his studies.

Tucson cleared away with the shovel the earth he had loosened, then again employed the pick. It was hard going, the earth was stony and packed hard. Perspiration commenced to soften the mud about his arms and shoulders. For a time he rested, one foot on the shovel, and studied Norquist.

Frieda Norquist appeared at her father's side,

stood talking to him, but received little attention. The girl was pretty, no doubt of that. Tucson couldn't blame Pete. She was fresh and young and boyishly built. Once she cast her level glance at Tucson. He saw that her eyes were a deep blue-violet. Tucson resumed work.

The girl gave him a second glance, then slowly sauntered closer and stood watching him. Finally she asked and her voice was sweetly curious, "You're Manuel, aren't you?"

Tucson kept his head down, continued working. *"Sí, señorita."*

"Why are you digging there?"

Tucson shrugged his shoulders and didn't reply.

"Don't you know?"

Tucson didn't lift his head. He said slowly, "No spik *Inglés, señorita."*

"What a memory," Frieda said sarcastically. "You spoke very good English yesterday."

Tucson said, "Oh, my gosh, it's no use." He stopped work and looked at the girl. He saw the look of wonder in the blue-violet eyes and the dawning look of surprise beneath the cornsilk hair. He saw that she noticed his gray eyes. He said quietly, "Don't talk about this to anyone else but Pete. And don't trust Janisary any farther than you can toss a bronc by the fore-laigs. You look to me as though you could take it. I'm trusting you to."

The girl said coolly, "I think I'd trust in you, mister."

"Thanks."

Frieda walked slowly away, heading for Pete. Tucson resumed work. Half an hour later the girl and Pete passed Tucson walking slowly. The girl looked paler than before, but composed. Tucson thought, "She don't stampede easy."

As he passed, Pete said, low-voiced, "Frieda's got it all. Keep up the bluff—and your nerve. Frieda won't talk. Listen, Janisary's headed this way. Keep your map out of sight."

"C'rect," Tucson grunted, between strokes of the pick. He didn't look up.

Frieda and Pete came to a halt near Norquist. Norquist wasn't wasting time looking up either. There was a look of bliss on the professor's face which now and then was replaced by one of extreme perplexity as his reading of the hieroglyphics encountered various knotty problems.

Janisary strode up, spoke to Frieda, touching the brim of his sombrero. He said to Pete meaningfully, "Lockhart, don't you think you should spend more time with your workers?"

Pete flushed and walked away.

Janisary suggested to Frieda, "Suppose we saddle up this afternoon and take a little ride out of the valley. I could show you the country hereabouts. You must be getting tired of the same scenery all the time."

"I like it here," Frieda said coolly. "I'm afraid the sun will be too hot for riding this afternoon. No, thanks, I don't care to go. I'm counting on a beauty nap this afternoon, as soon as we've eaten lunch."

She turned and walked away. Janisary looked after her with angry eyes. He seemed taken off his feet by the rebuff, not quite able to understand it.

He said to Norquist, "What's the matter with Frieda, off her feed?" He had to repeat the question twice before it penetrated Norquist's abstractions.

Norquist looked up, rather blankly, reluctantly, "What's that, Janisary?"

"I asked Frieda to go riding with me this afternoon. She refused. Doesn't she feel well?"

The professor shrugged his slight shoulders. "It is nothing. Girls are queer that way. When you know women better you will realize it. If I could read these stelae like I do Frieda, I'd be the world's greatest archaeologist. No, Frieda is all right. She just didn't care to go." He returned to his hieroglyphics, ignoring Janisary's presence.

Janisary appeared to be slightly mollified. He said, "How goes the reading? Learning anything new about your old Aztecs—"

"Aztecs!" Norquist's slender figure bristled as he rose to his feet. "I have told you one thousand times at least they were not Aztecs—"

"Mayas, then," Janisary said carelessly.

"I told you yesterday I was certain they were not Mayas." Norquist sounded irritated. "For the present I chose to call them an early Nahuatlan people; certainly not the true Aztec at present

191

known to students of archaeology. How they come here I do not know—"

"What do you know?" There was an edge to Janisary's tones.

"—except it is generally accepted," the professor continued, not noticing the interruption, "that a Toltec people once had a kingdom situated near the Gila River in Arizona. They migrated south and then southeast through Mexico, stopping for quite long periods at various spots to raise cities—their civilization antedates by many centuries the Christian era. The Singing Scorpion people may be of this race, but I do not think so. Certainly they are not true Toltecs. It is a great mystery I hope to unravel in time, but there is so much. Look, the trachytic rock used in building the pyramid. Where did it come from? There is no rock of that kind here. That's only one of the puzzles I have to solve. If I can only discover the key to some of these characters that continue to baffle my thought, I shall—"

But Janisary hadn't waited to hear more. Already he was on his way toward the southern end of the valley, lines of irritation tightening his features. Norquist finally realized that Janisary had gone. His eyes softened as he once more crouched down by the monument he had been attempting to read.

Tucson continued to work at the base of the stela. The earth had been firmly tamped down with fragments of rock for a fill. Pete Lockhart appeared at Tucson's side after a few minutes.

Tucson said, "Norquist and Frieda just gave Janisary the bum's rush—each in their own way."

"What do you mean?"

Tucson told about the girl refusing the riding invitation, adding, "The professor just plain out-talked him. Reckon Janisary ain't much interested in ancient tribe history."

Pete looked a trifle worried. "Janisary's been picking at him about locating some treasure. Norquist is getting tired of it. He's pretty mild as a rule, but I'm afraid one of these days he'll blow up and tell Janisary to mind his own business, then there will be hell to pay. . . . I gave Frieda the whole story. She took it like a thoroughbred. The kid's plumb scared though. S'help me, if I ever get her out of this—"

"You'll marry her I suppose."

"I hope so— "

"Just runnin' one risk after another, ain't you?" Tucson said dryly.

Pete smiled. "I feel a lot better, Tucson, since you arrived. You see, I sort of thought Frieda was falling for Janisary, but she isn't. She kind of had a hunch something was wrong, and has been trying to pump Janisary about your two pards who were brought in. She saw them arrive, knew Janisary had a couple of prisoners in one of the tents at the other end of the valley. Janisary put her off with some sort of story about them being a pair of horse-thieves. But Frieda has suspected things weren't just right from the start."

"Uh-huh." Tucson swung the pick twice more. "Say, I could work a heap better if I had some food. Nothin' to eat so far today—"

"I was going to mention that. It's nearly time now for the cook to give the dinner call. I can't bring you anything here, that would look queer. I reckon, Tucson," and Pete looked worried, "you'll just have to go along with the rest of the *peones* and carry your bluff on. God, I don't like it."

"I'll risk it," Tucson said quietly. "No use lookin' ahead for trouble. If we can just take one thing at a time as it shows up, mebbe we'll pull out of this scrape with whole skins."

He resumed work with the pick and was just at the top of his stroke when he heard the distant banging on a dishpan calling the laborers to dinner. Without finishing the stroke, Tucson dropped the tool and leaped out of the hole he had dug.

Pete chuckled, "That was worthy of any of our laborers, Tucson. Good luck."

Tucson didn't reply. He left the row of stelae, passed the three temples and headed down the valley. Four *peones* walked ahead of him some distance. Looking back, Tucson saw the laborers who had been engaged on the pyramid coming behind.

Ten minutes later he arrived near the cook set-up. The four laborers who had been ahead of him were forming the end of a line composed of Janisary's plug-uglies which was filing past the steaming pots of food, plates and cups in their hands. Boldly, Tucson went to a box containing tin dishes, helped himself, and got into the line. The other *peones* dropped in behind him. They looked at Tucson, but said nothing, though Tucson detected faint surprise in their eyes.

The line straggled nearer the pots of food. A Mexican cook and helper were engaged in dealing out beans, bread, bacon and coffee. Neither appeared to take any notice of Tucson as he received his food and passed on. Men were seated on the earth, all around, eating their dinners. The *peones* ate in silence. There was a great deal of conversation from the Janisary faction, seated by itself some short distance away. None of these took any notice of the *peones,* except to curse them, or cuff them out of the way if they came too near.

Tucson ate quickly, did not, like most of the men, return for a second helping of food. Searching in the pockets of the dead man's clothing he found corn-husk papers and some vile tobacco. He twisted a cigarette, Mex fashion, and lay back on the earth, resting on one elbow, to consider the situation. He noticed two or three of the *peones* watching him, but with a great appearance of nonchalance finally dropped back and pretended to sleep, as he saw many of the *peones* doing.

Undoubtedly, this being the heat of the day, there'd be a two-hour rest from labor. A great cottonwood tree spread its leafy branches above Tucson's head and he was grateful for the shade. He relaxed, with narrowed eyes, gazing at the row of five tents. The farthest one from Tucson's location was guarded by an ugly-looking individual with a rifle in the crook of his right arm. The tent flap was lowered.

Tucson mused, "Bet Lullaby and Stony are in that tent. Now how in the devil am I going to get past that guard?"

He raised up a trifle, looking around. Janisary's crew was sprawled on the earth, beyond the cook set-up: tables, pots, pans, an oven of rock construction. The cook and his assistant were engaged in stacking dirty dishes. With one exception, the *peones* were all dozing now. The one exception was walking back through the brush and trees, some distance away. Tucson slowly and cautiously commenced to edge over the trampled grass in the direction of the guarded tent.

He stopped suddenly, hearing the cook call out some words, after he had progressed a short distance. Now what? With a sigh of quick relief, Tucson saw that the cook was calling the tent guard to come for his dinner. Here, at last, was a break in the luck.

The guard called back angrily, "'Bout time. I was commencin' to think you'd forgot me."

196

"No forget," the cook replied shortly. "Come an' get eet."

The guard was already on his way, rifle cradled under one arm. He took no notice of Tucson as he slouched indolently past. Tucson waited until the guard had nearly arrived at the cook's tables, then he arose and slowly strolled into the high brush at his back. Once he felt sure of being out of sight, Tucson moved like a streak of lightning.

A moment later he had crossed to the rear of the row of canvas tents, turned sharply to the right to reach the front of the tent in which he hoped to find Lullaby and Stony. Casting a quick backward glance, he saw the guard engaged in conversation with the cook, just accepting dishes from the Mexican's hands. Boldly, Tucson pulled aside the tent flap and stepped inside.

A lurid volley of invective greeted the entrance. Tucson laughed silently, recognizing the voices of his pardners. He said shortly, "Shut your meat traps."

"Tucson!" in unison from Stony and Lullaby.

"*Will* you keep quiet? It's curtains if I'm caught here."

They fell silent. Tucson hesitated, getting his bearings. The tent interior seemed dim after the brilliant sunlight. In a moment, Tucson made out the forms of his pardners stretched on the earth. Their feet were bound, the ropes running behind them to knot about their wrists which were drawn up beneath their shoulder blades.

A soft step was heard outside. Tucson moved stealthily to the right side of the tent, waiting. But no one entered. He heard the clatter of dishes and judged the guard had brought back his dinner to eat in front of the tent.

No one dared speak. Gradually, Tucson made his way across the tent to Lullaby, stooped at his side and commenced to work on the knots at his bound wrists. The guard in front of the tent wasn't more than five or six yards distant. The knots that held Lullaby's wrists were tightly drawn, hard. Tucson was forced to work with the utmost caution, not daring to let even one grunt escape his tightly compressed mouth. It was a slow, nerve-straining procedure.

From time to time the sounds of dishes or smacking of lips reached Tucson's ears. Finally he heard the dishes being gathered up, then the guard's footsteps lazily receding.

"Tucson," Lullaby breathed softly at last. "You're safe!"

"How'd you get here?" from Stony across the tent.

"I'm askin' you?" Tucson said.

Lullaby said, "We got plumb mad when you didn't show up to meet us, outside Malpaisaño. Looked high and low for you. Finally we played a long chance, figuring Janisary must have you. So we started in askin', right and left, where Janisary could be found. First thing we knew, there was a dozen guns slung on us. We could have fought clear, mebbe, but that wouldn't get us to Janisary. We surrendered and were brought here. What kind of a layout is this?"

"*Shh!*" Tucson rose to his feet, crossed the tent floor and peered between the flaps. He had a plain view of the cook set-up. The guard was having his plate filled again. Watching, Tucson saw the man commence to eat without returning to the tent. He slipped back to Lullaby and the stubborn knots, told the pair again to keep quiet while he did the talking.

While he worked on the ropes, Tucson gave a brief recital of the various events leading up to his entering the tent. He concluded by telling them where he had left his guns.

"I don't dare untie these ropes all the way," he said to Lullaby. "But they're loose now and can be slipped off with a little effort. If you can break away, after dark, you get my guns pronto. I don't know whether I'll be able to get them myself first—I don't think so —gosh, suppose they come to feed you?"

"I don't reckon they will," Lullaby said, low-voiced. "We kicked up such a fuss last night when they untied us, that they said once a day was goin' to be enough from now on."

"They untied us for a few minutes this mornin'," Stony said softly, "fed us our breakfast. They said that would be the last for the day. God, I'm gettin' cramped layin' here—"

"I'll get at you in a minute," Tucson said. "Where's your guns?"

"Last I saw, Janisary had 'em," Lullaby said, and swore bitterly. "Gosh, this is the darndest place I ever saw," he added.

"You'n' me both," from Tucson.

"I don't reckon they'll pay any attention to us from now on," Lullaby continued.

"I hope they don't start to look at our ropes," Stony put in.

"The feller that tried that last night," Lullaby grinned, "got my feet in his belly. He left me alone then, though he did bruise his knuckles on my face, damn his hide!"

Stony asked, "If we can manage to get out, what next? Where will you be?"

"I ain't sure," Tucson said. "We can't plan that far ahead. We'll just have to meet things as they come. Keep as quiet as you can today, don't rile that guard, if you can help it. Just keep things peaceful so he won't have any excuse to come in here—"

"Shucks!" Lullaby said, "if we have to quit cursin' him and all his ancestors, he sure will think we're mighty contented of a sudden."

"Use your judgment, if you got any," Tucson said.

"Lullaby ain't," Stony snickered.

"Whatever you do," from Tucson, "don't try to make a break in daylight. Make sure the camp is asleep first. We can't lick the whole camp—"

"Gimme my guns and I'll try it," Lullaby said.

Tucson again went to the tent flap, peered out. He came quickly back, his face grim. "That damn guard is comin'," he whispered. "Cowboys, I'm sure trapped!"

From outside came Pete Lockhart's voice, rounding up his laborers, "Better get moving, boys."

"That means me," Tucson gritted. "That damn guard will see me, sure. If I don't show up, I'll be missed—"

"Mebbe you can wiggle under the back of the tent," Lullaby suggested. "Nev' mind Stony. I'll free him once I'm loose."

Tucson dived for the rear canvas, stretched the bottom, managed to get his head and shoulders through. *"Adios,"* he said softly.

He didn't catch any reply, but he heard the guard's footsteps at the front, then Stony's voice, "Hey, hombre, how about bringin' us a drink of water?"

Tucson heard the guard's brutal reply, "Shut your trap! You had a drink this mornin'."

At that, Lullaby and Stony joined voices to inform the guard he was a lousy, two-bit, gall-sored, wind-broken son of a something or other. Plainly the guard was hardened to such tirades as only his jeering laugh was heard in reply.

By this time, Tucson was clear of the tent, creeping low through the brush. He stopped on the edge of the clearing. Most of Janisary's gang were still sprawled on the ground, beyond the cooking equipment, but Tucson saw Tench Crawford approaching at a slow walk. Some distance away, the *peon* laborers were hurrying up the valley. Again Tucson was caught. If he hurried to join the *peones,* Crawford would be sure to notice the movement.

And then, Tucson pulled a greater bluff. Instead of rising, he lay back on the earth, one bare, muddy leg extending from the brush, his straw sombrero over his face. He waited, every nerve tense.

Crawford, sauntering along, caught sight of a bare leg. He stopped, and headed for the point where Tucson was sprawled on his back. Standing over Tucson he stood watching him. Tucson's breast rose and fell, as though he were deep in slumber. From beneath the straw sombrero issued a snore that was a cross between the sounds made by a locomotive puffing up a steep grade and someone tearing a rag.

Crawford laughed uglily, drew back one foot and kicked Tucson in the ribs. Tucson winced, rolled over, sombrero still low on his face, then scrambled up, sputtering excited Spanish.

"Get along to work, you lazy buzzard," Crawford grinned.

Tucson edged away, rubbing his eyes. *"Sí señor,"* he mumbled, keeping his hands before his face. He stumbled down the long gradual slope, heading after the other laborers who were now far ahead. Once he glanced back over his shoulder. Crawford was standing with the guard before the tent in which Lullaby and Stony were imprisoned. Tucson watched him anxiously. To his relief, Crawford didn't enter the tent, but strode back to join the rest of the gang.

Tucson rubbed his ribs where Crawford's boot had bruised the skin. "That's just somethin' else to square up, my bucko," he muttered savagely. "Just the same, one more narrow escape like that and I'll be ready for a nervous breakdown, or whatever it is folks gets when things get too tight for easy goin'. And it don't look like things is goin' to get any easier. From now on, things should start to poppin' plenty, or I ain't no judge."

# 16

## Janisary Shows His Teeth

The earth was finally removed from around the base of the stela. Tucson rested on his shovel while Pete Lockhart called several laborers to assist in removing the great stone from its centuries-old foundation. Crowbars and ropes were brought and the men set to work, under Lockhart's orders. Norquist hovered about on the edge of the group, emitting anxious clucks, in a manner that reminded Tucson of a worried mother hen, for fear the limestone monument would be dropped too suddenly, or dragged over gravelly earth, or in some manner chipped and damaged.

But no basis was found for his anxieties. By four o'clock that afternoon the stela lay flat on the earth, and Norquist gave a long sigh of relief as he had Lockhart order buckets, water and plaster of Paris brought from the supply tent.

"The day's nearly over," Lockhart commented. "You going to start casting now? There won't be any sun in a little while—"

"I wish, Peter," Norquist said frostily, "you'd take a little more interest instead of questioning my requests. I fear you haven't the true heart of the archaeologist. If there isn't sun, so much the better. The moulds will dry more slowly, lessening the danger of cracking. . . ."

Pete turned away, issued further orders. Several *peones* brought the supplies, then left to resume their excavating work. Lockhart put Tucson to work mixing the plaster of Paris. When a bucketful was ready, Lockhart carried it to Norquist. Carefully, almost tenderly, Norquist commenced to spread the wet plaster over the surface of the hieroglyphics, making certain that it penetrated to the bottom of each crack and crevice of the sculptured designs, using a stiff-bristled brush to force the semi-liquid mixture into the pictographs he wished to preserve and endeavoring to make certain that no air bubbles were included in the finished cast.

Norquist complained the first batch Tucson mixed was too dry. Buckets of water were sloshed over the stone and the useless plaster washed off. He demanded, with cold courtesy, that Lockhart make sure more water was added to the plaster of Paris. Tucson complied with the request and Norquist recommenced his labors.

Pete returned, toting empty buckets. Tucson got busy on a fresh batch. "What's the idea?" he asked, low-voiced as he worked.

"Practically impossible to carry these stones north," Pete explained, "at least for the present. Norquist is making moulds of the hieroglyphics. After the plaster has hardened, the cast will be removed and packed carefully in soft wadding of some kind. Norquist wants to send it to some brother archaeologist in Chicago to see if anything further can be done about the translation. Y'know, he expects to make casts of all these stelae."

"He's a glutton for punishment," Tucson observed.

"Why, he's having the time of his life."

"I suppose—but I wish we could get him interested in what's goin' on around him."

"It can't be done. Right now, for Norquist, there isn't anything to think about except what he's engaged in at present. He wouldn't listen if you tried to tell him. He's lost in a dream world of his own. Anything else is pure fancy."

"Mebbe so," Tucson said grimly, "but I aim to wake him up to a few facts." Ignoring Pete's protests, Tucson strode across to Norquist and stood at the side of the prone monument. Norquist didn't glance up, but kept on working, talking meanwhile to himself in a language Tucson didn't understand, a language that had to do with archaeology.

"Look here, prof," Tucson said briskly. He was forced to repeat the words before Norquist showed the least sign of hearing. He didn't look up as he said,

"Go away. I can't be bothered with that now," impatiently.

"Can't be bothered with what?" Tucson asked.

With apparently considerable effort, Norquist raised blank eyes to Tucson, struggling to bring his mind back to the present. Tucson went on,

"You've got to listen to me, prof. What you're doing is all very well, but I'm here to tell you you're in a tight, in great danger, savvy? Janisary's bluffed you from start to finish. He's one *malo hombre*, and you'll be lucky to get out of this valley with a whole skin, let alone dragging these old ruins with you. Can you understand that? Janisary ain't to be trusted. He's a bandit. You've got to snap out of this, get ready for a battle. . . ."

The fact that Tucson wasn't speaking the language of the *peones* apparently didn't register on

Norquist at all. Tucson caught the far-away dreamy expression in the blue eyes behind the thick lenses, and started in again,

"Did you ever use a gun, any? Do you think you could handle one, if we're lucky enough to—"

"Here," Norquist stooped down for an empty plaster bucket, handed it to Tucson, "Please, a little more water this time. The plaster is too thick."

Rather dumbly Tucson accepted the bucket, his jaw dropped a trifle.

"And don't keep me waiting," the professor continued, turning back to the stone.

A slow grin spread over Tucson's face as his gaze took in the wispy little figure stooped over the stela, then he turned back where Pete was mixing plaster. He said, ruefully, "Dam'd if he ain't the toughest proposition I ever run across."

Pete nodded. "Wouldn't he listen to reason?"

Tucson swore softly. "Listen? Hell, he didn't even hear me. I ain't sure he saw me. Pro'bly figured I was you. His mind ain't here, a-tall. Ten to one, it's way back in the dim ages when these toll-tax tribes was—"

"Toltec," Pete corrected.

"Does it make any difference?"

Pete shook his head. "I reckon not. When the blowup comes we'll just have to look after Norquist like a child. He'll probably yell like a child too when we take him away from his ancient playthings."

"Here comes a worse problem," Tucson cut in. "I'd like a chance to make that coyote yell. Where's Frieda?"

Pete glanced up and saw Janisary cutting across toward Norquist. "Frieda's in the living quarters in the temple. I haven't seen her or Zella Frost since dinner time. . . . Janisary sort of looks as if he had blood in his eye. I hope he hasn't turned ugly."

"He don't have to *turn*," Tucson said meaningfully. "He just hides it sometimes. . . . Listen, Pete, we don't know what's going to happen. You've got your gun, but don't use it unless they ain't no other way. I loosened Lullaby's bonds this noon. If we can stall off until night, mebbe we'll get some sort of break. If I get a chance, I'll go get my guns myself, but I told Lullaby and Stony where they were, and they can each use one, where I can't be in more than one place at once. Besides, if I head over to where I left my clothes I might be noticed—"

"Shh!" Pete said suddenly.

Janisary was standing ten yards away, talking, or rather trying to talk to Norquist. Norquist, engrossed in his plaster casting, didn't hear. Janisary's face grew red. "What in hell," he demanded roughly, "do you think you're doing now?" His hand reached out, seized Norquist's arm, jerked him upright.

Norquist shook his head indignantly, then commenced to sputter and fume. Janisary cut in on his heated protests to snap, "I asked what you were doing, Norquist."

Norquist jerked out, "Making casts as anyone not a nitwit could see. Look here, I can't be bothered with your imbecile questions. This is a necessary, an important, work. We can't remove these stones for some time. Ergo, it is necessary to make moulds and send them north where they may be studied by my colleagues—"

"I ain't interested in your colleges," Janisary said roughly. "You've wasted enough time, Norquist—"

"Wasted," Norquist snapped irritatedly, "wasted? My dear man, we have made remarkable progress—"

"I haven't seen any treasure yet."

Norquist's usually placid features reddened angrily. "Treasure! That's all you talk about. You have no cause for concern. The Mexican Government will receive its just and legal share when and if we discover anything of a monetary value. But it is far more important that I work on these stelae in an effort to discover the exact date at which the Singing Scorpion people raised these records of their time."

Launched forth on his favorite topic, some of the anger faded from the professor's features. He continued, "So far I have ascertained that the Scorpion people, like all primitive tribes of America, were sun worshippers. Of greater importance is the fact that they differed from the others by having for a god, or representative of the sun, a being known as the Singing Scorpion. Why 'singing' I do not know, but I shall probably learn before many weeks—"

"Weeks?" Janisary snarled.

"Don't bare your teeth at me, Janisary. It is only owing to your extreme ignorance that I waste the time explaining these things. You should be more appreciative. Yes, weeks! Don't you realize that a complete city lies buried beneath the earth of this valley? These temples and the great pyramid form only boundaries of a once busy plaza. Did you think that marvelously built tunnel was a work of modern man, or, perhaps of nature? The more fool you, then."

Even at this distance, Tucson caught the angry humming sound that arose on Janisary's lips. He looked quickly at Pete. Pete's right hand was inside his shirt, resting on gun-butt. Tucson nodded, said low-voiced, "Janisary's gettin' hot. If he reaches for his gun, plug him. We'll fight through—somehow—if we're lucky."

Pete nodded, didn't say anything. His eyes were on Janisary.

The professor was talking at length, thoroughly wound up in his subject, "And you ask for treasure, when I am uncovering these great facts to give to a waiting world—"

Janisary said, "Christ! You little—"

But Norquist had rushed on, unhearing, "Imagine

the sensation my discoveries will make in North America and Europe. Treasure! Great Scott, man! It's all around you, but not the sort you can turn into money. Have patience. The lesser things will come. When we have located the Green Eyes of Zexonteotl I suppose you will be satisfied—"

Janisary cut in, his voice dangerously cold, "What's this about the green eyes of somebody—"

"Zexonteotl—the Scorpion God—"

"Make it clear. You said something like that yesterday—"

Norquist said testily, "Must I repeat my statements over and over that they may penetrate your extremely thick head? If you had been listening closely you would have heard me translate from the stela. I spoke clearly, I believe: 'Whosoever shall possess the Green Eyes of Zexonteotl, holds in the hollow of his hand the fate of Quetzalcoatl—'"

"Talk sense," Janisary rasped.

"For anyone but a numbskull that is sense," Norquist bristled scornfully. "Zexonteotl—the Singing Scorpion, Quetzalcoatl—the Feathered Serpent. I explained this to you before, but you evidently weren't enough interested to listen. It is plain the Scorpion people were warriors, in continual bloody conflict with the tribes of the Feathered Serpent—"

"But what's this about green eyes—"

"Only a myth of course, or some primitive tribal belief—"

Janisary cursed Norquist. "Talk, dammit! What in hell do you mean by green eyes?"

"Probably jewels of some sort," Norquist replied carelessly. "I have learned through long experience that any primitive mention of eyes usually denotes precious stones."

Janisary endeavored to hold his temper in check. His humming vibrated with anger. "What about these jewels?" and his voice shook with mingled excitement and rage. "Where are they?"

The professor extended helpless hands. "Who knows? We may have to excavate the buried city—"

"In the pyramid, perhaps?" Janisary asked eagerly.

"Bah!" Disgust tinged Norquist's words. "The pyramid is only erected to the sun as a sign of devotion, the teocalli on top is the place of the sacrificial stone—"

"Teo—what was it? You mean that house up on top of the pyramid—?"

"It is only a walled chamber with an opening in the roof. It contains as you well know an altar of sacrifice. I've related how the ancient priests cut the heart from a human sacrifice at regular intervals—"

"By God! I'll cut your heart out if you don't quit talking and—" Janisary hesitated helplessly, then finished, "—and talk. What about these green jewels?"

"Eventually, when I have concluded the more important tasks, we shall look for them—"

"You don't say so?" sarcastically.

The tones were lost on the professor. "Of course. I'm sincerely interested in uncovering the Green Eyes of Zexonteotl. The Mexican Government will doubtless allow me to keep them, even should they prove to be jewels. If they are, there will be other valuable treasure, no doubt, to comprise its share. But the Green Eyes I wish to present to Frieda and Peter—"

"T'hell you say—"

"As a wedding present," the professor continued calmly. "I have decided to have Peter marry my daughter. He's a very handy man to have about—"

Pete repeated weakly to Tucson, "T'hell you say. That's sure news. I hope it comes true."

Tucson made a short warning gesture, muttered from the corner of his mouth, "Keep that gun handy." He was watching Janisary narrowly.

Janisary's face was scarlet with suppressed rage. "Where would be the most likely place to find these green jewels—?" His habit of low humming broke in on the words. It sounded evil, ominous, a hidden threat of death in the very tones. He flung back the serape that hung over one shoulder with a savage gesture. His hand commenced to edge down toward his holster.

"I couldn't state with any certainty," Norquist said icily, "but I should say in the temples on

213

either side of the temple we are employing as living quarters."

Janisary's eyes bulged. "You mean to say that you're wasting time with these old stones and uncovering that pyramid when there's treasure to be located—?"

"The old records are more important—"

The words weren't finished. Losing his temper, Janisary's arm lashed out and caught the little professor a back-handed slap across the face. Norquist staggered back, tripped and fell across the fresh plaster on the stone. His spectacles dropped from his nose.

Lockhart started to draw his gun. Tucson said low and sharp-voiced, "He ain't hurt. Hold it!" Lockhart relaxed slightly, nodding, "If I shoot it'll call the whole camp. Shall I cover him?"

"Too risky," Tucson jerked out. "Don't act unless he yanks his iron."

Norquist was down on hands and knees, fumbling around for his glasses, finally found them and arose, trembling with righteous anger. Placing the spectacles on his nose he quickly surveyed his plaster work which had been smeared in his fall. His voice rose to a high-pitched squeal of rage: "You see what you've done, Janisary? Ruined my plaster cast. Now it will all have to be done over—"

"To hell with that," Janisary snarled angrily.

Emotion overcame the little professor. He

rushed forward, swinging awkwardly at Janisary's face. Janisary stepped back, dodged the blow, struck Norquist again. His laugh was ugly. Norquist was scrambling up when Pete Lockhart stepped in between the two men.

"Can't you take it easy, Janisary?" he snapped, face white, "Do you want to hurt him?"

"You're damn right I do, the little double-crossin'—"

"He's been honest with you, doing his best," Pete interrupted. "And I'd think twice if I were you before I called anybody a double-crosser. You put him out of the way and you can whistle for your damned treasure. He's the only man who has the slightest idea where to locate it. We've got to work under his directions. If this excavating is rushed too much, the whole thing may cave in, and your treasure will be lost forever. Norquist has got to have a free hand. Can you understand that?"

There'd been considerable bluff in Pete's statements, but the bluff held. Janisary said angrily, "All right, I'll leave him alone, if he'll show some action on the treasure."

Tucson stood off a few yards, hat pulled low. Janisary was entirely ignoring his presence.

Norquist had been sadly contemplating the ruin of his plaster mould. He turned stiffly to Janisary, "The Mexican Government shall hear of this. No doubt it would be better to have a Mexican supervising the government's end of this business—"

Janisary laughed sneeringly, "The Mexican Government? That's a joke—"

"A very serious joke, you may learn to your regret," Norquist stated stiffly. His lower lip bled a trifle. "I am in charge of this expedition. Just as soon as I can spare the time to telegraph the government at Mexico City, you shall be relieved by a more capable man. I have influence—"

"That's a good laugh," Janisary sneered.

"I shall complain to the government—"

"I," Janisary bragged, "*am* the government."

"You?" Norquist said scornfully. "Are you insane—?"

"It's only a matter of time until I will be president," Janisary stated confidently. "There's a revolution coming—"

"You *are* crazy," Norquist nodded understandingly.

Janisary laughed softly. "You wouldn't say that if you could see the following I have in Chihuahua and Sonora and Coahuila. At a snap of my finger a hundred thousand natives are ready to obey my orders. They think I will lead them to better conditions." He shrugged. "*Quien sabe?* Perhaps I may, but first the revolution must be financed. The treasure—"

Norquist's short laugh sounded as though he were trying to humor a demented person. "This is absurd, preposterous, unheard of! Have you a fever? Let me take your pulse."

"You'll take it across you face in about a minute," Janisary snapped impatiently. "If you don't believe me, ask Lockhart."

Norquist turned inquiring eyes on Pete. Lockhart nodded grimly, "There's truth in a lot Janisary's said," reluctantly. "I didn't tell you before because—"

"But, Peter, this is calamitous! What is to become of the work?"

"I reckon," Pete replied, "this bandit has the answer to that—him and his coyote crew. Better take it easy, professor. There's Frieda to think of—"

"But does this mean," Norquist faltered, "that I must discontinue the work on the stelae?"

Tucson considered making a rush for Janisary, calling to Pete to cover the bandit with his gun. Then he rejected the idea. Doubtless, Janisary might be captured, but his men at the other end of the valley would be roused. It would mean a fight against overwhelming odds. In addition, there was the risk to Stony and Lullaby who were not free. At the first sign of trouble they would be employed as hostages in return for Janisary.

Janisary stood glaring angrily at Norquist and Pete. "Damn your old rocks," Janisary rasped. "Look here, you locate that treasure for me—those green eyes—and you can have all the time you want to work on your rocks. That a bargain?"

Renewed hope showed behind the thick lenses

of Norquist's glasses, but he said, "We are making all progress possible. Do you expect me to swing a pick with the laborers?"

Janisary glanced at the slight form, shook his head.

"You wouldn't be any damn good. But look here, you got a heap of men working on that pyramid, just clearing away earth. Why can't they get busy on these other two temples? You haven't even started on one of 'em yet; the work's lagging on the other. That pyramid stuff ain't important."

Norquist winced, but held his temper. "Too many workmen would get in each other's way," he stated icily. "There is much of this work that must be accomplished carefully. Too many men tramping around might step on old pottery—" he corrected himself, "—might trample treasure stones into the earth." Norquist, fully awake now to the seriousness of the situation was doing a little bluffing on his own account. He flashed a warning glance to Pete, and went on, "If you understood more fully the various problems to be encountered, I wouldn't have to explain so often just what is—"

"Look here," Janisary sounded impatient. "That temple to the west, there, is only partly excavated. The one to the east of our living quarters hasn't been touched. I have only your word there is a temple beneath all that earth. Now, listen, I want some action on those two temples, or there'll be hell to pay, see?"

"But we're working every day—"

"You better start working nights then, too—say, that's an idea. Why can't you put a night force on?" Janisary looked as though he had discovered a great idea.

Norquist shook his head. "The men won't work at night. They'd strike first—"

"They'll work if I hold guns on 'em," Janisary snapped.

Norquist said sarcastically, "And you, personally, would direct operations, I suppose?"

Janisary was silent.

"And run the risk of ruining everything?" The professor laughed scornfully.

"I'm still holding out for that night work idea," Janisary said stubbornly.

Norquist considered, then said to Pete, "Peter, how many men have we who would be willing to work the night shift?"

Pete shrugged his shoulders. "Half a dozen perhaps—for extra pay."

Norquist nodded, turned to Janisary. "If I give my word to go ahead tonight on the two temples, have I your permission to continue my labor on the stelae? Peter would be in charge of the night crew, of course."

Janisary said grudgingly, "All right, it's a bargain."

Pete said, "Don't blame us if it don't turn out the way you want it to, Janisary. Remember, this night work is your own idea. I'm against it, myself—"

"Professor Norquist's runnin' your part of the show," Janisary said roughly. "How long do you think you'll be before you can get into that west temple, Lockhart?"

Pete considered, said cautiously, "Maybe sometime tomorrow night. We're far enough along so we'll have to be mighty careful."

"Tomorrow, eh?" Janisary nodded triumphantly. "That's better than I hoped for. All right, get busy. And no tricks, mind you. I want to see the inside of that west temple by tomorrow night. You can have a coupla days longer on the east mound."

He swung arrogantly around and strode away. Norquist looked after the retreating form for some moments. "I do not believe," he stated suspiciously, "that man is to be trusted. . . . I fear his crude manners have ruined my plaster cast." He sighed. "Now it is all to be done over."

Pete Lockhart walked back to where Tucson waited. "We're getting a break," he said triumphantly. "I'll put four laborers to work excavating that east temple. I know just about where we'll find the entrance to the west temple, I think. I've been stalling along. You and I, tonight, will handle the west temple, Tucson."

"Good. It will give us a chance to talk, make plans—"

"You better not risk going up to supper tonight. You had good luck today. It might not happen again. You go over and start pushing your shovel on that west temple. I'll have your supper brought to you."

Lockhart walked over to the four laborers working on the west temple, talked to them a few minutes. They picked up their tools and started for the mound on the eastern side of the living quarters. Tucson arrived and commenced shoveling earth and rubble as Lockhart and the laborers left.

The sun dropped lower. A long shadow cast by the western wall of the valley slowly edged across Tucson's toiling form. The cook's call to supper sounded. Tucson kept on working. Once, when he looked up, he saw Norquist fussing with plaster of Paris over the hieroglyphics of the stone stela.

"Seems like," Tucson mused, "if he can read those writin's, he should be able to tell fortunes, or somethin'. I'd sure like to know what's ahead. I ain't feelin' right in my bones, somehow."

A little later he saw Lockhart bringing food for him and the four other night-shift laborers.

# 17

# The Green Eyes of Zexonteotl

"The idea being," Pete Lockhart was saying later that night, as he and Tucson toiled over clods of earth and broken masonry, "that if we can find treasure of some sort, I want to cache most of it away, where it can be found later. Give Janisary just a few bits at a time to stall him along. So long as he thinks I'm useful to him, he won't do anything drastic."

"You think we'll get inside this temple by tomorrow night?" Tucson asked.

Pete laughed softly. "Cowboy, if we don't enter tonight, I'll be a heap surprised."

"Tonight?" in surprise. "But I thought you told Janisary—"

"Sure I did. Look here, all the earth doesn't have to be cleared away before we can locate the entrance—or one of the entrances. I've talked to Norquist. He's taken measurements and told me just about where to cut in. You see, he learned quite a bit when we uncovered that temple they're using for living quarters—"

"Janisary's in there now, isn't he?"

Pete nodded. "I had a few minutes with Frieda and I asked her to employ all her wiles to keep him there tonight. The coyote! He's clean gone on Frieda, damn him! It's one thing I don't blame him for though. Frieda has promised to be as nice to him as possible. Professor Norquist has promised to talk treasure to him, all evening. If we're lucky, some time after Janisary is asleep, you'n' me will reach a walled-up entrance. Then, we'll get inside and see what's what."

The light of three lanterns standing a few feet away on a fragment of volcanic rock, picked out highlights on Tucson's sweat-streaked features

222

and glistened snakily as it coursed down his face. Lockhart too was bathed in perspiration. Despite the coolness that arrived with evening, the work of clearing away the débris on the north side of this particular temple was tiring and hot. The sun-dried mud was rapidly disappearing from Tucson's skin.

Some distance away, working on the earth packed against the temple on the opposite side of the living quarters, could be heard the picks and shovels of four laborers, as they toiled through the night by the light of several lanterns.

Tucson said, "Any chance of those *peones* gettin' inside their temple tonight?"

Lockhart shook his head. "I told them just to clear away the earth. They've got a job ahead, but it will satisfy Janisary, so long as he thinks they may uncover treasure. As a matter of fact, I wouldn't be surprised if we didn't find a damn thing."

"That won't make Janisary feel any better," Tucson commented. "I wonder where Stony and Lullaby are—still in the tent, or—"

"Pro'bly haven't made a break yet. Ten to one they'll wait until the camp quiets down and gets to sleep. Don't get impatient, cowboy. It isn't nine o'clock yet."

"I'd like to get movin', if things will only break that way."

"After you've been held in this valley as long as I have, a few hours more or less won't make any difference."

"You're right, at that," Tucson nodded, resuming his picking operations. Again he stopped, "Trouble is, we can't be sure if Lullaby and Stony will get loose tonight. It's just a long chance. I kind of figured if they did show up with my guns we might be able to capture Janisary and make some sort of terms."

"We'll have to see how it works out."

Tucson swung his pick, loosened a chunk of granite, jerked it to one side. Pete shoveled the earth and rock away as Tucson broke it up. Far down the valley could be seen the light of the outlaws' campfire. Even at this distance, Tucson could hear voices plainly. Now and then he caught the nickering of horses in the corral near the bandits' camp. Gradually the moon edged up above the eastern wall of the valley, flooding the great pyramid and surrounding country with silver light.

Tucson stopped for a rest. He laughed shortly, "It's a wonder to me the professor isn't out plasterin' his stella or whatever you call it. I don't see how he could bear to leave it."

Pete chuckled. "He finished it before he ate supper. Otherwise he'd probably be out working by lantern light. He's counting on doing the second one tomorrow—shh!"

Tucson swung his pick, grunting between strokes. He heard voices: Norquist's and Janisary's. The two men approached nearer. Janisary's voice was blustering, threatening. When he deigned to reply, Norquist's tones were icily polite—no more.

Janisary said bluntly: "Lockhart, if we ain't in that temple in twenty-four hours there's going to be a lot of trouble you won't like."

Lockhart suppressed the angry retort that rose to his lips. "I'm not backin' down from the statement I made today. If this was as big as the center temple, I wouldn't be so sure, but there's no wall around this—"

"How do you know?" Janisary snapped.

"If there had been," Norquist said coldly, "they'd have struck it by this time."

"Then there's nothing to do but push ahead for the entrance?" Janisary asked, somewhat mollified.

"That is all," flatly from Norquist. "If by any chance you know exactly where the entrance is, beneath all this earth and rock, you can expedite operations by taking us into your confidence."

"You know damn well," Janisary flared, "that I don't know—"

"Very well then," Norquist declared triumphantly. "Such an admission should prove to your complete satisfaction what, to us, has been very obvious from the first, namely, that your utter ignorance is a hindrance rather than an aid in our exploring."

Tucson whistled a soft "Phew!" that was lost in the steady thudding of the steel pick.

Janisary's voice shook with rage. "Don't crowd me too far, Norquist. I'm trying to be patient—"

"Yes, trying to be patient that I may serve your ends," Norquist cut in sharply. "Undoubtedly, Janisary, you possess certain advantages, but not all. Allow me to remind you that without me you may lose everything. In short, if I may be allowed to employ your own terminology, 'Don't crowd *me* too far.'"

Janisary swore at him, then turned and walked off in the darkness.

Pete said in worried tones, "Look here, professor, I wouldn't anger him if I were you."

The little professor emitted something that resembled a chuckle. "Nonsense, Peter! One must talk up to such swine. I have been bored with his imbecilities from the first, but suffered them in silence so long as I imagined he was a representative of the Mexican Government. Now that I know him for an impostor, I take great pleasure in reminding him I hold what is known as the whip hand—that is, to a certain degree. . . . Good night, Peter. I'll go in and keep an eye on Mr. Janisary." The lantern light gleamed on his bald pate.

"For heaven's sake, don't put him on the prod."

"I think I know what you mean, Peter, but may I remind you that your diction isn't all it might be? . . . Again, good night."

Tucson laughed softly as the slight form passed

beyond the ray of the lanterns and disappeared inside the wall surrounding the center temple.

"I was afraid of his temper," Pete sighed.

Tucson said, "The prof put an edge on his words to Janisary, eh? I'll bet he'd make a good little fighting machine, at that, if he was aroused enough. He doesn't realize, even now, what we're up against."

"Oh, he's human as the devil," Pete answered, "once his mind's off archaeology—but it doesn't often happen. . . ."

An hour passed, with the two men working steadily. "Dang it," Tucson grunted once, "we ought to be getting some place soon."

Pete replied, "If I've calculated correctly, you should strike a walled-up entrance before long. That'll be a job, getting out the blocks of stone. After that, we'll be getting some place."

They were driving straight through solid earth and nests of packed rock in the northern slope of the mound. Above him, Tucson could see the moon-bathed sky; on either side an earthen wall rose above his head.

The pick was encountering more rock than earth now. Tucson grunted as he stooped down and lifted a weighty chunk of volcanic rock in his hands, rolled it behind him.

"Seems like," he panted to Pete, "there ain't nothin' but rock here—hello!" as the point of the steel pick flashed down, entered a crevice and failed to encounter resistance, "I've struck a hole, or somethin', here."

"What!" Pete hurried to fetch a lantern. Tucson jerked out the pick, bringing with it a small fragment of stone. Pete held the lantern to the spot; nothing beyond but inky blackness. Pete set down the lantern. For a moment he didn't speak.

Tucson rested on the pick handle, said, "Well?"

"We're in luck, Tucson. This entrance isn't walled up—I mean, it's not fitted with cubic blocks of stone, mortared together. The Scorpion people, maybe, left in a hurry, and just piled rock up against the entrance. Norquist has told me of such cases. We'll be inside in another ten minutes. Notice any gas or anything of the kind from that hole?"

Tucson said no. "Smells sorta musty, mebbe."

"The temple hasn't been completely airtight, though that's not always the case—"

"C'mon," Tucson interrupted, "let's clear this entrance."

His pick rose and fell, loosening the rocks that barred the entrance to the temple. The hole grew larger and larger as he lifted out big chunks of rock and rolled them back for Pete to dispose of. The two men were working feverishly now.

Tucson was soaked in perspiration. Before him was an irregularly shaped opening, plenty large enough for a man to enter through. He dropped the pick.

"We're in," he said shortly. "Grab a coupla lanterns and come on." Before he had finished speaking, he had thrust one leg through the entrance. The other followed a moment later. Pete, carrying two lanterns was right on his heels.

The two men stood upright inside the temple. For a moment neither spoke, too overcome with awe and the mystery of the ancient crypt. Tucson and Pete found themselves in a vaulted chamber, with keystoned arches supporting a ceiling of closely-fitted slabs of stone. At either end of the room was a slope-sided doorway leading to another dark chamber beyond.

"Probably only three chambers in this one," Pete murmured, half absent-mindedly comparing this smaller structure with the center temple. "What do you think of it, cowboy?"

"Man," Tucson exclaimed, "I've never seen the like. . . ."

Forgotten for the moment was all thought of Janisary and the dangers to be encountered. Tucson was lost in an admiration of the long-buried chamber. Frescoes and elaborate carvings adorned the walls. Queer designs and symbols were sculptured into solid rock at spots, all in clearly-cut relief, though somewhat dust-covered at present. It had been in its highest hour of civilization, a place of lavish magnificence, one of the tombs of a vanished race.

Dust lay thickly underfoot in the chamber,

which was approximately fifteen by twenty-five feet in size. The lanterns, standing on the floor, cast a pale, weird light about the walls and floor. A group of pottery stood at one side, gray with the deposit of centuries. There were urns, pots, shallow dishes, mugs. With his bandanna Pete removed the dust from a bowl-shaped dish. The action revealed a face painted in red and yellow and black on the surface of the bowl.

Pete said quietly, "Sometimes they left food when they buried their dead. Probably these open dishes contained the *tortillas* of those days, who knows?"

"What's that?" Tucson indicated a long block of rock at least three feet high, six long and three wide, ranged along one wall.

"Sarcophagus—coffin," Pete said shortly. "There were several in that center temple when we entered it."

The long coffin appeared to Tucson to be of solid rock, but, examining it, after brushing away a half inch of dust, he saw that it was covered with flat slabs of stone, fitted closely together.

"Look here," Pete said excitedly.

Tucson crossed the room to Pete's side. Pete had removed a circular, flat cover of jade from one of the pottery urns and turned it on its side. There came a faint metallic clatter in the stillness as a torrent of small jewelry poured forth on the dusty floor. There were gold and silver rings of various sizes, earrings and pendants of the same metals and of turquoise. Bangles and anklets appeared, gleaming dully in the lantern light. A number of silver beads and tiny golden bells, ringed at the top, probably once strung in a necklace, were among the other objects. Three tiny, exquisitely carved scorpions of rock crystal caught Tucson's eye.

"Reckon I'll keep one of those for a souvenir," he said, almost speaking in a whisper. The greater part of the jewelry was made up of gold, silver and turquoise, though a few opal-set rings appeared.

"My gosh!" Pete's voice trembled with awe. "Can you imagine—what's the matter?"

Tucson had suddenly gained his feet and went to the entrance. He stood listening a moment. Some short distance away he could hear the ringing strokes of *peones'* picks, at work on the farther temple.

He came back to the center of the chamber. "Didn't want to forget ourselves," he explained. "Thought I better give a listen."

"Hear anything?"

"All quiet along the firin' line," Tucson said quietly.

Pete didn't answer. He was again lost in contemplation of the discovered jewelry and in opening a second urn. After a moment he crowded the trinkets back into their receptacles and stood up.

"No green eyes around, anyway," he commented. "I'd sort of like to find those for Frieda. . . . Let's give a look at this sarcophagus, cowboy." He gestured toward the long stone coffin.

The sarcophagus was covered with six slabs of rock, three feet by one, and at least two inches thick, their edges being fitted closely together. "They haven't been mortared," Pete commented as he and Tucson carefully lifted off the slabs and laid them to one side. When the last one had been removed, Pete seized a lantern and hurried back. Neither of the men spoke for several minutes, as they gazed silently into the long-buried tomb of some ancient ruler.

The long coffin had been cut from solid rock. A few fragments of bone, even now disintegrating, lay on the bottom, which was thickly covered with dust. Here were more trinkets, necklaces from which the stringing had long since disappeared, several rings set with opal and turquoise, some sort of fanciful headdress of beaten gold as thin as cardboard. A long plume, or feather, carved from a solid bar of gold, lay at one end partly covered by the bone dust. Two silver goblets with an exquisitely chased design about the sides lay at the upper end, near the skull.

It was the skull that held the attention of the men longest. At first, Tucson took it to be only a replica of a human skull. It was completely covered with a mosaic of flat, closely-fitted bits of turquoise, the even, grinning teeth being covered with beaten silver.

"Small skull," Tucson commented. His voice shook a trifle.

"Woman's, I reckon. Probably a princess of the Scorpion people."

Tucson exclaimed, "Look! What's happening?"

The turquoise surface of the skull seemed to be moving. Pete held the lantern higher. "What the hell!" he cried.

No doubt about it: the tiny flat bits of turquoise that formed the mosaic seemed to be separating. Thin gleams of light flashed as they moved. The dust covering of ages shifted under the heavy breathing of the two men as they bent near to watch. Now from the eye sockets gleamed two beams of greenish light that were caught but a moment in the yellow rays of the lantern Pete held over the tomb.

Then, quite suddenly, the skull seemed to collapse. With a tiny glassy clatter the hundreds of bits of turquoise separated and dropped to the bottom of the coffin. Of the skull all that remained was a handful of dust, flat segments of turquoise, heaped in confusion, and two objects that shone bright green under the lantern.

"The skull's gone!" Tucson said.

"Spooky for a minute, eh?" Pete's voice wasn't steady. "Sort of jolted me, too, for a moment. That turquoise covering preserved it a little longer than would ordinarily have been the case. Perhaps the skull, beneath, had already dissolved to dust, or the fresh air completed the process. Maybe it needed only our breathing on it, to shatter the mosaic shell—"

"Those green stones—" Tucson commenced.

But Pete had already started to reach down into the coffin. He hesitated, drew back his arm, then again stretched his fingers toward the stones that had filled the eye sockets of the skull, and raised them to the light to blow off the dust.

"The Green Eyes!" Pete gasped.

"They look like glass—"

"Bet they ain't just glass, cowboy."

The stones were circular in form, one surface having been carved to represent an eye, though whether human or reptile Tucson couldn't determine. A sort of iris and pupil were to be recognized. The reverse surface had been cunningly cut in hundreds of tiny facets, so arranged as to capture and reflect the slightest light. As the stones gleamed in Pete's trembling fingers they seemed to burn with strange green fires that lived and leaped and quivered at the least movement.

Pete and Tucson exchanged glances, grinned nervously. Neither spoke. Both men were covered with dust and perspiration. Long since the mud had vanished from Tucson's hair and coursed in tiny rivulets down his face and neck. His straw sombrero had been doffed for additional comfort and his hair showed bright red in the lantern light.

At a sound from the entrance, the two men whirled around, then drew quick breaths of relief. Professor Norquist stepped through the opening. "You broke through quicker than I expected," he said.

Pete said quickly, "Where did you leave Janisary?"

"Always you worry about Janisary. An hour since he left for his bed. I have not seen him. What have you found—?"

"Look, professor," Pete said excitedly. His speech failed as he extended the twin green stones.

Norquist accepted the discovery calmly enough. "Ah, the Green Eyes of Zexonteotl. Where did you find them? Emeralds, of course. If flawless, and I believe they are, they are more precious than diamonds. Enough wealth in them to finance Janisary's revolution—"

"That coffin over there," Pete extended one forefinger. "And look, there's jewelry in those urns—"

"Always jewelry," Norquist said impatiently. "Peter, you are as incorrigible as Janisary." He added, "I'll keep the Green Eyes. They are to be yours and Frieda's—after I have made a notation in my records. But what else have you found in the tomb?"

"We hadn't finished looking," Pete said. He started to tell about the turquoise skull, but Norquist had impatiently seized a lantern and was bending over the ancient coffin. A moment later he gave a sharp cry of delight, and whirled back to the center of the chamber, holding an oblong slab of obsidian glass, not much larger than a child's slate, into which had been cut several rows of hieroglyphics similar in appearance to those on the stelae, but in miniature form.

The professor was speechless with joy. Finally he found his voice, "Look at this. It is the most perfect small stela I have ever seen. Gaze at that exquisite carving, as sharply formed as the day it was made. This is wonderful, wonderful! Now at last I should learn when the Scorpion people lived. This is sure to bear the date at which the occupant of the tomb was interred."

Tucson grinned as the little professor capered about in an almost childish glee.

"—the greatest find I have ever made, Peter," Norquist was exclaiming. "I must make a cast of this at once. If I wait for tomorrow, Janisary may do something to prevent me; I shall get to work at once. Here, boy," to Tucson, "hurry out like a good fellow and get me plaster and water. You'll find them near the stela I finished today." He turned away, and again commenced to examine the coffin.

Tucson and Pete exchanged grins. "Even red hair doesn't register on him, when he's this way," Pete said. "Better go get what he wants, or we'll lose time explaining matters."

Tucson pushed through the opening and stepped into the open air. The moon had swung far to the west now. He looked around. No one was to be seen, but from the other temple came the blows of workmen's tools.

Tucson hastened to secure the plaster of Paris, buckets and water. He hurried back and entered the tomb. The professor was still stooped over the coffin, talking to himself in a technical language Tucson didn't comprehend and to which Pete was paying no attention, as he stood in the doorway of one of the adjoining rooms, holding the lantern and looking about.

Tucson dropped on his knees and commenced mixing the plaster with water. Finally, the task done, he mentioned this fact to Norquist. The professor didn't hear the words. Pete came back into the room, saying, "There are two more sarcophagi in that next chamber, Professor Norquist. Shall we go ahead and open them?"

He was forced to repeat the question, before Norquist finally replied, "There is sufficient here to keep me occupied for a time."

"Maybe," Pete speculated, "we might find some more of those green eyes. What do you think?"

"I feel sure," Norquist said firmly, "the ones we have constitute the only pair. Peter, I repeat, you are as bad as Janisary. Until you have removed from your thoughts all ideas regarding the monetary value of treasure, you will never be an archaeologist. You already have the Green Eyes of Zexonteotl, and should be contented."

Pete chuckled, "Just one of those emeralds would content me, not to mention two."

Tucson was still in a kneeling position at the side of the bucket of mixed plaster, his head cocked to one side, listening.

Pete said, "What's up? Think you heard something?" Tucson made a gesture to remain quiet, even as Pete continued, "Maybe it would be a good idea to watch that entrance, just in case—"

He didn't finish the words as a new voice cut in with the reply, "It's too late for that now, Lockhart. Claw high, you hombres!"

# 18

## "Take Him Alive!"

Tucson, kneeling at the side of the bucket of plaster, slowly raised his hands in the air and rose to his feet, his heart sinking with disappointment. Pete's hands were up, too. Norquist, the order having failed to penetrate his consciousness, was still engrossed with the contents of the coffin.

Tucson had recognized Gage Janisary's voice, but couldn't see the man's face in the entrance. The interior of the temple chamber was well lighted by the lanterns, and Tucson realized it would do no good to resist now. All of the odds were with Janisary.

Janisary's laugh was ugly as he continued, "Get

inside there, Crawford. I'll keep 'em covered, then follow you in."

Tench Crawford pushed his way through the entrance, grinning nastily, a gun in either hand. He motioned Pete and Tucson over against the back wall just as Norquist straightened up, blinking his eyes at the unexpected sight.

"Bless me!" Norquist ejaculated. "Gun! What's all this—"

"Get over with your pals there, Norquist," Tench Crawford snapped. "One bad move and you're a dead man—"

"And we're in no mood to take any back talk, either," Janisary interrupted in ugly tones, as he stepped into the room, guns in fists. "Get movin', Norquist." Norquist moved slowly away from the coffin. Janisary spoke over his shoulder to someone outside, "Keep 'em covered through this opening. We'll have 'em out in a few minutes."

Tucson wondered how many men were outside, considered making a break for the entrance and fighting his way through, but in the next moment rejected that plan. With men outside and Janisary and Crawford in the temple, he'd be shot down at the first move.

Janisary's dark eyes gleamed triumphantly as he said to Pete, "Figured you were right smart didn't you, Lockhart? I thought it was dang queer you being so willing to work nights. Just kind of figured you were double-crossing me when you said you couldn't get in here for another twenty-four hours—"

"Now look here, Janisary," the little professor commenced, "I've told you before—"

"Shut up!" Janisary snarled. "I'm not trusting any of you hombres. That's just why I left word for Crawford to come and get me at midnight tonight and bring a couple of men—" Janisary's tones dwindled off to a shocked silence as he focused his gaze on Tucson's red hair. "My God! Smith!" he fairly yelled.

"You got the name correct, Scorpion," Tucson said easily.

Janisary recovered from his first surprise, laughed harshly, "Cripes! This is almost too good to be true." He crossed the floor in quick strides, looking Tucson over from head to foot. "Fixed up like one of the laborers, eh? Say, how long you been in here—"

"We just dug through about an hour ago—" Tucson began.

"Cut it, Smith! You know I'm talking about the valley. How'd you get in? When did you get in?"

"Just arrived on a shootin' star," Tucson drawled.

"Don't want to talk, eh? You'll talk plenty and pronto before I'm through with you. I suppose you know I got your pals tied up."

"Is that so?" Tucson affected surprise. "I was wonderin' where they were."

"You aren't going to do much more wondering on this earth," Janisary snarled. "I've had just about enough of your interference. Eventually, when I put the screws on, you're going to be damn glad to tell me how you learned about this valley."

Tucson said insolently, "I bought a gun once. Anybody but a nitwit could have got directions from that."

Janisary cursed. "I don't believe it."

Tucson clasped his hands across the top of his head to rest his arms. "That's where you make your mistakes, Janisary. You don't believe in truth and going straight and—"

Janisary swore some more. "I had a man watching you. How'd you get past him—you and your pards—?"

"Rode past—"

"Don't try to be funny. Porky didn't show up. I had two men out watching the trail. When they told me three hombres carryin' the descriptions of you and your pals were on the way—well, I sort of prepared for your arrival—"

"With doped beer, eh?"

"One way or another," Janisary bragged, "I find a way of stopping my enemies. Oh, you're going to be regretful you ever set foot in this valley—"

Norquist cut in icily. "I think we've had enough talk, Janisary. Apparently, this laborer is known to you. However—"

"I told you to shut up once," Janisary snarled. "Where's the treasure?"

Lockhart cut in quickly, "I haven't said we found any treasure."

"You don't need to say anything," Janisary snapped. "We heard you talking about it."

"Oh, that," Pete bluffed. He gestured toward the pottery urns standing near the wall. "You'll find a few things in there."

Janisary's eyes lighted up. He hummed softly to himself, broke off to jerk over his shoulder, "Watch 'em, boys."

"We got 'em covered, chief," from outside the entrance.

Tench Crawford said in ugly tones, "They won't start nothin' while I got these hawg-laigs trained on 'em. I'm just itchin' to pull trigger."

Janisary strode across the chamber, knelt by the urns containing the jewelry, quickly tipped the contents out on the floor. His hands shook with excitement as he examined the treasure. His delighted humming vibrated through the room. Now his motions became slower. Finally he rose to his feet, face angry.

"The Green Eyes aren't here," he stated in hot tones. "There isn't an emerald in the bunch."

Lockhart said coolly, "Aren't you satisfied with what you've got?"

"Don't stall," Janisary snapped. "I want those emeralds."

Tucson laughed scornfully, "Where'd you get the idea we found any emeralds?"

Janisary said again, "Don't stall. I heard you hombres talking about them, just before we come in and got the drop on you."

Tucson said, "Check," hopelessly.

"Think I don't know," Janisary laughed. "I'm one move ahead of you all the time—"

"Not on guns you ain't," Tucson grinned.

Janisary's face reddened. "Dammit," he demanded, "I want those emeralds."

As he stepped forward, his foot smashed down on one of the pottery dishes near the treasure urns. An angry squeal left the professor's lips as he rushed on Janisary.

"You clumsy swine!" he cried, clenched fist shaking in Janisary's face. "Do you realize you've damaged that piece beyond repair? You and your treasure! Bah! You don't recognize real value—"

Janisary's left gun made a short sidewise sweep, the barrel of the weapon striking Norquist across the chest. There was enough power behind the blow to send the little man sprawling to the floor.

Janisary swore as Tucson started forward, shoved his other gun against Tucson's middle. "It's up to you, Smith," he snarled, "whether I pull this trigger or not."

"Get back, Lockhart!" Crawford snapped, "Back!"

"And keep them hands up, you galoots!" came a rough voice from outside the entrance.

243

Tucson and Pete again backed toward the wall, hands high. Norquist was just stumbling to his feet. Janisary's laugh was triumphant as he said, "You damn near got it then, Smith. I'd just as soon let you have it as not. I don't trust you. You're too tricky—you and your pals." He added cruelly, "Maybe you'd like to hear that one of your pards almost got away tonight. Somehow, he'd wiggled his ropes loose. It was just through luck that we found out."

Tucson's heart sank as his final hope went glimmering, but he said bravely, "You sure got to work fast to keep ahead of those two."

Janisary turned back to Norquist. "I've stood just about enough from you, Norquist. It's going to be awful easy to let daylight through your skinny ribs if you don't come across with those green emeralds."

"I haven't got them," the professor declared.

"One of you three's got 'em," from Janisary. "Come across."

"You can search me," Tucson said coldly.

Janisary jerked out. "Hand 'em over, Lockhart."

Pete laughed coolly. "No savvy."

"Don't get funny," Janisary snapped.

"Hell," Pete said, "I can't give you something I haven't got."

Janisary's lips came together like a rat trap. "Stubborn, eh?" He eyed the three men threateningly, then "Keep 'em covered, Tench. I figure to see which of these three is the worst liar."

He thrust his guns back into holsters, stepped to the professor and started to search his pockets. The little man submitted to the indignity in silence, laughing scornfully when Janisary had finished. Scowling, Janisary next went to Lockhart. Here, while he didn't find the green stones, he did locate Pete's gun, hidden inside his shirt. Pete's face fell as Janisary drew out the gun. Janisary cursed at sight of the weapon and at his failure to locate the green eyes.

Tucson jeered, "The initials on that Colt-gun is P.E.L., Scorpion. Ever see it before?"

Janisary was white with anger. Thrusting the gun into his waistband he crossed to Tucson, commenced to search the pockets of the dead *peon.*

"You're just wasting time, Janisary. We don't know anything about any emeralds." At the same time, Tucson was wondering what had become of them. He was sure he had seen Norquist place them in his pocket. But Janisary had made a thorough search.

Janisary said, "Dammit! I heard you hombres say you found those stones. I want 'em and I want 'em quick."

"You must be mistaken," Tucson laughed.

Janisary cursed him, struck him across the face.

Tucson said steadily, "There's something else I'll have to settle with you."

Fighting to hold his temper, Janisary again searched the three men, questioned them persistently. The emeralds weren't produced, and Janisary couldn't locate them. Finally he gave up for the moment. "All right," he said. "We'll let it go now. Tomorrow when I stake you three smart hombres out on an anthill I bet you'll be damn glad to tell me where those stones are."

There was some further talk made by Janisary, then he said, "I'll be keeping you hombres under guard." He called to the men outside the temple, "I'm sending these men out. Keep 'em covered when they come. We'll tie 'em up later." Then to Tucson, "All right, Smith. Outside. And move plumb cautious. You'll get a slug if you try anything."

Tucson nodded, moved carelessly to the entrance. Without a backward glance he stepped through to the outside. Two men awaited him with drawn guns. The channel leading to the opening in the temple wasn't wide enough for Tucson to pass, so long as they stood in his way. He mentioned this fact and the men stepped slowly back.

Suddenly, Tucson went into action. He dived low at the two men before him, heard their guns roar as they exploded over his head. His left shoulder struck one man on the hip, bowling him over. His right fist swung with considerable force to the groin of the other man.

Behind him he heard Janisary cursing, caught

the rush of feet. Somewhere, near the other end of the valley he heard shouts. The two men were down in front of him now. Tucson was on his knees. He scrambled up, as the other two rose to meet his rush. His fists swung right and left. Again the men went down. Tucson started to leap over them, when one of them reached up and caught his foot.

Tucson stumbled, hit the ground with a heavy thud. The other two closed with him. Over and over the three rolled, kicking, gouging, scratching. It was too close to use guns now. Through the melee Tucson caught Janisary's shouts, "Take him alive! He's got to tell where those emeralds are! Take him alive."

Tench Crawford was yelling something about having Norquist and Lockhart covered. A heavy body struck Tucson, a fist was slung against his ear. His left fist flailed out and he had the satisfaction of hearing a yelp of pain.

But Janisary had added his own strength to the fray now. Twice Tucson fought to his feet, carrying the striking weight of the three men on his back, and twice he was forced to his knees again. He twisted sidewise, endeavoring to get in a clean blow at the head nearest him. At that moment, Janisary struck again. Tucson's head cracked down, struck a fragment of rock. Momentarily stunned, he wilted to the earth and lay quiet.

Janisary and his two men rose wearily from his prone form. Janisary backed away, gun at ready.

"Get up, Smith," he panted, "and don't try that again. I can't take any more chances with you."

Tucson staggered to his feet. The moon was low now, but there was enough light to gleam on the extended barrel of Janisary's six-shooter. Tucson raised his arms in the air and remained silent.

Janisary said to the other two, "Go back and help Tench with Norquist and Lockhart. I'll watch Smith."

Two minutes later, Pete and the professor appeared in the open air, their hands high. Shouts sounded along the valley, as a knot of Janisary's followers came running up to lend a hand if necessary. They circled around Tucson and the other two captives, asking questions. Janisary and his men explained briefly.

"Dad, what's wrong!" Frieda pushed through the circle of men, throwing her arms around her father's neck. "I heard shots—"

"Keep out of this, Frieda," Norquist said steadily. "Go back in the house."

"Not until you tell me—" She broke off, appealing to Janisary, "What does this mean, Mr. Janisary—?"

Janisary said angrily. "Take your father's advice. Get back in your living quarters—"

"I won't do it until you explain what this means—"

"Get back, do you hear!" Janisary gave the girl a rough push.

*Smack!* Frieda's open palm landed against Janisary's mouth. Janisary swore savagely. Pete took one step forward. One of the outlaws struck him across the face, two more closed in. Janisary took a firm hold on the girl's wrists, snapped angry orders, "Take this girl to her living quarters. If Zella can't tie her up without help, go as far as you like. You needn't be gentle on my account. From now on I get what I want, or somebody suffers—plenty!"

# 19

# Tribal Law for Traitors

Two o'clock in the morning. Silence had again settled over the valley, except for the sounds of a night-bird some distance away. Tucson had been taken to the temple that served as living quarters and was seated on a chair, bound hand and foot, the ropes running around the back of the chair. He was a sorry sight. His face was bruised. His flimsy garments had been nearly torn from his body in his fight to escape. Only one shoulder and sleeve remained of the shirt. Half a trousers leg was missing. His bare, muscular back was crossed with bloody scratches, streaked with mud and perspiration. His eyes were weary as they roved about the room.

The walls and ceiling of this temple were decorated in similar fashion to the smaller one Tucson and Lockhart had entered a scant two hours before. Tucson had learned there were seven rooms in this structure, the one he occupied at present opening off the front entrance to the temple. At his back a curtained doorway gave into a narrow passage off which were entrances to smaller rooms used as sleeping quarters.

In one of the smaller rooms, at the back of the temple, Tucson knew Frieda was held captive, trussed with ropes like himself. Where Norquist and Lockhart had been taken, Tucson didn't know. After an hour of threatening, cajoling, bargaining in the hope of learning the whereabouts of the Green Eyes of Zexonteotl, Janisary had flown into a rage and taken Pete and the professor away, their hands bound behind their backs, and Tench Crawford herding them along.

Idly, for lack of something better to do, Tucson surveyed the big room where he was held. Walls of huge stone blocks were fitted so closely together they seemed to be solid elevations. Designs and symbols, animals, scorpions, faces, formed a sculptured frieze which ran around the four sides of the room, near the ceiling. Below this, cut into the rock, was a fretwork band in red and black.

This temple didn't arouse in Tucson the same feeling of awe he had experienced upon entering the other temple with Lockhart. Probably the furniture and other signs of habitation had something to do with this. Goatskins and Indian rugs were spread on the floor. There were several wooden chairs, including the one to which Tucson was bound with tightly tied ropes. A lighted oil lamp burned on a heavy oaken table, casting its illumination to all but the most remote corners of the big chamber which stretched the front width of the temple.

Opposite Tucson, in the center of the wall, was the entrance, at present hung with a huge *chimayo* blanket woven in blue and red and yellow. To one side of this makeshift door, on a chair tilted back against the wall, sat one of Janisary's outlaws, a cocked six-shooter in hand. He was a narrow-browed, brutish-looking individual with unshaven jowls and shifty eyes. His arms were long, his shoulders bulky; he reminded Tucson, to no small extent, of a gorilla.

"I tell you I got my orders," he growled reply to a request Tucson had made sometime before and which had necessitated considerable thought. "You ain't to have nothin'—"

Tucson persisted, "All you got to do is stick the cigarette in my mouth and light it, after it's rolled—"

"Nothin' doin'. Gage said I wasn't to go near you. That's flat!"

"All right." Tucson subsided, then a minute later, "Any objection to tellin' where he and Crawford took Lockhart and the professor?"

"Well," dubiously, "I guess not. Gage didn't say not to—"

"Where'd they go?"

"Back to that other temple. Gage is still tryin' to locate those emeralds. He took Lockhart and Norquist with him so he can question them about the price he might get for that other jewelry."

Tucson laughed coldly. "He won't get much out of those two. Pete doesn't know, and the prof won't do any talking—"

"No, no?" the guard jeered. "My name ain't Zink Freeling if Norquist don't get a sudden urge to talk plenty and pronto, when Gage commences to screw down on him. Some of these Yaqui Injuns Gage has got in the valley shore knows some neat ideas in torture. And don't get no idea you'll be forgotten. The Scorpion's plumb persuasive when he gets his mind sot on anythin'."

Tucson laughed scornfully, said, "Let's talk about that smoke."

"Nothin' doin'. You don't get no cigarette from me."

The *chimayo* blanket was pushed aside and the woman known as Zella Frost entered. At the first sound, the guard had swung up to his feet. Now he backed away a pace, a smirky smile on his simian features. "Oh, it's you, Miz' Frost."

Zella Frost nodded shortly, her gaze meeting Tucson's. After a moment a slow flush flooded the woman's features and she looked away. Tucson didn't say anything. There was something warm and vital, and at the same time hard, about Zella Frost. She was tall and slim, with hazel eyes and full red lips. Her heavy chestnut hair was coiled neatly to form a frame for her attractive features. She couldn't have been more than thirty, Tucson knew; she appeared younger. Every line of the trim figure in divided riding skirt and mannish flannel shirt spoke of superb physical condition.

Zella Frost's voice was a throaty contralto, warm and vibrant as she said to Zink Freeling, "Did I hear your prisoner asking for a cigarette, Zink?"

"Yes, ma'am, Miz' Frost."

"It isn't much to ask."

"It's against orders. Gage said—"

"I'm not under Gage's orders. Look here—"

"Mebbe not under his orders," the guard said slyly, "but you—"

The woman's color heightened. "Never mind that, Zink. Look here, you go outside. This man can't escape. I'll give him his smoke—"

"Good Gawd, Miz' Frost, I daren't—"

Zella Frost looked steadily at the guard. "Gage doesn't need to know. It may be the last cigarette this man will ever have. You can't refuse that much. Suppose you were in his boots—"

"But I ain't. An' I ain't goin' to risk my own skin—"

"Zink, you've been after me a long time to teach you that triple shuffle. I'll do it, if—"

Eagerly Freeling produced from a pocket a deck of greasy cards. "You mean that? Straight goods?"

"Straight goods—tomorrow. It would take too long now."

"All right, Miz' Frost—only be careful. Don't breathe a word to Gage, neither. He'd skin me alive."

"You can watch for Gage yourself. Outside. Stand near the entrance in the wall. Keep your eyes open. You'll have plenty of time to see him before he can get here. You better hurry though."

The guard withdrew, still somewhat reluctantly. Zella Frost looked steadily at Tucson as the man's footsteps died away. She said lightly, "That's what comes of being an inveterate gambler. I've showed Freeling a few tricks with the cards in odd moments. He'd sell his soul— black as it is—to learn more."

Tucson said, and his voice sounded strained, "Looks thataway."

Zella Frost smiled wistfully. "For once, my profession can be turned to a good use." She crossed the room, plucked from the table a sack of Durham and papers, rolled deftly two cigarettes, one of which she placed in Tucson's mouth, the other between her own lips. The scratch of a match sounded abnormally loud in the silence of the big chamber. She stood close to Tucson in lighting his cigarette. Tucson's eyes were on hers every moment. As she withdrew the flame to ignite her own tobacco, the back of her hand brushed Tucson's cheek. There was something soft, caressing, in the touch.

Cigarette smoke drifted between them as Zella Frost, still standing close, searched every line of Tucson's bronzed features, not missing his wide, firm mouth. Gradually a softer light, though they hadn't been hard before, entered the hazel eyes.

Tucson said quietly, his lips twisting in a wry smile, "I could do with some cleaning up."

"I was looking *inside,*" the girl said. "You've lived mighty clean, Tucson."

Tucson said, "I've tried. Sometimes I've wondered—"

"There's never been any real need of that," Zella Frost said swiftly. "*You* couldn't go wrong. . . . It's been a long time, Tucson."

Tucson said something about ten years, adding, "I didn't recognize you at first. Then, when Pete Lockhart mentioned your name—"

The girl's laugh sounded rueful. "So you'd forgotten me?"

Tucson said quietly, "I don't reckon a man ever forgets a woman he's asked to marry him. We were foolish to quarrel, Zella—"

"It wasn't your fault," the woman said swiftly, passionately. "I was the fool—with a lot of kid ideas. I wanted to see life and I wanted money—"

"Nobody'd blame you, Zella, for not wanting to tie yourself to a cowpuncher's forty a month.

Certainly, I don't. I don't know but what you were wise. Until recent, I've never had more than a few dollars to rub together at the same time."

Zella suppressed the fierce exclamation that rose to her lips, and said, "I've learned there's more to life than money, Tucson. I've wished more than once that I hadn't refused you. Well, considering the life I've led, that was certainly a break for the Christians." Her short laugh wasn't as careless as she tried to make it.

Slow smoke curled in spirals from Tucson's nostrils. He said, as quietly as before, "What I asked ten years ago, Zella, still holds good. There never has been anybody else to take your place."

The girl's hazel eyes widened. She looked searchingly at Tucson. After a time she said, and her voice broke a little, "That's a trifle more than I can take in, all at once, Tucson Smith. And I never did know you to be a liar."

"You don't love Janisary." It was a statement of fact, rather than a question.

Zella's laugh was scornful. "I thought I did once—five years ago. Then I learned what he was. I left him. A few months ago I met him again. He lied about his activities, got me to come down here. Don't ask me why I came, Tucson—"

"No woman should be asked to explain her reasons for doing anything. I'm not asking, Zella—not anything, about the last ten years."

"I guess I don't know—myself," Zella continued, "why I came to this valley. I was tired of life, as it was. Maybe I was looking for excitement, a new type of adventure. *Quien sabe?*" She shrugged her shoulders. "Anyway, I came. Janisary told me he was working for the Mexican Government here. Then one day, Pete Lockhart found an opportunity to tell me a few things. I couldn't leave then. I wanted to see Frieda and her father and Pete safe first. I've tried to work out something, but Janisary has been too smart, so far. He thinks I'm jealous of the girl. Sometimes he isn't so smart—"

"Look here, Zella, if we get out of this, what I said ten years ago still holds good."

The girl's eyes were misty now. She shook her head, smiling through tears. "It's too late for that, Tucson, not after what I've—well, I've drifted. That's a short way of saying it. I've dealt faro from here to the Canadian border—"

Tucson said again, "I'm not asking anything, Zella, about the past ten years."

His cigarette had burned down. The girl removed the butt from his lips, again touching his cheek lightly, as before. She stepped back reluctantly, shaking her head. "It's too late for that, Tucson. You don't know—"

Tucson repeated Zella's own words of a few minutes before, "I've been looking *inside,* girl. Nothing makes any difference—now or any time."

Zella shook her head. It was an effort to hold

her voice steady as she said, "We're wasting time talking, Tucson. I've got to get you out of this. Shall I untie you now—"

"Not any time," Tucson said quickly. "I can't allow you to run that risk. Freeling would tell Janisary he left you with me. No, we can't chance that. But, I've got two pards in this camp. If you could find a way to—"

"Do you think I'm afraid to run any risk?" Zella said.

"Not afraid, girl." Tucson shook his head. "I know your nerve."

"Listen, I'll untie you. Then I can get a gun— two guns—"

"No, Zella—"

"You can't help yourself," the girl laughed warmly. She stepped around to the back of the chair, reached to the knots.

There was a step at the *chimayo* blanket. Zink Freeling said, hard-voiced, "What you doin', Miz' Frost?"

Zella stepped back from the chair. She said calmly, "These ropes seem a bit loose, Zink."

Freeling said suspiciously, "Better let Gage 'tend to that. He'll be here in a minute." He looked narrowly at Zella, "I reckon I'll have to tell Gage about you—"

Zella's laugh was hard. She still held her cigarette butt in her hand. With a deft flick of finger and thumb she sent it winging at Freeling's head, saying calmly, "I would if I were you, Zink. At the same time you can tell him about leaving the room."

Freeling scratched his head. He didn't say anything.

Steps were heard outside. Norquist and Pete were shoved into the room, hands still tied behind them. Janisary and Crawford pushed in at their heels. Janisary looked angry. He said, "What you doing here, Zella?"

Zella said defiantly, "Getting acquainted with your prisoner."

Janisary's eyes narrowed. "Hope you enjoyed yourself."

"He's pretty much of a man, Gage. More than you will ever be."

"Oh, like that, eh?" Gage whistled softly. "I reckon I'll—"

"Look here, Scorpion," Tucson cut in. "You've got no call to get rough. All Miss Frost did was light a cigarette and stick it in my mouth."

Janisary's face went as black as a thundercloud. "T'hell you say," he snarled. "I reckon, Zella, you've gone too far this time. I gave orders—"

"I'm not subject to your orders, Gage." The girl's chin was up, her face white.

"No?" Janisary sneered. "I'll teach you different." He whirled around on Zink Freeling, "What were Smith and Zella talking about?"

Freeling gulped and said feebly, "Nothin'. She just rolled him a cigarette—"

"Don't lie, Zink!"

"Well, I—er, you see, chief, I don't know. I—"

Janisary was quick to comprehend. "In other words," sarcastically, "she persuaded you to leave the room. You damn fool!"

"It was just for a minute—"

"Yes, and if I hadn't come when I did—" Slowly, a new idea was forming in Janisary's mind. He looked at the girl, "You know, Zella, I've wondered a long time how Lockhart's gun got out of this valley. It's just occurred to me—"

"How anything could occur," Zella said coldly, "to that thick skull of yours, Gage, is more than I can comprehend."

Janisary flushed scarlet. For a moment he couldn't speak. When he found his voice the words trembled with cruel rage, "A traitor right in my own camp, eh? Well, there's a few Yaqui Indians at the other end of the valley. They have rules of their own regarding traitors—especially women traitors."

He broke off to speak swift orders to Freeling and Crawford. Norquist and Pete were backed against a wall, a short distance from Tucson. Then, Janisary continued, "I'll watch these hombres. Crawford, you and Freeling take Zella down the valley to Shigandi Joe. Tell him to work a little tribal law on her. Explain that she nearly put the whole camp in danger of capture. After Shigandi Joe gets through with her—" Janisary's upper lip curled in a snarl of hate, "—I reckon we won't have any more traitors. Joe teaches the sort of lesson that ain't forgot soon!"

Norquist and Lockhart were protesting, trying to wrench their arms free. The veins on Tucson's forehead stood out in great knots as he struggled to break his bonds. Janisary laughed triumphantly, his guns out. Freeling and Crawford had seized Zella's arms. The girl didn't falter, didn't show any resistance, but every vestige of color was drained from her face.

Janisary snapped, "Get movin'! We got work ahead. It looks as though we're going to need a little of Shigandi's help in making these three stubborn hombres talk about emeralds too!"

# 20

# A Long Gamble

Crawford and Freeling tightened their grips on Zella's arms, turned toward the door. Then they stopped short, released the girl, hands darting toward holsters. But the move came too late.

"Claw for the sky, you scuts!"

Grim-faced, Stony and Lullaby stood just inside the doorway, their backs to the *chimayo* blanket. Each held one of Tucson's guns, covering Janisary and his two henchmen. Further words weren't necessary. The stern features of the two cowboys spoke volumes that Janisary didn't dare ignore. A curse broke from his lips, as he dropped his guns to the floor and raised his arms into the air. Freeling and Tench Crawford were quick to follow suit.

Stony flipped his gun to Lullaby. "Watch 'em! I'll get their guns."

Lullaby said grimly, "I hope their arms get tired, or somethin'."

Janisary took a step forward as Stony tossed his gun to Lullaby. The weapon landed solidly in Lullaby's fist, bearing on Janisary. Lullaby laughed with genial savagery, "Come right ahead, Scorpion."

Janisary's arms shot skyward again, he glared at his two henchmen, who hadn't made a move, and fell back muttering. Tucson was speechless with delight. Finally he found his voice, grinned widely, "You two rannies sure are one welcome sight. I was beginnin' to think you weren't—"

Norquist and Lockhart were making anxious queries regarding Frieda. Zella had darted across the room to untie Tucson. She spoke over her shoulder, "Frieda's not harmed. I'll release her in a minute." She fumbled feverishly at the knots.

Pete said, "There's a knife in my hip-pocket, Zella."

Zella procured the knife, turned back to Tucson. Meantime, Stony had scooped Janisary's guns from the floor, plucked the weapons from the holsters of Crawford and Freeling. He backed away, a gun in either hand, his waistband holding other weapons.

Tucson said, "I don't suppose you hombres thought to bring my clothes, when you grabbed my guns—"

"Wrong again," Lullaby drawled. "Your raiment is just outside the front door, rolled in your cartridge belts." Piously, he added, "I should think you'd be ashamed to sit around half-naked this way."

"Which situation," Tucson chuckled, "was more or less forced on me. I'll remedy it in a few jerks of a yearlin's tail."

"Look here, Smith," Janisary finally found his tongue. "You may hold the upper hand right now, but you ain't got a dawg's chance of getting out of this valley alive. You can't get horses without arousing the whole camp. Mebbe we can make a bargain—"

"I'll tend to that part," Tucson said shortly. The last ropes fell from his body. He stood up, stretched his muscles, then, shortly, "Put up your dukes, Janisary!"

Janisary said, "What do you mean?" at the same time raising his fists. Tucson struck him in the face, followed up and hit him again. Janisary crashed to the floor and lay still, blood running from his nose. Lullaby and Stony set up a faint cheer.

Tucson smiled sheepishly, "You and your tribal law," he snapped scornfully at the prone Janisary. "Get up, you ain't hurt." Tucson turned to the others, "There's a lot I'll stand for on my own account, that won't go down when it applies to—to—" He broke off, meeting Zella's eyes. Zella was using the knife on Lockhart's bonds. She glanced up, signaled to Tucson to hurry.

Tucson nodded, said to Lullaby and Stony, "Get these coyotes tied up. I'll get my clothes, give a look-see around and be back pronto. Then we'll go into action. Let me have my guns. You got plenty now." He seized the weapons and whirled through the doorway to the outside. A second later, he stuck his head past the *chimayo* blanket. "Lullaby, let Zella leave to release Frieda when she gets through there."

Lullaby said, "Right," looked surprised. Tucson disappeared.

Outside Tucson found his clothing. Some water in a bucket stood nearby. He splashed it over his body and dressed hurriedly, then strapped on his gun belts and stepped outside the surrounding wall to look around.

The moon had dropped from sight now. The valley was quiet. At the southern end, Tucson could see a faint red glow that denoted the outlaws' campfire. "Nearly out," Tucson muttered. "Darker it is, the better." The *peones* were thudding desultory picks on the other temple.

264

He pushed back through the opening wall, reentered the big chamber. Janisary, Crawford and Freeling lay on the floor, bound hand and foot. Frieda had joined the group now. She stood at one side talking to Pete and her father. Lullaby and Stony were waiting impatiently.

Tucson said to Frieda, "Where's Zella?"

"She'll be back in a minute," Frieda said. "She's gone to get some guns from Janisary's room—"

"Mine and Stony's," Lullaby put in. "Say, Tucson, how about this Zella girl—"

"You can trust her," Tucson said quickly.

Stony asked, "Now we're free, how we goin' to get out?"

"That's had me going too," Pete put in.

Norquist asked blandly, "Is it going to be necessary to leave—at once—before my work is finished? I don't understand—"

Frieda said swiftly, "I'll explain later, Dad. We've got to move in a hurry."

"Here's the plan," Tucson spoke in clipped sentences. "There's two guards at the outside end of the tunnel. Pete, it's up to you and Stony to put the silencer on 'em. When we come through with horses, we'll be coming fast. We won't have any time to be held up by guards. Can you do it?"

Stony nodded carelessly. Pete said, "Do our darndest."

"For God's sake don't raise an alarm," Tucson said earnestly.

"But how you goin' to get horses?" Pete wanted to know. "Tucson, they'll catch you sure—"

"I'll have Lullaby to help—"

"But even two of you—"

"—not to mention the Scorpion himself," Tucson finished with a grim smile. He swung back to Frieda, "Listen, girl, it's going to be up to you and your father to watch the men we leave here. No matter what they say or do, don't untie 'em. Zella will be back in a minute. Trust her. You've used guns, haven't you?" and at the girl's quick, affirmative nod, he continued, "Hold a gun on 'em every minute. If they so much as wiggle a finger, warn 'em once. Shoot the second time. We won't be gone long. I don't think anybody will come, but if any blasted outlaw sticks his nose in here, let him have it and talk later."

"Okay, Tucson," the girl smiled faintly. Tucson could see she was frightened.

Janisary spoke from his position on the floor, "You don't get any help from me, Smith. You're up against a cold deck. You'll all die if you try to get out of this valley. Maybe we can make a deal."

Tucson said, "Last time I acted gentle with a scorpion, it stung me. I don't take any more chances with that breed." He crossed the floor to Janisary, knelt down, untied the man's feet. Seizing Janisary's collar he jerked him upright. "You'n' me and Lullaby is goin' for a walk," he stated shortly. "C'mon."

"I refuse to move one step—" Janisary commenced.

Tucson jabbed a gun barrel in his back. "Walk, I said!" His tones were like a breath from the Arctic. Janisary obediently started for the door. Tucson said to Frieda, "Tell Zella I'll be back *pronto.*"

Followed by Lullaby, Stony and Pete, Tucson herded Janisary to the outside. The valley was still quiet. Tucson spoke briefly to Stony and Pete, then the pair cut across the valley in the direction of the tunnel, moving at a run through the darkness.

Tucson said, "C'mon, Janisary."

Janisary hung back. "Where you takin' me?"

"You'll know soon enough." Another prod of the gun barrel. Janisary started off. Tucson said, "Faster, you skunk," and jabbed him again. Hands bound behind him, Janisary started off at a reluctant walk as Tucson and Lullaby fell in a pace behind.

In a few minutes the temples had been left to the rear. Down the valley gleamed the outlaws' campfire. There was no sign of movement near it. Tucson figured a walk of six or seven minutes would bring him as near as he wanted to go.

"Listen, Singin' Skunk," Lullaby said to Janisary. "Don't try any sudden dashes for freedom. We're too close for that. You see, we don't dare let you go."

267

"I got sense," Janisary growled as he trudged along.

"I sort of doubt that, too," Tucson commented, then to Lullaby, "I'd sure give up hope of seeing you and Stony. This Janisary coyote said it had been discovered that your ropes was loose and—"

"That was Stony. After you loosened my ropes, Stony was plumb impatient. He squirmed and wiggled around and finally managed to loosen his own ropes, but he made so much noise about it that the guard come in to see what was up. Naturally, he found out, when he noticed that Stony had moved around considerable. Me, layin' quiet, he never suspected, though he did take a brief look at my ropes. Trouble was, it was too brief, and he didn't notice they was loose."

"I was expecting you earlier in the evening."

"We couldn't get goin' before. The feller guardin' our tent was plumb suspicious and kept lookin' inside every once in a while. Finally he fell asleep—"

Janisary cursed bitterly.

Lullaby laughed and said, "Hell, Janisary, your guards spend most of their time sleepin'. You ought to speak to 'em about it. . . . Anyway, Tucson, just as we got ready to leave, there was some shootin' and yelling arose down this way. That woke the guard up—"

"That was when I was puttin' up my fight—"

"Yeah, they told Stony and me you'd nigh broke

loose. Eventually the noise died down. Our guard started to snore again. I slipped my ropes, then untied Stony. We sneaked out under the back of the tent, got your guns where you had left 'em, and—well, you know the rest, how we found the correct address just in time—"

"Say," Janisary fumed, "how long is this foolishness goin' to continue? You can't escape."

"Shut up more and walk faster," Tucson snapped. Janisary felt the gun barrel boring against his spine and quickened pace. They were nearly halfway to the outlaw camp now, almost within hailing distance.

A few yards more and Tucson called for a halt. It was too dark to see the scowl that gathered on Janisary's face, as Tucson talked, but there wasn't any doubt in Tucson's mind as to how Janisary received the plan.

"I'm dam'd if I'll do it!" Janisary snapped. "Do you think I'm a total fool—"

"I'll know you're a total fool if you raise your voice like that again," Tucson said, cold-voiced. "We're not taking any chances, Scorpion. We're playing a long gamble. If we've got to die, we're taking you with us. I'm offering you life for seven horses—"

"Seven, did you say?" Lullaby broke in. "There's only six of—"

"Seven," Tucson cut in. Lullaby fell silent. Tucson went on, "Go ahead, Janisary, hail the camp—"

"Cripes! You can't get away with it. They'll think it's funny if I don't come all the way to camp—"

"Oh, yeah?" Tucson's voice was grim. "You can tell your hawss wrangler that you been yellin' ever since you left back there. Bawl him out for not bein' on the job." Tucson stated other words Janisary was to use.

Janisary shook his head. "I'm dam'd if I will," he declared stubbornly.

Tucson sighed heavily. "When I say 'three' Lullaby, let him have it." Tucson's tones were grim, hard. "I'll be pluggin' him at the same time—"

"All right, all right," Janisary said hastily. "I'll do it."

"And you'll do it damn fast," Tucson snapped. "I'm losing patience, Scorpion. You're makin' us lose time. If we don't get movin' right soon, dawn will be here, and there won't be any use tryin', then. But don't stall for that. It's goin' to depend on just how fast we get those horses, whether we leave you alive or dead when we pull out."

Lullaby added to the bluff. He said hopelessly, "Hell, Tucson, our chance is gone, I reckon. Let's plug this snake and do the best we can without him. Somethin' else will turn up—" He stopped and pressed the muzzle of his gun against Janisary's side.

Janisary shrank back. "For God's sake, don't shoot. I'll do it."

"Do it right then, just like I told you," Tucson growled. "Any funny business and I'm finishin' you, *pronto*. And don't say anythin' but what I told you to say. Get busy, or get ready for hot lead!"

Janisary raised his voice, "Hey, Monroe!"

The voice carried down the valley. There wasn't any reply.

"Let him have a hot slug, Tucson," Lullaby urged in bloodthirsty accents.

"No, no," Janisary said frantically, "I'll make him hear. He's probably asleep." Again he lifted his voice, "Hey, Monroe!"

There was some movement near the small campfire, the length of a city block distant. Then a sleepy voice replied, "That you, chief?"

Tucson prodded Janisary with the gun barrel. Janisary yelled, "Dammit, have I got to come all the way down there? Can't you hear? I been yelling for the last ten minutes—"

"I was asleep," came the reply. "What's up?"

More prods from the gun barrel. Janisary squirmed nervously. "I want seven horses—saddled—"

"What you want seven horses for? What's wrong?"

"Oh, hell," Lullaby growled. "I knew it wouldn't work." His gun barrel was searching out a soft spot under Janisary's heart.

Janisary gave a quick gasp of fear that exploded

in a violent oath of exasperation at the man's curiosity and slowness. "Damn your hide, Monroe, if I have to come all the way down there, you'll regret it—"

"You don't, chief, you don't," Monroe called back hastily. "I was just wonderin'—"

"Well, quit your damn wonderin' and get busy," Janisary yelled angrily. Tucson whispered to him and he went on, "We're loading some of that treasure. Me'n' Crawford and Freeling and the four *peones* back there are taking it into Malpaisaño in the morning."

"Right, seven horses. I'll be along *pronto*."

"Make it faster'n that," Tucson whispered.

Janisary repeated obediently, "Make it faster than that, Monroe."

"Right, chief."

Janisary swore bitterly. "You'll never make it, just the same—"

"Shut up!" from Tucson. He stood listening. Sounds carried clearly in the silent night air. He could hear a certain amount of commotion from the direction of the corral. Someone else raised a sleepy voice to ask, "What's wrong, Monroe?"

Monroe said something about horses and transporting treasure. The other man said, "Reckon I'll go look at that treasure." Tucson heard Monroe call back from the corral. "Take my advice and stay where you are. The chief sounded proddy. Reckon he ain't got them emeralds yet."

The camp fell into silence again. Tucson could hear the soft thudding of hoofs from the corral and heard a horse snort as a saddle cinch was tightened.

Tucson said softly, "You may live a little longer at that, Janisary. Good thing that hombre decided not to come down here."

Janisary cursed him, not daring to raise his voice. Lullaby told the man to shut up. The three started back for the temple at a quick pace. Nearing the three temples Tucson heard voices near the easternmost structure, then the sounds of picks striking against rock and earth: it was the *peon* laborers. Tucson judged they had been idling on the job; probably sleeping a good deal during the night. Anyway, regardless what happened, the *peones* would have no part in the action to come.

Tucson and Lullaby, with their prisoner, arrived back to find conditions as they had left them. Frieda stood near the doorway, gun in hand. Her father was seated on a chair, a stunned expression on his features as though he couldn't quite comprehend the swift changes that had occurred. Crawford and Zink Freeling still lay, bound, on the floor. Their eyes sought Janisary's as Tucson pushed the bandit chief into the room, but Janisary didn't meet their gaze.

Janisary objected to having his feet bound again, but Lullaby got busy and a minute later, the bandit lay on the floor, a few yards from his henchmen.

Lullaby said, "Think we ought to gag 'em?"

Tucson shook his head. "They know better than to yelp, while we're here. After we're gone a gag wouldn't do much good anyway." To Frieda he said, "Where's Zella?"

The girl replied, "I don't know. She brought those guns and belts from Janisary's room—" pointing to some weapons on the table, holsters, belts, and two rifles standing nearby.

"There's my hawg-laigs," Lullaby said joyously. "Stony's too." He crossed quickly to the table and effected a change of guns.

"—then she went out," Frieda finished. "She didn't say where."

"Pro'bly be back in a minute," Tucson nodded. To Lullaby, "I'll go out and keep an eye open for those horses. Stony and Pete ought to be along with some news right soon, too. Sit tight, unless I yell. If Janisary kicks up a fuss, bat him down."

Tucson stepped out of the house. He called twice softly to Zella without receiving a reply. "Maybe she's in her room in the living quarters," he muttered.

The minutes seemed to drag. From down the valley came the movements of horses. Now and then a voice reached Tucson. The strain was commencing to tell. He paced impatiently back and forth. The eastern sky was graying a little. The last stars had died out of the west. A morning breeze ruffled through the valley.

Abruptly, Tucson heard the thudding of horses' hoofs from near the corral. "Here comes the hawsses," he said to himself. "Hope that Monroe hombre brings 'em alone. Dammit! Where's Stony and Pete? They should be back by this time—if they're comin'."

He turned and ran back in the living quarters, called to Lullaby, then leaped outside again. Lullaby appeared at his side, "What's up?"

"Janisary and his skunks are safe for the time bein'. There may be more than one man with the horses. We don't want to fight if it can be prevented. He's sure to smell a mouse—Monroe, I mean—"

Tucson stopped suddenly. Footsteps thudded through the night. Pete and Stony, with two captives being pushed ahead of guns, took form in the darkness.

"You Stony—Pete?" Tucson asked quickly.

"It's us—with a coupla stubborn hombres that wouldn't run, until we'd persuaded 'em they had to hurry—that we didn't have time to waste pickin' wild flowers," Stony panted.

Pete was replying to Lullaby's question, "No, we didn't have any trouble. These guards were sitting with their backs toward us, when we come through the tunnel. We got the drop. Stony tied their hands behind 'em with their bandannas. They didn't want to come, but after Stony bent a gun barrel over one of their heads, they was right

275

amenable to reason. Thought we better bring 'em along—"

"Take 'em inside," Tucson said quickly. "Tie 'em up tight, then bring Frieda and Norquist out here— Zella too. Stony, grab those guns in there. Your hawg-laigs are among 'em. Hurry! The hawsses are on the way."

Pete and Stony didn't stop to ask questions but hurried their captives inside the living quarters. The horses sounded nearer, now. Monroe, riding one horse and holding the reins of half a dozen more, came trotting up. Tucson breathed a sigh of relief at seeing him alone. He said, low-voiced, "You get the reins of those six broncs, Lullaby."

Monroe's eyes tried to pierce the shadows in the darkness. "Hey, chief, where are you? Here's your horses—"

He stopped suddenly, seeing Tucson at his side. "What the—"

"I'll take those horses," Tucson said quietly.

"Who's this?" Monroe asked suspiciously. "I don't know that voice—"

"Mebbe you recognize this then," Tucson laughed grimly, jabbing one gun against Monroe's side. "Quiet now! Not a word. Keep still and you won't be hurt—"

"I got the reins, pard," from Lullaby.

"Good. Monroe, get down off that bronc."

Frieda and the rest were emerging from the temple, now. Monroe, stiff with fear, slid down

276

from the saddle. Pete and Stony jerked the bandanna off his neck, bound his hands and rushed him toward the living quarters.

Tucson said, "Where's Zella?" anxiously.

"She hasn't returned," Frieda said. "I don't know where—"

Tucson didn't wait to hear more, but rushed after Pete and Stony, found them in the big chamber, tying Monroe to a chair, while Janisary and his other henchmen glared in silence.

"Shore makin' a collection of skunks," Stony grinned.

Tucson dashed through the various rooms but couldn't find any sign of Zella. He left the temple, got outside in time to find all but two horses unmounted.

"We better slope, pard," Lullaby was saying.

Before Tucson had an opportunity to reply, a wild yell came from the outlaws' camp, "Brooke and Joslin ain't here!" More excited shouts, then, "Them two punchers is gone!"

Stony laughed, "Reckon our guard waked up an' discovered his charges was missin'—"

"Janisary! Hey, chief!" More shouting from the outlaws' camp.

Lullaby snapped, "For God's sake, Tucson, come on!"

The outlaws' camp was a flurry of excitement now. Pete, in the lead, was already getting Norquist and Frieda on the move.

"C'mon, Tucson," Stony urged. "We'll be cut off in another minute. Them outlaws is saddling up."

"Get going," Tucson jerked out. He swung up to the saddle, holding the reins of the horse he had intended for Zella. The horses got under way with a leap. Men on foot were coming at a run down the valley, now, yelling for Janisary.

Tucson dug in his spurs. The others were already ten yards in the lead. Stony and Lullaby held back, one riding on either side of Tucson, urging him to drop the reins of the horse he was leading. The riders were strung out after a minute, Tucson last, racing for the tunnel. The whole valley echoed with sound. Somebody cut loose with a gun in the general direction of the escaping horses. The bullet screamed far wide of finding a mark. But that started it: guns commenced to flame through the valley. Tucson yelled, "Hold your fire, fellers! No use wastin' lead. Another minute and we'll be at the tunnel!"

Frieda and her father were in the lead. Pete rode close behind. Then came Stony and Lullaby, followed by Tucson who still led the riderless horse. The ponies were running like mad now, their flashing hoofs reeling off yard after receding yard. Abruptly, in the darkness, the high eastern wall of the valley loomed high overhead. Tucson urged his pony up until its nose was even with that of Lullaby's horse, and called through the fierce rush of wind, "Nothin' to do but ride 'em, now, Lullaby. Swing wide of Malpaisaño. Too many Janisary followers there. Head for San Valerio—"

Lullaby yelled, "What you aimin' to do?"

The wind tore words from Tucson's mouth. "I'm headin' back. I thought I might be needed this far, but you're clear for a spell. Get Frieda and Norquist to San Valerio. I'll follow later."

He sensed, rather than saw the twisted look that appeared on Lullaby's leathery features. Lullaby ripped out one word: "Zella."

Tucson called back, "Zella."

"Like that, eh?" from Lullaby.

Tucson replied steadily, "Like that, pard. I can't leave her. We'll be coming along after Janisary and his gang leave the valley chasin' you. Give 'em a run. We'll meet you in San Valerio."

" 'Right," Lullaby said reluctantly. "If you don't hit our trail *pronto,* me'n' Stony will be comin' back. *Adios, amigo.*"

His words were lost in the pounding of thundering hoofs as Tucson slowed pace and allowed himself to fall behind. He saw Lullaby spur up to Stony's side, noted the momentary hesitation of the two riders, before they again plunged ahead. As Tucson finally pulled to a halt, he heard the hollow echoes flung back from the tunnel as the horses were urged into the big opening. After a few moments these sounds died away.

Tucson wheeled his horse toward a clump of cottonwoods. Here he dismounted, holding the reins of both ponies, his gaze ranging across the valley floor. Voices near the outlaw camp were shouting wildly for Janisary. A shower of sparks made brilliant pinpoints of crimson through the gloom as someone threw fresh wood on the campfire, causing it to flare high. Tucson could see now, several ponies, saddled and waiting near the corral. Men were running wildly back and forth, their forms silhouetted against the fire.

Running feet and angry yells made more noise near the three temples now. Two minutes later, Tucson heard Janisary cursing like one insane as he plunged from the living quarters and headed down the valley at a desperate run. The staccato *clop-clop* of horses' hoofs sounded as somebody brought Janisary a horse. The mad flow of angry sound swiftly moved toward the outlaw camp.

Tucson laughed silently. "We sure upset the Scorpion's apple-cart this time," he mused.

Through the bedlam of noise at the outlaw camp came the voice of Janisary, raging like a madman. Everyone seemed to be yelling at once for horses or guns, getting in each other's way, swearing violent oaths. Eventually a certain order issued from the chaotic situation, as Janisary managed to make his voice heard through all the excitement.

There came a swift drumming of hoofs as the mounted outlaws came sweeping along the valley floor. Tucson crouched among the cottonwoods, motionless, until the bandits had crowded their way into the tunnel in pursuit of their escaping prisoners. The sounds finally drifted off to silence, though once Tucson imagined he heard faint yells from the other side of the valley wall; of this he couldn't be certain.

Tucson waited five minutes longer. From near the opposite end of the valley he heard several remarks in Spanish and made out the voices of the *peon* laborers talking excitedly among themselves regarding the departure of the outlaws. Beyond this, there didn't seem to be a sound in the valley.

Tucson mounted and, leading the extra horse, headed for the living quarters in the temple. "Outguessed again, Janisary," he muttered softly. "I reckon you've nigh reached the end of your rope—and that will come the first time your trail cuts mine."

# 21

# Trapped!

As he neared the three temples, Tucson moved cautiously, prompted by some vague premonition of evil. His brow furrowed in thought. He was unable to shake off the feeling of a warning sent to him by that extra sense men sometimes possess in times of danger. There was nothing to be seen nor heard, except the chattering of the *peon* laborers which reached him faintly from the far

end of the valley. The four laborers who constituted the night shift on the easternmost temple
had ceased work. Tucson didn't know where they
were but judged they had joined their brother
*peones.* At any rate he knew the laborers would
take neither side in the valley troubles.

He looked about for Zella, but no sign of the
girl was to be seen. The horses walked slowly
past the temple. Tucson pulled to a halt, then
struck with another idea, started the two horses
again: it might be best to conceal the ponies in the
brush beyond the temple he and Pete had entered
the previous night. It was now nearing dawn.
Some of the *peones* might take a fancy to leave
and help themselves to Tucson's mounts. He
wanted to be sure of having two horses handy.

"Though I reckon," Tucson muttered, "if those
laborers want to pull out, there's still plenty
horses in that big corral. Everyone rode a horse
into this valley. There's pack horses besides."

At that moment, a long shrill neighing from the
corral, followed by the piercing hee-haw of a mule
floated along the valley. "Yep, plenty mounts if
they're wanted," Tucson nodded. "Still, there
might not be saddles. I know these horses I got
are all right. Reckon I better hide 'em."

He dismounted in the thick brush, tethering the
two beasts to a low-hanging mesquite limb. Then
he started back for the living quarters where he
had last seen Zella.

There wasn't a sound about the temple as he approached, despite the uncanny prickling of danger that ruffled the hair at the back of his neck. He passed silently through the opening in the wall that surrounded the temple. Ahead of him, only the heavy *chimayo* blanket barred his entrance. Yellow light showed beneath its woven bottom edge. At least the oil lamp was still burning inside.

Tucson stepped to the blanket, pulled it aside a fraction of an inch and peered inside the big chamber. Furniture met his eye. On the floor lay pieces of rope and knotted bandannas which had been cut from the feet and wrists of the bandits held there a short time before. The lamp burned with a steady flame on the oaken table. Tucson thought the room was empty until he heard a slight sound. It sounded like a muffled sob.

Shifting his gaze to another part of the room he saw Zella seated on a stack of Navajo blankets which had served as a low divan. The girl was dry-eyed, her face white. She sat, long fingers clasped about one knee, gazing blankly at the floor. The light from the oil lamp touched bronze highlights of color on her chestnut hair.

Tucson drew aside the curtain and stepped quietly into the room. Zella looked up. Warm joyous color flowed into her face. "Tucson, oh, Tucson," she breathed, "you came back!"

"Gosh, girl," and Tucson choked a little, "did

283

you think I was gone? I just wanted to make sure the others got safe to the tunnel. I couldn't leave you—"

"But Janisary—and the others—"

"They've left. Lullaby, Stony and the rest will beat them to San Valerio. I said we'd meet them there."

Unconsciously, the man and girl had been approaching each other. Tucson's arms lifted to find Zella's shoulders. The girl came close, a long sigh of mingled pain and peace on her lips. Tucson was holding her warm body tightly to his own. He felt her heart beating against his breast as he stilled the protests on her lips with his mouth.

After a minute she drew back, her eyes misty, "It can't be, Tucson," she said steadily, "not ever. I know best. But, oh, it's good to know that you came back, that you really cared enough—"

"Shh!" Tucson smiled fondly. "I've got horses waiting. Hurry! We've got to slope pronto, girl—"

"I can't let you do this, Tucson." Zella's hands came up to Tucson's face. Her eyes, filled with an infinite tenderness searched his gray ones, finding further contentment in what she saw there. "Don't you understand that—"

Tucson's voice wasn't quite steady. "I was afraid you'd run away when we pulled out. I figured to come back. I called to you—"

"I heard you. I was hiding in that temple where

the treasure was discovered. Oh, it was hard not to answer, not to come when you called. I think it will always be hard not to come when you call, Tucson *mio*. But don't you see—" She fought to hold her voice hard and light, "—that sort of happiness isn't for me, ever—"

"Zella, don't say such things—"

"I'm looking farther ahead than you, Tucson." The girl nestled in his arms, her eyes hungry on his own. "I told you I'd drifted—more isn't needed—you realize what that means—"

Tucson broke in doggedly, "It means nothing at all. We're aheadin' across the Border—you and me—headin' far north—Wyoming, Montana, the Dakotas—wherever you'll be happiest. We'll have our own outfit, Zella. Oh, girl of mine," his voice shook with the joy of the moment, "there's ten years to make up. Ten years to forget other things—and more than ten—"

The girl swallowed hard, shook her head. "Don't! You're making it hard. Don't, Tucson—!" Her tones were miserable.

"I'll make you see it my way," Tucson persisted.

The girl shook her head, blinded by tears. "All this—all this happiness—coming at once, Tucson. It's—it's—but don't ask me. I can't. It wouldn't be fair."

She broke away from his enfolding arms, stepped back. Tucson took one step toward her, then stopped, frozen to a sudden silence.

A voice at his rear, at the back of the big chamber, sneered, "Put 'em up fast, Smith! Hate to interrupt these tender moments, but—"

Tucson spun on one foot, reaching and drawing as he moved. He shot by pure instinct, the gun kicking twice in his hand to drown out the roar of a single shot that passed over his head.

For just a moment, Tench Crawford stood framed in the doorway, his body stiffening. The gun wavered in his hand a moment, then dropped from nerveless fingers as he pitched headlong and lay still.

Zella gave a little cry of fright. "I didn't know he was here, Tucson. I came in only five minutes before you. Quick. There may be others—"

Tucson nodded. "Right, we've got to drift *pronto,* Zella—"

He saw Zella's eyes widen with horror. He started to turn, and at the same moment felt a gun barrel jammed against the small of his back.

"Hold it, Smith!" came Janisary's cold tones. "You, Zella, get back near that far wall—away from Smith. I'm not taking any chances. I'd just as soon plug you as not. Smith, put that gun in your holster! Quick!"

The gun barrel was hard against Tucson's back. It all flashed through his mind in a second: Crawford had been placed at the inner door of the chamber to draw Tucson's attention while Janisary came past the *chimayo* blanket at the

286

entrance. Tucson slipped his gun back in holster, waiting for an opportunity to turn.

"Unbuckle your belts, Smith," Janisary rasped in ugly tones. "I don't trust you with 'em on."

Tucson obeyed the order. Belts and weapons dropped to the floor.

Janisary continued, "Watch the girl, Zink. I'll take care of Smith."

Tucson hadn't heard Zink Freeling enter. His mind worked swiftly. Two against one. It had been three. Tench Crawford was done for. At the first opportunity, Tucson speculated, he'd make a rush for Janisary and—

"Don't count on it, Smith," Janisary had guessed what was in Tucson's mind. "I'm watching you close. I'll pull trigger at the first sign."

He removed the gun barrel from Tucson's back, stepped warily around him, keeping fully five yards' distance between them. Tucson's eyes met Janisary's now, saw the triumphant lights in the Scorpion's cruel gaze.

"Get over near the wall, near Zella," Janisary snapped. "And move plumb cautious."

Every sense alert for the first chance that might come his way, Tucson crossed to Zella's side. Now he saw Freeling, grinning nastily, near the *chimayo* blanket.

Janisary sneered. "You two sure made it up in quick fashion, Zella. Nice double-crosser you turned out to be—"

"Scorpion," Tucson's voice was hard, "talk to me if you got anythin' to say." He eyed the gun in Janisary's right fist, noted the second six-shooter at the bandit's left hip.

"I'll talk to you, right enough," the outlaw sneered. "Zella will come in for some talkin' too. I never thought—"

"And you never will think clearly, Janisary," Zella stated cooly. "If you did, you'd realize Tucson Smith for the man he is—more of a man that you ever could be, you killer, you thief, you—"

Janisary's face clouded with anger. He took one step forward, then regained control of himself. "I'll talk to you later, Zella. Right now, Smith and me have things to talk over."

"Get to it," Tucson said easily. "What's on your mind."

"I want those emeralds."

"You can have 'em for all of me," Tucson said carelessly.

"Where are they?"

"Ask somebody that knows—I don't—"

"Smith, it won't do you any good to lie now—"

"I ain't lyin', Scorpion."

Zink Freeling snapped, "Bet he is, Gage."

Tucson shot a quick glance at Freeling. "Shut your mouth, louse."

Freeling started a hot reply. He stepped toward Tucson but Janisary waved him back, "I'll handle this tough cowpoke, Zink. You keep your eye on the girl."

288

Freeling tilted his gun a trifle. "Go on, make a break, sister."

Zella looked her contempt at the man, didn't deign to reply.

Janisary said impatiently, "By God, Smith, I'm through bothering with you. I want those emeralds. You know where they are—"

"That's where you're all wrong—"

Janisary's gun barrel lifted a trifle. "This is your last chance, Smith. Either tell me or—"

"I tell you I don't know. Last I saw of 'em, Professor Norquist had 'em. Then you broke in on us. You searched him, searched all of us. I don't know what became of the emeralds."

Tucson met Janisary's searching gaze with steady eyes, even managed a careless laugh. "You're licked, Scorpion," he said. "I don't know where those green eyes went to."

It finally dawned on Janisary that Tucson was speaking truth. "By God!" he exclaimed disappointedly, "I don't believe you do know."

"I'm tellin' you," Tucson laughed. He felt Zella's hand on his arm, reached over and patted her fingers softly.

A harsh laugh left Janisary's lips. "That being the case," he rasped, "I don't see any use lettin' you live any longer, Smith. You've interrupted my plans from start to finish. I think I might just as well end your meddling right now."

He raised his gun, held it steady on Tucson's

heart. Zella saw the light of murder burning in his cruel eyes. She saw Janisary's finger slowly tighten about the trigger of the heavy forty- five. A wild sobbing scream left her lips as she threw herself in front of Tucson.

The gun roared savagely. Tucson felt the girl go limp in his arms. For the moment Janisary, Freeling, everything else, was forgotten as Tucson gathered the girl close to his breast, searching her white face, speaking the same thought over and over.

Zella's eyes fluttered open after a moment. She murmured, "I said it couldn't be, Tucson *mio,* but it's been good to be so happy just for—just for a little—"

There was a faraway look in the girl's eyes now. Her voice drifted off to silence. Slowly her long lashes settled softly on the white cheeks. A sob broke from Tucson's tense lips as he lifted his head, saw Janisary through a swimming mist of emotion.

Janisary had backed away a step, the gun still in his hand; his own eyes wide with shocked surprise at what had happened. Freeling gasped out something about shooting a woman. Neither Janisary nor Tucson heard him. Janisary backed another step, slowly lowering his gun.

Tucson's movements were very deliberate now, as though he were alone with Zella's still form. He gathered the girl's body in his arms, turned and deposited it gently on the stacked heap of Navajo blankets which she had been seated on such a little time before.

Then Tucson straightened up and turned to face Janisary. Janisary looked at the cowboy and backed another step. Tucson's were the eyes of a madman now, his features were set in a grim, determined mask. He took two steps toward Janisary.

Janisary said hoarsely, "I didn't—I swear I didn't mean that, Smith. I—I—"

Tucson didn't reply. His advance across the room was deliberate, as though no power on earth could halt it. Only the fingers of his muscular hands gave sign of his intentions. They clenched and unclenched convulsively. His steps were steady on the stone floor of the big chamber. Freeling was forgotten. Tucson had eyes only for Gage Janisary, eyes that burned relentlessly deeper and deeper into the very core of the bandit's black heart.

Janisary lifted his gun, still backing away. His hand shook like a man with ague. He felt now that nothing ever would stop Tucson until those strong muscular fingers had closed on his throat. Janisary choked out an order to Freeling. With a supreme effort the outlaw leader fought to hold his gun steady on Tucson's body. The gun roared in the close chamber.

A fragment of rock chipped off the far wall. Still

Tucson came on and on and on. Janisary pulled trigger again, and again missed. The very foundations of his nerve were shaken now. A cold fear of Tucson Smith chilled his spine, made his legs powerless to retreat farther. A third time he fired and saw the leaden slug whine wide of its aim.

Then Tucson leaped—leaped through the air with the swift strength of a cougar seeking its prey. Janisary cried out in stark fear, backing away. He dropped his gun, both hands raising to shield his throat. He felt his hands brushed down as though they were straws, felt Tucson's fingers reaching for his neck, realized the terrible cold anger that was forcing those fingers in and in.

Janisary's face commenced to purple, his tongue appeared between the lips of his open mouth. Then, just as he was about to gasp a dying breath, the fingers were reluctantly released. Air flowed into his lungs. As from far away, he heard Freeling's trembling voice,

"Gawd, chief, he nearly had you that time. I had to hit him three times before he'd let go. Even had to pry one hand loose. He was plumb crazy."

Janisary staggered to his feet, braced himself against one wall and gazed down at Tucson, sprawled on the floor. A spot of red matted the hair on the left side of Tucson's head. Tucson didn't move.

Janisary said unsteadily, "Yes—plumb crazy, I guess."

# 22

# The Glass of Death

Tucson recovered consciousness slowly. Red-hot irons seemed to be beating on his head. With an effort he opened his eyes and found himself looking at a flat ceiling of stone overhead in which was a large square opening. Limitless distances beyond, a perfect sky of turquoise blue met his gaze. He twisted his head a trifle, despite the pain the action cost him, and saw that he was in a small stone chamber, with square openings in each wall. Sky through these openings too, though from one window he caught a glimpse of the high rock wall surrounding the valley.

Directly opposite his head was a narrow entrance. More sky and rocks. A *zopilote* floated on lazy wings some distance away. Tucson guessed he was in the small building he had noticed on top of the pyramid. He wondered how he got there, tried to move, and discovered that his hands, stretched back of his head, and feet were firmly secured.

"Spread-eagled," was the thought that flashed through his mind.

But why, where? His eyes roved aimlessly around the four walls—by craning his neck back he could see the walls behind him. Their surfaces were covered with sculptured figures and hieroglyphics. Other facts penetrated his consciousness after a few minutes. He could twist his aching head a little to either side. He was spread-eagled on a huge table-like altar made of closely-fitted blocks of volcanic rock. The altar must have been close to ten feet in length. Tucson lifted his head a trifle, saw rawhide thongs stretching from his ankles to steel tent-stakes driven deep into the cracks between the blocks of rock. He judged his arms were held in the same manner.

Clearer thought flooded Tucson's head after a few minutes. He wasn't lying flat on the altar. Something hard was under the small of his back; he couldn't determine what it was. His head and shoulders felt damp. Where were Janisary and Zink Freeling? A wave of pain clutched Tucson's heart when he thought of Zella.

Steps sounded outside the entrance to the chamber. Tucson closed his eyes again. He heard Freeling's panting, grumbling voice,

"Dammit, chief, if you think it's easy work luggin' this water up them steps, you got another guess comin'. I don't see what difference it makes if he comes to, or not. It was a bad enough job totin' Smith 'way up here. S'help me, if this don't bring him to I'd say t'hell with it. We ought to be leavin' to catch up with Shigandi Joe—"

"You'll do exactly as I say, Zink," Janisary's cruel tones cut in. "Hell, I want Smith to know what's happenin' to him. If I'd wanted to put him out while he was unconscious I could have shot him. . . . All right, give him that bucket."

The steps came nearer. A wave of water struck Tucson's head and shoulders, splashed over the altar stone. Tucson winced a trifle and opened his eyes. Water ran over his face and arms.

Janisary said, "Give him the other bucket, Zink—no, wait! He's awake."

Tucson heard Janisary's cruel, amused humming, then saw the bandit's face bending over his own. "How do you feel, Smith?"

"Like batting you down plenty, if you'd let me loose a minute."

"I ain't li'ble to do that. I had a taste of you on the warpath last night. You weren't sane, Smith. Freeling nearly ruined his gun barrel on your head."

Freeling came near. He looked a trifle drawn. He looked at Tucson a minute, then backed away. He said uncomfortably, "If that's all, chief, mebbe I better be on my way. I'd like to catch up and—"

Janisary swore good-naturedly. "Get out you yellow-livered scut. Catch up. I'll be with you at the kill. Get goin'."

Freeling passed from Tucson's view. His retreating footsteps were heard outside. He appeared to be running from something.

Janisary said, "Zink is sort of chicken-hearted about some things. He don't like dynamite."

"Dynamite?" Tucson's face was impassive.

Janisary nodded. "That roll of dynamite sticks we found among Norquist's supplies. Oh, Professor Norquist has been very handy to me. Don't you feel something under your back?"

"Oh, that," Tucson forced a thin smile. "I thought it was a cushion for my lumbago, you cowardly skunk."

Janisary shook his head. "It's no go, Smith. You can't make me mad enough to shoot you outright. Say, you've no idea how much trouble you've caused Freeling and me—aside from last night, I mean. Do you realize it's going on to ten in the morning. Lovely day, too. Not a cloud in sight anywhere—"

"What is this, a weather report?"

Janisary nodded. "I want you to remember, as long as you can, what a beautiful day it is. There isn't even a fleck of a cloud—oh, yes, the annoyance you caused us. You know, Freeling is pretty strong, but he complained it was quite a task carrying you up here. I suppose you know where you are."

"In that little buildin' atop the pyramid, I suppose."

"Bless me, Smith," Janisary imitated Norquist's manner of speaking, "you'll never become an archaeologist. This is known as the *teocalli,* or sacrificial temple. This is where those old Scorpion priests made their human sacrifices to the Sun- God. They had a neat little way of ripping out a victim's heart. Well, it's nice there's so much sun today."

Tucson said grimly, "With your dynamite, it won't be so neat. When's it due to go off?"

"Around noon. We've a little time to talk yet. I was telling how much bother you caused us. After we got you spread out and tied here, you refused to regain consciousness. I sent Freeling for two buckets of water. You didn't make a move when I drenched your head. Then I had to send for two more. You were sleeping soundly, Smith. I suppose it's a shame to wake you up—"

"Only," Tucson said easily, "you couldn't resist watchin' me for a spell. Mister, I hate to think what will happen to you, when Stony and Lullaby—"

"Bah!" Janisary laughed scornfully. "Ten to one they're prisoners of Shigandi Joe and the other men right now. The minute they hit Malpaisaño my men there would—"

He stopped short at Tucson's contemptuous laugh. Tucson said, "Think we didn't think of that? Hell, Scorpion, they ain't headed for Malpaisaño. They're riding for San Valerio."

"So much the better." Janisary's face lighted up. "That's farther. Shigandi Joe's a hound on a trail too. Just to make things interesting I don't mind telling you that Monroe handed you a lame horse, by mistake, last night. Your friends won't travel any faster than that lame pony, so my men will catch up—"

"They'll catch a flock of lead too," Tucson interrupted.

Janisary shook his head triumphantly. "You can't beat me, Smith. Too many men have tried and failed. I've outsmarted you from start to finish. You poor deluded simple cowhand. If you'd used your head you'd have realized I heard you last night, running around like a sick calf, bawling for Zella. I heard your outfit talking about it, in front of the living quarters, begging you to hurry. I guessed you'd come back for her. That's why I stayed, with Freeling and Tench Crawford—"

"Cut it, Janisary," Tucson's eyes bored into the outlaw's. "The less you say about her, well—yes, that's something else I'll live to square with you."

*El Escorpión* looked amused. "Yes, I think you're still out of your head. Don't you realize you have less than two hours to live?"

Tucson said steadily, "Mebbe, but I don't feel that way about it."

Janisary hummed delightedly to himself a moment, then, "Listen, Smith, you know how dynamite works? You attach a fulminating cap to a stick—in your case I have several sticks bound together—then run a fuse from the cap—"

"And scratch a match, touch the fuse and run like hell," Tucson interrupted.

"You're right about the fuse and the fulminating cap. I'm not going to scratch a match though. You know, Smith, Norquist told me the ancient priests always made their sacrifices at noon—when the sun was directly overhead, streaming down through that square opening you see up there. At that minute this whole altar and floor will be covered with sunlight—"

Tucson said wearily, "Cut out the gab about sunlight and cloudless skies. Touch your fuse and get out—"

"Now, Smith, don't get impatient. The fuse is all attached—right length—to a neat bundle of No. 2 dynamite sticks. You can't see the fuse without getting up—and I can't allow that—but it runs from the dynamite under your back, down on the floor. The end rests beneath one of the nicest burning glasses I've ever seen. It's arranged on a sort of tripod with a swivel frame so it can be turned in any direction. Norquist took it out of his supply kit and showed it to me one time."

Tucson didn't reply. Janisary went on, "Don't you know what a burning glass is? Well, to be real exact," imitating Norquist's tones, "the professor explained it to me as a convex lens for producing extreme heat by converging the sun's rays. You see, the end of the fuse rests beneath the burning glass. Eventually the sun will reach the correct point where its rays may be focused on the end of the fuse. The fuse will get hot, ignite and—well, Smith, there won't be any more."

Tucson gazed steadily at his tormentor. "And you've got the nerve to say I'm insane?"

Janisary's jaw dropped a trifle. He had expected Tucson to show fear, to beg and plead for release, or even faint with fright. Suddenly a cold chill coursed Janisary's spine. Tucson had laughed at him, actually laughed. The tones filled the chamber.

"You don't believe me?" Janisary asked in amazement.

"Certain I believe you, skunk. It's the sort of thing you'd do. You and your burning glass—"

"You think it won't work, eh?" Janisary commenced to lose his temper. "Hell, Norquist told me he had carried it for years in his exploring. It came handy in lighting fires when his matches were gone, or had become wet—"

"Get out of here," Tucson snapped. "I believe you, all right. Let me die in quiet—which is more than you'll ever do, Janisary."

"Oh, I'm going all right. In a very few minutes. It's getting along toward noon. Why don't you beg off, Smith. Mebbe I—"

"Beg anything of *you?*" Again that cold laugh of Tucson's.

"Oh, you think after I'm gone, some of those *peones* will release you? Not a chance, Smith. They all grabbed nags and high-tailed it out of the valley shortly after dawn. They didn't like the way things were going."

Tucson said wearily, "Oh, shut your trap. Go ahead, join your coyote crew. But your time will come, Janisary."

He closed his eyes. For some time Janisary tried to rouse him with conversation, endeavoring to spur him into tormented retorts. The outlaw stood at the side of the atlar, gloating over his victim. Once, the cowboy's unbroken nerve roused Janisary's anger to the point where he sent his fist crashing against Tucson's face. Tucson rolled his head with the blow. Blood ran from his nose. He opened his eyes, stared steadily at Janisary. Something cold and hard and relentless in those eyes. Janisary commenced to back away, a feeling of awe at such courage entering his heart.

Fifteen minutes passed. Janisary stood against the wall, staring at the closed eyes of the cowboy. Tucson might have been asleep, judging by the calm rise and fall of his chest. Janisary looked closer. Dammit! Had the man fainted or something? Janisary didn't want that. He wanted Tucson conscious, trembling with fear, when the moment of death was flung from the sun through the burning glass.

Janisary swore, strode across the floor for the bucket of water that hadn't been used before. His worried humming filled the room as he raised the bucket and dashed the contents over Tucson.

Tucson blinked through the dripping, said quietly, "I was hopin' you'd do that, Janisary. It eases my head a heap."

For five minutes Janisary stood and cursed him, ending, "And if you think any of that water wet the dynamite, you're mistaken. I was plumb careful."

Tucson said calmly, "Don't be a downright fool, Scorpion."

Janisary went white with helpless rage. He took a step forward, fists raised. Tucson eyed the man steadily. With a final oath, Janisary turned and almost ran from the building. Tucson heard his steps clattering down the stairs that ascended the pyramid.

After a long time he heard the thudding of horse's hoofs. The sounds grew fainter and fainter until they had died out in the silence that enveloped the Valley of the Singing Scorpion.

For the first time Tucson realized that his body was trembling. He gathered his nerve to await death. . . .

# 23

# No Surrender

Meantime, death in another form was drawing closer and closer to Lullaby, Stony, Lockhart, Norquist and his daughter. By dawn the party, pushing its horses to the utmost, had swept far wide of Malpaisaño and headed for the town of San Valerio, still farther to the east. Some time had been lost getting directions straightened around. It hadn't been long until, far in the rear, they heard faintly the shouts of the outlaw horde.

Then, Frieda's pony had gone lame and commenced to drop behind. A quick stop had been made, while Lullaby had examined the horse. His face had looked hopeless when he glanced up: there was nothing to be done. The animal had done its best and was now slowly breaking down. They mounted again and went on, but at a slower pace.

The sun rose, shedding waves of scorifying heat to still further beat down the resistance of the little party. They were traveling through semi-desert country now—sand, alkali, cactus of various sorts. In addition to the plant growth, a quantity of red rock of all sizes and shapes dotted the landscape. Great fragments of this crimson stone lay heaped about or reared grotesque forms in gigantic upthrusts yards higher than a rider's head.

And through it all the inexorable heat beat relentlessly down, searching out every crack and crevice, causing even the lizards and other forms of reptile life to seek shelter beneath the darkest corners of the red rocks.

Hour after hour, Stony and Lullaby urged their friends to greater efforts. The professor was proving difficult: he refused to believe the outlaws were as thoroughly bad as Lullaby claimed them to be. He couldn't, he argued, see the sense in this running away when there was archaeological work to be done in the valley. It had been a mistake to leave in the first place. No doubt Janisary had his ugly moments but by pushing work on the treasure hunt the man might have been pacified. "After all," Norquist had maintained, "this is a modern day and age. Men are civilized, no longer barbarians—"

"This," Pete Lockhart had cut in, "is Mexico." And added, "You keep riding like hell, professor."

They had kept on and on. Then, Frieda's horse had given out altogether. It was no use trying to urge the poor beast further. Frieda had mounted behind Pete, and released the lame animal. Now only four horses remained to do the work of five. From time to time, a stop was made while Frieda rode behind either Stony or Lullaby as a relief for Pete's horse. Norquist was having all he could do to manage his own horse without taking on an extra burden.

Then, the horses commenced to tire. There were no water canteens on the saddles. Now and then, when the wind was right, Lullaby could catch the sounds of the outlaws behind them. The outlaws were nearer now. Once, when Lullaby and his party were sweeping down a long sandy slope, the bandits had sighted them, and spurred into swifter motion with loud yells of triumph.

Stony and Lullaby looked anxious. Both were looking for a spot to hole up and make a stand-off fight. Finally, such a spot was sighted. It was on a small rise of ground and covered with a confused jumble of red boulders. Lullaby and Stony had spurred up ahead of the others, then led the way.

For several hours now, the siege had gone on. Lullaby, Stony, and the others were lying full length behind a breastwork of red rock in a saucer-shaped hollow, watching with anxious eyes the outlaw horde of nearly two dozen men, scattered all around them, hiding behind boulders, and keeping up a steady fire. There were only two rifles in the Norquist party. These, Lullaby and Stony kept hot, but their Winchester ammunition was growing low. Pete and Frieda were using six-shooters, firing at outlaw forms whenever one made a momentary appearance from behind a rock or clump of prickly pear. Even the professor, by this time fully aroused to the danger, was doing his best with a Colt's forty-five, but his best consisted largely in wasting cartridges.

By degrees the outlaws were growing closer and closer. They hadn't entirely escaped: four dead bodies lay sprawled on the sand within short view of the little body of defenders. Other outlaws had been wounded. Their horses were farther back. Now and then two or three of them would mount and, riding Indian fashion, circle the besieged, and spatter the rock breastwork with hot lead that whined and ricochetted in all directions.

Once, Stony had spotted a lone outlaw ride up and join the others, taking a place behind a stunted mesquite shrub from which a steady firing commenced to emanate. "My God," Stony groaned, "they're gettin' reinforcements."

His clothing had been clipped in a dozen places, his Stetson punctured half a dozen times. Lullaby had a bloody smear across one cheek where a flying bullet had creased him. Pete had a bandanna knotted just below his left elbow for the same reason. Even Frieda had a shallow furrow beneath the stained bandanna on her right shoulder, this caused from a ricochetting slug that, fortunately, was nearly spent when it touched the girl. Only the professor remained, miraculously, untouched. He exposed himself recklessly between moments spent in bewailing the fate that had driven him from his beloved ruins.

Once an outlaw, speaking in a mixture of Yaqui, Apache, and American, had offered a truce to talk terms of surrender. This, Stony and Lullaby had refused. "You know what they'd do, once they'd caught us," Lullaby had declared grim-voiced, and he glanced momentarily at Frieda, whose face was pale but composed. "Nope, no surrender. We fight this out to the last ditch."

The time dragged slowly to the accompaniment of whining cartridge slugs and heat. Just before noon, the outlaws increased their fire to a steady drumming. The guns roared and snarled and belched smoke and flame. There wasn't a breath of air. Powder smoke drifted lazily in a thick haze between the little rock barrier and the attacking outlaws. Now and then a bandit yelped with pain as the raiding horde crept from brush to rock, coming ever closer.

Lullaby felt the barrel of the Winchester grow hot to the touch. Ragged fire spurted steadily around the top of the rock barrier. A bullet clipped a lock of yellow hair from beneath the rim of Frieda's stiff-brimmed Stetson. The girl forced a nervous laugh and shoved fresh loads into the cylinder of her six-shooter.

For half an hour the outlaws' fire was intense. Then, realizing they were wasting lead, they fell back, resumed their sniping tactics from behind rocks. Pete panted, "Beat 'em back again, but God knows for how long." His face was streaked with sweat and powder grime.

Norquist said something about water, and the others became increasingly conscious of their own torturing thirst. Their tongues were liked scorched leather against their parched lips now. One o'clock came. Then two. Three o'clock dragged along on hot sluggish feet. The sun was reaching toward the far-flung ridges of the San Federico Range. But there didn't seem any let-up to the punishment offered by the sun's rays. They beat fiercely down, reflected torrid waves from the surrounding rocks which seemed white-hot to the touch.

Suddenly Lullaby discovered his cartridges were gone. The Winchester shells had given out some time before, when he had changed to six-shooter. He borrowed some cartridges from Pete who had a scant dozen still remaining. The others' supply was seriously depleted too.

Lullaby mopped the incrustations of salt and alkali from his face and looked at Stony. Stony returned the look, smiled wryly. Words weren't needed between the two. Lullaby left his place behind a block of red rock, crawled, crouching low, to where Pete was sprawled out behind three upstanding pads of prickly-pear growing out of a stony ledge.

Lullaby said, low-voiced, "Pete, tell Frieda to save one ca'tridge for herself. We all better do the same."

Pete nodded, grim-faced, wiped the coursing lines of perspiration from his forehead. "The finish, eh?" he said sententiously.

Lullaby said, half absent-mindedly, "I wish Tucson was here—no, I reckon I don't at that. Only I'd like to see him before—"

He paused. Frieda a few feet away ducked involuntarily as a leaden slug whined overhead and said to Lullaby, "Did I hear you mention Tucson?" Lullaby nodded. The girl said, "I wonder where he is?"

Lullaby forced a short laugh. "I'm lookin' for him to catch up at any minute. Pro'bly have help with him."

Which was something Lullaby had relinquished hope of long since. He knew something had happened. Janisary hadn't been once spotted among the outlaws. Probably he and others had stayed behind to capture Tucson. That must have been what happened. It was three o'clock and after now. If all had gone well, Tucson would have joined them long since.

Frieda looked a little relieved at Lullaby's words, then, "But where would he get help?" she wanted to know.

Lullaby pretended not to hear. He was already on his way back to join Stony. Stony met him calmly, peering over the top of the rock barrier. The outlaws' fire had died down somewhat. Stony pointed to several forms moving past the rocks and plant growth.

"Looks like," he said easily to Lullaby, "they're bunchin' up to rush us. There'll be hell to pay—"

"And no pitch to pay it with," Lullaby said grim-voiced. "No ca'tridges to meet a rush with, except just a few—"

"We'll have to make every shot count—"

"Except one for ourselves—"

Stony laughed harshly. "And we better make that count, cowboy."

"Oh, hell, we can't any more than die once."

"But how they would drag out that dyin'."

The two men exchanged glances, didn't say anything.

Pete called suddenly, "It looks like a rush!"

"We been expectin' it," from Lullaby.

He crouched low behind the rocks, gun raised, holding his fire until he could make sure of each shot.

The outlaws were coming nearer now, dodging from rock to rock, spreading out. A ragged fire started in, then came more steadily. The defenders crouched behind their breastwork putting off a reply until the last thing. No bullets to waste now.

The guns were roaring with sharp staccato thunder. Flying lead splashed and flattened against red rock. Powder smoke rose in thin clouds to hang in the hot breathless air over the terrain that separated the outlaws from the tiny defending force. The outlaws were closing at a run now.

Lullaby's gun was jumping like mad in his hand. He saw one outlaw sprawl down. A second twisted queerly in mid-stride before crashing to the dust. A third dropped, but still they came. Once Lullaby heard Frieda scream. He glanced toward the girl. She smiled a thin white-faced smile of shame at her fright, lifted her gun.

Lullaby suddenly discovered his six-shooter hammer was falling on empty shells. He'd used his last cartridge.

He yelled to Stony, "Looks like the end, old beetle."

Stony grunted, "Not while I can use this Winchester for a club. I'll get me a couple skunks yet."

Then suddenly the firing commenced to increase again. Stony and Lullaby couldn't understand it.

The outlaws were turning back, scattering, fleeing wildly in all directions. Over the nearest rise of ground poured a number of riders, khaki-clad riders, in the uniforms of Mexican cavalry. More and more followed, until the landscape seemed crowded with uniforms and horses. Lullaby spied a man in American cowboy togs, then another— a wild yell of joy left Lullaby's throat.

The firing was already dying down as the uniformed riders, carrying smoking carbines, commenced to form a rough circle to round up the outlaws and make captive those who were left alive.

Lullaby saw a big man on a horse break from the group. He wore the clothing of a western cowman. "By God!" he yelled at Stony, "that's Rufus Lockhart!"

"S'help me, it's ol' Rufe himself!"

Lullaby bawled at Pete, "Hey, Pete, there's your dad—" and broke off suddenly. Frieda was just disengaging herself from Pete's arms, her face a flaming red of embarrassment. Pete leaped over the rock barrier, dragging Frieda by the hand. From some place Buck Patton appeared.

Then they were gathered in a small group, shaking hands, everyone talking at once—even the professor who was calmly insisting on telling Rufus Lockhart of the great archaeological discovery he had made.

"—and I was too impatient to wait longer," the

elder Lockhart was saying, a broad smile beaming on his face, his arms about the shoulders of Frieda and young Pete. "Shucks! I was feeling good again, even if Buck did keep remindin' me of doctor's orders—"

"Damn! I held you down as long as I could," Buck Patton grinned.

"Anyway," the elder Lockhart continued, "I pulled some wires, got in touch with the Mexican Government, then Buck and I jumped a train and come as near to here as we could by rail. When we got off the train, there was two companies of Mexican cavalry, waiting, put at my disposal. We started out—"

Lockhart stopped, seeing Lullaby reach to his saddle for the canteen of water carried there. Lullaby removed the stopper. The canteen passed around the group.

"—and couldn't learn anything when we passed through Malpaisaño," Rufus Lockhart was continuing. "We pushed on without stopping, then halted at the rancho of a young Mexican who knew Tucson Smith. He told us a few things, offered to go along and show the way to Cathedral Rock. We started out. A mile farther on, we thought we heard firing over this way. The Mexican cavalry captain said we better investigate and—well, here we are. But where's Tucson—?"

"That's what we're wondering," Lullaby said, serious-faced.

Rufus Lockhart said, "Say, here's Esteban Mercado now—y'know the Mexican who claims he helped Tucson get into the Valley of the Scorpion."

It was a serious-faced Esteban who had approached accompanied by a *Capitan* of Mexican cavalry. The two talked to Lockhart for some minutes. Lullaby caught the trend of the conversation and went white.

The elder Lockhart turned back to the group, "Janisary's still going strong in his old way. One of those captive outlaws told Esteban that he left Janisary and Tucson in the valley—"

Esteban broke in, "Theese man, Zink Freeling, he's say that Janisary hav' arrange dynamite—"

"—got Tucson tied up tight with a bundle of dynamite under him. Fuse running from the dynamite to lay under a burning glass," Lockhart was saying, white-faced. "When the sun's rays hit the burning glass, the fuse will ignite and—"

"Good God!" Lullaby groaned.

"When was it to explode?" Stony asked, his lips trembling.

"Esteban says at noon—"

Lullaby wilted, an expression of pain crossing his face. He turned to Stony. Together the two men walked off by themselves.

Pete Lockhart gulped, "That's nearly four hours ago. It's—it's all over now. Poor Tucson. He was a man if there ever was one."

Esteban's eyes were full of tears. He was talking to the two Lockharts in a broken voice telling what he had learned from the captive Zink Freeling. Stony and Lullaby rejoined the group.

Lullaby said, "If you'll let us have fresh horses, Stony and me aim to head for the valley. Mebbe Zella was able to save Tucson or—"

"Didn't you hear Esteban?" Pete broke in, choking a little. "Janisary killed Zella. There's no doubt of that. The *peon* laborers had left. Tucson was alone. He met his death that way, like the brave hombre he is."

"I—I reckon," Stony gulped, "we want to go back, anyway—you know, see the place, and—and—" He couldn't go on.

"You see," Lullaby said miserably, "there's just a slim chance that Janisary was only trying to scare Tucson. Mebbe he really wouldn't go through with—with—" And his voice broke in a half sob.

Buck Patton and Rufus Lockhart exchanged glances. Buck started to say, "No chance of Janisary not goin' through—" Then he stopped. No use making matters any tougher for Lullaby and Stony.

Rufus Lockhart conferred with the Mexican *Capitan* of Cavalry. Horses and saddles were changed. One company of soldiers set off with the outlaw captives. The other accompanied the Lockharts, Frieda and her father (who was anxious to get back to the valley), Esteban Mercado, Stony and Lullaby. Buck Patton and Esteban rode ahead of the soldiers, trying to keep up with Stony and Lullaby. The cavalry, headed by an army lieutenant, was strung out at the rear. A long cloud of desert dust lifted across the plain, as the riders got into motion, drifted on the slight breeze that had come up, then settled, as it had done for a thousand years, on the heaped boulders of red rock. The sun was reaching far to the west now. . . .

# 24

# Fate of the Sun-God

As the hoofbeats of Janisary's horse faded from Tucson's ears, the red-headed cowboy realized every nerve in his body was a-tremble. With a supreme effort of his will he forced himself to lie quietly on the huge stone altar. Spread-eagled as he was, arms and legs stretched to their full extent, it was impossible to be comfortable, especially with the bundled sticks of dynamite beneath the small of his back.

He strained at the bonds that held his wrists, felt the rawhide cut cruelly into his flesh. For a moment he struggled uselessly, before getting a hold on his nerves again.

"Dammit," he said sheepishly, "I'm makin' a plumb fool of myself." His voice fell to a whisper, "I'm afraid. I'm afraid. Might as well admit that. But I'm plumb glad I didn't show the Scorpion how scared I was. Noon, he said. Must be nearly that now."

Tucson's gaze roved toward the ceiling, saw the brilliant shaft of sunlight pouring almost vertically through the square opening, saw the bright blue sky overhead—and wondered how many more minutes of life were left to view that same spread of rich turquoise. After a time he could pick out the tiny dust motes swimming in the ray of light that poured down and commenced to envelop his body. The sacrificial chamber was brighter now, bathed in a great golden light.

The sun's ray was creeping nearer and ever nearer to the burning glass, inch by inch, inexorable. In imagination, Tucson saw the sun strike the burning glass, the fuse end, frayed, beneath: Gradually the light would spread over the glass, then slowly concentrate into a single, white-hot beam to touch the fuse. Thin, tiny spirals of smoke ascended from the fuse. Then another and another. A thread end of fuse glowed red, went out, caught again, then spread swiftly to other thread ends. There was a sudden vicious sputtering as the fire traveled quickly along the fuse, up the side of the altar, to the dynamite, then—

A groan burst from Tucson's lips. He strained against his bonds like a crazy man, writhing and twisting. For a moment he thought he would go insane. In that brief second of time he was near to losing his reason. His eyes bulged angrily at the bright blue sky overhead. Not a trace of fleecy white anywhere. God! If he could only see a cloud. . . . But, no, nothing but brilliant sunlight. . . . Janisary had said, just before he left, there wasn't a cloud in the sky. . . .

With a supreme effort, Tucson regained control. "I'm actin' like a damn cowardly skunk," he muttered angrily. "Cripes! Lettin' my imagination run off with me thataway. It's plumb disgustin'. Look here, Tucson Smith, it won't be much longer to wait. Meet it like a man. It'll come sudden— and then it will be over. You can't die but once."

A certain calmness stole over his being. He closed his eyes, forced himself to relax. Many pictures passed through his mind: Zella, Lullaby, Stony. He remembered the days when he had first met Zella—and Stony—and Lullaby, and the many adventures he and his pardners had been through. They had all been in tight spots before and pulled out with whole skins. But this was different: now he was unable to help Stony and Lullaby and the rest, if what Janisary had said about a lame horse was true, and it probably was.

Tucson made swift calculations. Even at this moment it was possible that the outlaws had Stony and Lullaby holed up some place, making a last stand. "And I can't be there," Tucson muttered. "But maybe they'll get through, someway. I sort of feel they will."

A kind of peace settled over Tucson, as he lay,

eyes closed, calmly awaiting death. Some inner voice kept repeating over and over, "Any minute now. Any minute now." But Tucson refused to listen.

His mind turned to the thousands of victims who had met death on this very altar: human sacrifices to the Sun-God—the Sun-God who had held the fate of so many in those dead ancient days. But there were others who worshipped the Sun-God who died natural deaths. That was a Sun-God fate too. And these others far out-numbered those who had died as part of a bloody ritual of worship.

Thoughts after innumerable thoughts drifted through Tucson's mind. The minutes sped swiftly along, changing into quarter-hours, and then a half, while Tucson waited, peacefully now, for the final moment when a breath would change to a dying gasp. He could feel the beating of his heart. Steady, now; no sign of fear; no mad racing against despair.

It was thirst that dragged Tucson up, reluctantly, from a well of deep abstractions. He didn't know—never did know—how long his eyes had been closed while countless images and incidents paraded across his consciousness. He had almost forgotten he was to die any instant. But, now, thirst was to be added to his misery. He remembered the buckets of water dashed over him, almost wished for Janisary's return with further buckets.

The sky was still blue in the opening overhead, the sunlight just as brilliant.

Tucson gave a sudden inner start. Could it be? The wall at one side was less bright than it had been the last time he looked. The shaft of sunlight, pouring through the opening in the ceiling, was coming at a decided angle now.

What had happened? The sun had passed meridian. The sun glass hadn't ignited the fuse! And never would this day.

A trembling of relief shook Tucson's limbs. Something had thwarted Janisary's fiendish plan. Was the Sun-God being merciful this day? Tucson asked himself. Was the fate of Zexonteotl for the cowboy to be different than he had contemplated?

"By gosh!" Tucson exclaimed. "The old Sun-God is giving me a break. Reckon—but wait! Here I am trussed up like a wild steer. Have I got to stay here and starve to death instead?"

Again he commenced to tug at his bonds. To his surprise the thong about the right wrist seemed to give a trifle. Tucson renewed the fight. It was slipping! Then Tucson remembered: wet rawhide stretches. The buckets of water Janisary had thrown on him had splashed on the rawhide thongs, soaked in. . . .

Five minutes of furious struggle ensued before Tucson worked his right wrist free, the flesh scraped and cut and bleeding. But it was free!

Tucson laughed joyously. "Janisary, I've beat

you again! Your time is coming, Scorpion!" He half rose, twisting his body, working on the left wrist with the cramped fingers of his right. Once he glanced at the floor, saw the fuse-end beneath the burning glass and laughed shakily.

"Dam'd if I know why it didn't ignite, but it didn't. I got a break, that's all."

Ten minutes later he had unknotted the bonds that held his ankles and shoved his legs over the edge of the altar, stepped to the stone floor. For a moment he could scarcely stand, his limbs were so cramped. He staggered, a sorry sight, to the doorway of the sacrificial temple. His knees shook. Blood and grime smeared one side of his face where the water hadn't washed it clean. A brown spot matted his hair at one side where the skin was broken.

Out on the terraced landing Tucson stepped. Now the whole valley lay stretched out before him as he walked about, stretching his legs and breathing great gulps of fresh air. His eyes swept the heavens above the valley wall and he shook his head in perplexity: not a wisp of a cloud in sight. But why hadn't the burning glass ignited the fuse?

"Reckon I'll just have to leave it to the fate the Sun-God picked for me," Tucson muttered.

His gaze swept down the countless stone steps ascending to the top of the pyramid. Here at the top he noticed that five terraces broke the steep ascent. His eyes picked out the row of standing stelae, roved beyond to the three temples in a row: one only partly excavated, the other entered the previous night. Green Eyes of Zexonteotl. The emeralds lingered in his mind a moment:

"And I wonder where they went to?"

His gaze lingered longest on the center temple. Zella would still be there. Tucson's eyes softened, then hardened again at thought of the Scorpion. For a last time he gazed the length of the valley. Not a sign of a human anywhere, though off to the right a trifle, almost hidden by brush and trees, he caught sight of the two horses he had left there last night.

Tucson flexed his muscles. They worked easily now. Then he turned and reentered the sacrificial temple. When he emerged he carried the bundled sticks of dynamite. A brief examination had brought no explanation for the failure of the explosion to occur. Apparently, all was in order.

Ten minutes later, Tucson had set the dynamite and fuse on the earth, near the temple where the green emeralds had been found. He entered the brush, brought out the two waiting horses who neighed joyously at sight of the cowboy, leaving them standing not far from the dynamite, reins dangling on the earth.

With steady stride, Tucson turned and headed for the temple that had served as living quarters. Arriving, he pushed aside the *chimayo* blanket, then held it back that light might enter the dim, windowless interior. His guns and belts lay on the floor as he had unbuckled and dropped them the previous night. His sombrero was nearby. Beyond, on a stacked heap of Navajo blankets, Zella lay, peaceful in death. Tucson dropped the curtain and stepped inside. . . .

When he emerged he carried the cold, still form gently in his arms. Crossing to the temple his pick had opened the night before, he murmured softly, "The coffin of a princess, Pete said it was. I can lift back those slabs of rock, cover her up." He closed his eyes in pain, strode to the entrance, stepped through, holding his burden close. . . .

A short time later he again stepped into the open air, sombrero in hand. Placing the hat on his head, he brought the dynamite, then arranged rocks cunningly about the opening in the temple that they might fall in the correct position. A half hour passed while he toiled near the entrance to the tomb.

At last he stepped back, uncoiling the fuse, stretched it on the earth and scratched a match. The fuse caught, sputtered. . . .

Unhurriedly, Tucson stepped back to the horses, gathered the reins of one, climbed to the saddle of the other. Only two words left his grimly tightened lips as he turned the ponies toward the tunnel: "Now—Janisary."

He was nearly to the tunnel when the explosion

came at his rear. He didn't look back. One hand came up, brushed futilely at his eyes. As he urged the horses into the tunnel he said softly, "The tomb of a princess . . . sealed up . . . until . . ." His eyes closed on the thought. . . .

Emerging from the tunnel, he drove in sharp spurs. The horses leaped ahead, running recklessly over the broken rock that lay scattered near the tunnel entrance.

# 25

# Roaring Forty-Fives!

For two hours Tucson drove the ponies at a furious gait, changing from one to the other without pausing to stop, a matter of drawing the lead horse up until its saddle was even with his own, and then vaulting to its back, finding stirrups and changing hands on the reins. On and on he forced the tired beasts. Their coats were streaked with perspiration and alkali dust, their withers foam-flecked. Tucson's face was set in grim determined lines, his hard eyes constantly on the changing horizon ahead.

There was a trail to follow, hoof-chopped by the feet of many horses. What lay ahead, Tucson didn't know, except that these were outlaw tracks and Janisary had gone to join his men. The way was breaking down into more open country now. Vast flats of alkali and sand, cactus-dotted, stretched out before him, spotted here and there by outcroppings of reddish rock.

Monotonously, mile after mile, the two horses flashed along the trail, four-footed messengers of six-gun nemesis. Tucson's bronzed features were set in hard, straight lines, his eyes narrowed to thin slits of hate. Five more miles were pounded off and still Tucson didn't sight his prey. He urged the horses to a faster gait, coaxing, pleading with them, a prayer on his lips. Alkali dust settled a gray coating on his lean form.

Once a light of pity entered his burning eyes as he thought of the faithful horses, tearing out their hearts to answer his demand for speed and still more speed. "God, what a poundin' to give a decent pair of hawsses," he muttered.

The San Federico Mountains were growing hazy at his back, the sun winging westward, when Tucson's searching eyes finally spied a rider still far ahead and going fast. The man was too far away to be clearly distinguished, but Tucson knew in his heart it was Janisary. He breathed a fervent prayer of thanks, bent low in the saddle and plunged on.

The figure seemed to grow larger within the next ten minutes. Tucson knew he was gaining. Then, Janisary happened to look back. The bandit chief halted a moment to learn who was following him. Perhaps in that moment he realized a premonition of death, for he jerked his horse frantically around, dug in cruel spurs.

"God," Tucson breathed, "don't let him escape me now."

For a moment the race stood even, then Tucson's horse commenced to falter. He felt the poor beast stumble, regain its step and plunge on. Tucson called on its last ounce of strength. A quarter of a mile the noble beast gave everything it had, then it stumbled again.

A minute later he had leaped to the saddle of the fresher horse, loosing his grip on the reins of the exhausted animal. A rush of wind tore words from his mouth: "Thanks, old hawss. Take your rest. Somebody will pick you up."

He looked back once. The tired pony at his rear had stopped, head down, straddle-legged, almost ready to drop.

"It's up to you, pony," Tucson said, pleading with the horse he was riding. "C'mon, little horse. We're gainin' again. Don't let that coyote escape me this time."

His heart went out to the pony, its legs moving in smooth rhythmic strides over the earth. Its tongue was out now, its eyes distended, but there was nothing but pure grit in its movements. On and on, horse and man drove across the cactus-dotted landscape. The rush of wind nearly tore Tucson's breath away. The country through which he was riding had changed to a swiftly unreeling

325

kaleidoscope of blurry gray and green and red that flashed past his gaze with the swiftness of the wind.

Tucson could see Janisary plainly now. The man's arm rose and fell as he beat the horse over the head in an effort to get still more speed out of it. But it was no use. Only a quarter mile lay between the two riders now. Tucson leaned over, whispering to the horse. The animal responded gamely to the request. The quarter mile lessened to half that distance. A grim light of triumph lighted Tucson's steely grey eyes. One hand strayed toward his right-hand gun, unconsciously patted the holster.

Suddenly Janisary pulled his pony to a long sliding stop in a scattering of dust and gravel. He forced the horse to be still, reached to saddle boot for his rifle. Tucson saw him level the rifle across the horse's back, caught the puff of powder smoke, heard the *ping-g-g* of the bullet as it screamed dangerously close to his body.

Tucson didn't slack speed for an instant. He came on, full tilt, rapidly closing the distance between himself and Janisary. Not more than twenty yards separated the two men now.

The rifle spoke again. Tucson felt his horse falter. His own gun was out. He thumbed one swift shot as the pony swerved and went to its knees. Tucson jerked his feet from stirrups, leaped wide as the pony went down, dead before it crashed to the earth.

Again, Janisary threw killing lead from the rifle, the bullet ripping through the handkerchief at Tucson's neck. A lance-like spurt of flame roared from Tucson's gun as he closed in at a swift run.

Janisary vented a curse of dismay, tossed the rifle to one side and reached for his six-shooters.

"Bet I hit the mechanism of that Winchester," was the thought that flashed through Tucson's head, as a third shot roared from his Colt-gun.

Janisary's twin six-shooters were belching lead and flame, but Tucson was moving too fast to make an accurate mark. Less than ten yards separated the two men.

Now Tucson reached for his left gun. Three reports blended into one continuous volume of sound. Janisary spun half around, righted himself, one arm dangling at his side. His other hand spat sharp flashes of white fire.

Tucson had thrown himself to the earth, even as Janisary cut loose his murderous lead; one of the cowboy's guns was empty before he struck the ground.

Janisary halted in mid-stride. His remaining gun dropped from his hand. He wavered on uncertain legs a moment, then crashed full length on the sand and lay quiet.

Powder smoke stung Tucson's throat and nostrils with its acrid fumes as he rose to his feet. He stood gazing at the silent figure a few yards away. Methodically he plugged out his empty shells, shoved fresh cartridges into his cylinders, thrust the Colt-guns back into holsters.

Striding across the sand, he stood gazing down on the dead Scorpion a few moments while his fingers searched for and found Bull Durham and cigarette papers. He rolled a smoke, stuck it between his lips. A match crackled in the silence. Tucson inhaled deeply.

Slow smoke curled from his nostrils. His voice was steady as he said, "I reckon that's all." His voice sounded curiously flat in the abrupt quiet that followed the roaring forty-fives. He glanced at the sky. Turquoise sky and sunlight slowly fading on many red rocks. A pair of *zopilotes* side-slipped and soared on motionless wings high above.

His own horse dead, Tucson set about catching up Janisary's mount which strayed near. It didn't prove difficult. The horse had been pushed too hard to make any sudden dashes. Tucson put foot in stirrup. A wave of weariness engulfed him as he settled to the saddle. There were still tracks to follow. . . .

Fifteen minutes later, as he topped a rise of ground, he saw Lullaby and Stony sweeping up the slope to meet him. Joyous cowboy yells greeted his appearance. Behind his pardners rode Frieda and Pete and Norquist, other men too, and a long line of Mexican cavalrymen.

The horses came drumming up the slope, as Tucson raced to meet his friends. The lowering rays of the sun picked out Rufus Lockhart, Buck Patton and Esteban.

And then they were all dismounted, gathering around. Everyone was laughing and shaking hands, exchanging stories. The Mexican soldiers chatted excitedly with many white-toothed smiles.

"And when you get as good as us, cowboy," Stony was grinning at Tucson, "maybe the army will come to your help too."

"That's how important we are," Lullaby drawled. "We get in a tight and they send real cavalrymen to pull us out."

"Me, I count on my luck, and the Sun-God," Tucson chuckled. It was good to be with his friends again, exchanging their experiences. The worst of griefs would pass in such company.

Pete said laughingly, "So you credit the Sun-God—old Zexonteotl, eh, Tucson?"

"Somethin' like that," Tucson laughed. "Though he didn't tell me what he did with those emeralds. I was hopin' to locate 'em for you and Frieda."

Frieda said, "It's far better to locate you again, Tucson."

Tucson blushed, started to say something and was interrupted by Professor Norquist. "Treasure! Emeralds!" the little man said impatiently. "That's all you think of. The emeralds are where I can get them."

"What?" half dozen voices asked.

Norquist nodded. "The night in the temple, when

329

Janisary knocked me down. While he was watching Tucson and Pete I dropped the emeralds into the bucket of plaster. They'll be there until—"

"What I want to know," Lullaby puzzled, "is why that burning glass stunt didn't work?"

Tucson said, "You got me. Something wrong with the glass mebbe."

Norquist looked insulted. "That is the finest glass money can buy. I have lighted fires with it dozens of times—"

"Eet was the Sun-God," Esteban nodded solemnly. "He withhold hees rays for sake of a *buen hombre*—"

"Bosh!" Norquist exploded. He halted suddenly. An expression of exasperation flooded his features. "Why, bless me, bless me! Today was the day. I meant to make an observation of scientific interest. I'm sure that—" He broke off, produced a notebook from his pocket, riffled certain pages, peering through his thick lenses. Then he looked up, "Why, of course, Tucson. That explains it."

"What does?" Tucson looked amused.

"A solar eclipse occurred today at noon—"

"An eclipse of the sun!" Frieda exclaimed. "And just at the right time to save Tucson's life."

"Tut, tut," Norquist was perturbed. "I should have noticed that, but at that time, we were unduly busy. The Janisary forces kept us occupied. If I recollect correctly there was a faint haze in the air. I credited it to powder smoke—"

"And I lay there, waitin'," Tucson smiled, "with my eyes closed. Didn't even know the sun wa'n't doin' its duty as usual. Sun-God luck! An eclipse of the sun. Can you beat that?" He laughed scornfully at Stony and Lullaby, "Huh! You and your army! How about me and my eclipse?"

Everyone laughed. Dusk was settling over Mexico. Norquist was insisting that Rufus Lockhart return with him and see the wonders in the Valley of the Singing Scorpion. Some remark was made about Frieda and Pete riding to San Valerio, not only to hire more laborers but with a view to returning to a honeymoon in the valley.

No one noticed Tucson and Stony and Lullaby steal off in the gathering darkness and lead their horses away from the group. A few minutes later, Rufus Lockhart mentioned that he hadn't thanked Tucson and his pards for all they had done.

Buck Patton said, "They ain't the sort that want to hear thanks, Rufe. You'll have a job makin' 'em listen."

Muffled hoofbeats thudded across the sand, departing at a good lope. Silence fell over the group as they listened. No one spoke for a minute. Then Esteban touched Lockhart's arm. Without words he pointed toward the north.

There, sky-lighted on a rise of ground, the Three Mesquiteers had pulled their ponies to a halt and whirled for a last look at the group standing down in the hollow. Lullaby was on Tucson's right, Stony on the left. The three sat motionless a moment, then as the final rays of the dying sun flung an aura of golden light over the trio, Tucson raised one arm, palm outward, in the Indian sign of peace.

Crimson banners waved but a brief minute in the western sky, changed quickly to mauve, then gray, which in turn faded swiftly, with the three figures, from view. A long-drawn *"Adios, amigos-s-s"* floated clearly down the slope through the gathering purple twilight. Darkness dropped like a great soft blanket over the land. Then through the desert night came the steady drumming of horses' hoofs, the sounds growing fainter and ever fainter, until the muted beats had blended imperceptibly into the gentle breeze that ruffled the sagebrush. . . .

**(Allan) William Colt MacDonald** was born in Detroit, Michigan in 1891. His formal education concluded after his first three months of high school when he went to work as a lathe operator for Dodge Brothers' Motor Company. His first commercial writing consisted of advertising copy and articles for trade publications. While working in the advertising industry, MacDonald began contributing stories of varying lengths to pulp magazines and his first novel, a Western story, was published by Clayton House in *Ace-high Magazine* in 1925. MacDonald later commented that when this first novel appeared in book form as *Restless Guns* in 1929, 'I quit my job cold.' From the time of that decision on, MacDonald's career became a long string of successes in pulp magazines, hardcover books, films, and eventually original and reprint paperback editions. The Three Mesquiteers, MacDonald's most famous characters, were introduced in 1933 in *Law of the Forty-fives*. His other most famous character creation was Gregory Quist, a railroad detective. Some of MacDonald's finest work occurs outside his series, especially the well researched *Stir Up The Dust* which was published first in a British edition in 1950 and *The Mad Marshal* in 1958. MacDonald's only son, Wallace, recalled how much fun his father had writing Western fiction. It is an apt observation since countless readers have enjoyed his stories now for nearly three quarters of a century.

**Center Point Publishing**
600 Brooks Road ● PO Box 1
Thorndike ME 04986-0001 USA

(207) 568-3717

US & Canada:
1 800 929-9108
www.centerpointlargeprint.com

LA